Fix

Sex, Lies & Banking

Lily Temperley

D1158813

Published by Clink Street Publishing 2014

Copyright © 2014 Lily Temperley

First edition.

The author asserts the moral right under the Copyright, Designs and
Patents Act 1988 to be identified as the author of this work.

All rights reserved. No part of this publication may be reproduced,
stored in a retrieval system or transmitted, in any form or by any
means without the prior consent of the author, nor be otherwise circu-
lated in any form of binding or cover other than that which it is published and without a similar condition being imposed on the
subsequent purchaser.

ISBN: 978-1-909477-01-8
Ebook: 978-1-909477-03-2

For P Rabbit

Acknowledgments

I would like to thank my sister and my first editor. I owe you a huge debt of gratitude. My Mum and my Dad. My best friend in the world to whom I owe much. My friend and 'brother' who is always there for advice and guidance. Likewise my Zen friend in Northern Ireland.

To those I have mentioned in this first book if only by name or trait as a means to show that you've helped me along the way and I appreciate it. Susie, Elle Mas, Kirby, Finkster, JME, TMM, and Josephina.

Very special thanks to my hairdresser and his husband – the best confidantes a girl could wish for. To Angela, Angie, Ms Eccles-S, Penny, Gerald, Izza, Tess, Krys and Lise thanks for believing I could write a book.

To the other angels in my life, Snezha, Jean, Sara and Bern who taught me so much about life.

And to the people who helped me get this to print, Daniel, Stephanie, Becky, Lucy, Gareth and Chris.

And finally, to the people who use words in ways that inspire me and make me laugh, Eva, Katherine J, MM, JJ, 1D, Alec, Tina, Charlie and Seth.

Thank you.

'You own everything that happened to you. Tell your stories. If people wanted you to write warmly about them they should've behaved better.'

Anne Lamott

I stare at the brown paper envelope and feel sick to my stomach. It contains large colour photographs, slightly blurred and grainy but crystal clear in what they portray. Me, naked in a variety of different sexual positions with a number of different women. Their faces are indistinguishable but I know who they are and what they are. Hookers. Other pictures show me entering and leaving establishments that a man in my position shouldn't be associated with. Too late for that.

The sender has not included a note. Scrawly handwriting across the envelope refers to the contents as 'The Harrington Sexual Misdeeds Dossier'. I am clueless as to the intention of the sender. They have not asked for money. Or anything else, for that matter. Is it a veiled threat to ruin my reputation, and along with it, my dreams of ever becoming Caldwell Bank's next CEO?

I run my hands through my hair and wonder, which one of the countless women I have slept with could possibly be behind this? I found the envelope wedged into the mail slot of my front door. It was hand delivered to my house. Could it be a work associate? I know I have burned my fair share of bridges and stepped on plenty of toes in my time. Who hates me enough to go to these lengths to do this to me?

Alexandra

It started out as a normal day. I think to myself, *I will be spending my precious leisure time working. Again.*

I have made my way into the offices of Caldwell Bank, a gleaming glass tower that stands amongst other similar structures in the mini-city that is Canary Wharf in London's Docklands. Usually a hive of activity during the week, the Wharf has a distinctly eerie feel at the weekend when, other than security, there is seldom a soul around.

The Caldwell building is lavish and impressive, with a marble floored lobby decorated with expensive sculptures, Italian leather sofas and beautiful exotic flowers in oversized glass vases. In the earlier days of working for the company, I used to walk in and get a thrill from the ambience of success. Now, I have to remind myself to appreciate the architectural beauty of the building and all the amenities the firm provides. Food is available to order around the clock, sleeping pods can be booked for a nap and a variety of services are housed on various floors of the building, from coffee bars to a hairdresser and a store, which sells toiletries, and work attire. It is set up in such a way that you have no reason to leave. They don't go as far as removing the door handles.

As I move through the lobby, the decadence on display causes me to have an unpleasant physical reaction in the pit of my stomach. The office represents shackles to me on so many levels. I sigh; work makes me feel as trapped as home does at present.

I glance at my reflection in the lift mirrors and acknowledge to myself that I haven't tried very hard with my appearance today. It is February in London. Days are typified by brooding weather, rolling dark clouds in angry skies, perpetual drizzle and icy winds that bite at your lips and make your eyes water. Today is no exception, it is dank, cold and grey, and my mood reflects this. My honey-coloured hair looks dull, a bit lacklustre and is, as ever, unruly. My skin is a little ruddy.

Not wanting to see myself, I close my eyes and listen to the mechanics of the elevator as it climbs to the forty-second floor, home to the Caldwell Executive Team. I step out of the lift and round the corner heading towards my desk. I feel the dull ache behind my eyes as they adjust to the lights and inwardly curse myself for drinking so much the night before.

The lights. They are on. I know from my early weekday starts and often being the first person to arrive onto level forty-two that it takes someone moving onto the floor to activate the motion sensors that trigger the lights turning on overhead as you walk.

It is a Sunday and I was expecting the office to be empty. My plan, to go in and get a head start on the coming week's pile of work, now seems like a bad idea. The excess of the previous night hangs over me. The fruity, peachy smell of a Bellini still too recent for me to have even considered having breakfast this morning.

I stop short and take a deep breath. I am in no state to be making small talk and being on the Executive floor of one of Britain's largest companies means that whilst I am unsure of whom it is I will run into, I am fairly certain it will be someone important. This is unlikely to be a pleasant encounter for me, particularly given the state I am in. I had dressed in haste this morning. I feel a sense of foreboding as I glance down at my snug black v-neck, showing a little more cleavage than I would ordinarily, when in my right mind, consider for this environment. I am in my ever-comfortable much worn ripped Diesel jeans. Hurriedly, I had pulled on my old faithful scuffed knee-high boots as I headed out the door of my flat. I fervently hope that whoever is on the floor is not one of the Executives.

I gingerly make my way past the kitchen door and the coat cupboards and stop behind a row of filing cabinets. Without revealing myself I peer around the corner and across the open plan desks. The interior of the building is the height of contemporary design. Simplicity, subtle sophistication, texture and clean lines. The Executive Suite is no exception. It is sleek and luxurious with thick carpets, bold colour blocks on the walls, high ceilings, and geometric shapes in wall art and sculpture thoughtfully positioned around the floor. The external windows are bare, floor to ceiling, maximising natural light and the stunning views over Canary Wharf and beyond.

I hear the faint strains of pop music coming from one of the offices and as my eyes travel towards its source, my heart skips a beat as I realise who it is that has also decided to come into work today.

I stay where I am and squint. This only serves to intensify my ever-present hangover. I am tempted to spin on my heel and leave but I am captivated. He is sitting in his glass office, oblivious to the fact that I am watching him. He is dressed in faded jeans and a casual checked shirt, rolled up to his elbows. This is a stark contrast to the exquisitely tailored Savile Row suits, Hermes ties and hand-made Italian shoes I am used to seeing him in. He is leaning back in his chair holding papers in front of him. It looks like he is reading something important and he is deep in thought. But I am not that interested in what he is doing. I am delighted to have this opportunity to study him and realise that I am barely breathing and my heart is hammering a tattoo in my chest.

My senses are on high alert and the music floats across the open space. I am momentarily mesmerised, my hangover forgotten. Patrick Harrington is quite possibly the most beautiful man I have ever seen. Tall, with sandy brown hair that flops mischievously into his eyes. Eyes of steely blue, as piercing as they are enticing. He is beguiling. Everything about him, from his good looks to his physical presence, screams power and authority. This is a man who commands attention. And to top it all off, there is his accent. The soft, sexy lilt of a man who has lived in several countries, softening the broad edged sounds of his Irish background.

I had known whom Patrick Harrington was for as long as I had been with the firm. Everyone knew who he was. He had recently been promoted into a top job, Head of Investment Banking, and joined the elite Executive ranks of Caldwell Bank to help run the company. The press release was still vivid in my memory, as much for the news it brought as the handsome photograph of Patrick Harrington alongside the editorial.

"Caldwell Banking plc are pleased to announce the appointment of Patrick Harrington to Head of Investment Banking and Capital Markets. Patrick will join the Caldwell Executive Team and will report directly to CEO, Bradford T. Stone. Previously, Mr. Harrington was a Senior Managing Director, Head of Caldwell's Global Markets businesses. Before this post, Mr Harrington was a specialist in Derivatives Products, responsible for the Bank's European business. Mr. Harrington joined Caldwell Bank's Capital Markets operations as a graduate. Mr. Harrington holds a bachelor's degree in Biochemistry from St Peters College Oxford and a MBA from the Wharton School, University of Pennsylvania."

Almost six months before today, I had been in the Bank's Park Lane New York offices with my boss, ahead of an Executive Team meeting that both she and Patrick had flown in to attend. Exuding charisma and with charm that he was legendary for, he had stopped by the desk I was occupying and introduced himself. Not that it was necessary, as I had followed his career long before the press release. I cringe a little as I think about how nervous and girlish I was that day, giggling and stammering while trying to string a sentence together under the intensity of his attention. I was inhaling the very scent of him; my senses were scintillated with hints of sandalwood and bergamot. He smelled masculine and clean.

Every day since then I had longed for further encounters with the illustrious Patrick Harrington. I was consumed by infatuation and the lure of this intoxicating man. My days went by in anticipation, feeling as if I was in a constant state of vigilance, awaiting another chance to be near him.

Upon his promotion, Mr Harrington had been allocated a coveted office in the Executive Suite and had swept onto the top floor of the bank's Canary Wharf headquarters with his entourage of support staff in tow. His reputation as a charismatic leader, shrewd businessman and, probably most importantly, a notorious ladies man, preceded him. In the weeks leading up to Patrick Harrington moving in, everyone on the forty-second floor was talking about his imminent arrival. I had been teased mercilessly about his penchant for young blondes.

My boss is Eloise Little, a hard-nosed businesswoman, with connections across all the divisions of the company. Her name may be Little but her persona is anything but.

Back in London, after Patrick had made his official introduction in New York, Eloise had seen the two of us talking one Monday morning. Patrick was poised at my desk and I was trying hard not to gaze up at him, knowing that if I did I would get lost in his penetrating blue eyes and become a mumbling mess again. Moments after he had left, I was summoned into her office and without so much as a hello she barked, "What were you talking to THAT man about?"

Reeling, I stammered that he was asking me about my weekend. I could see the beginnings of a sneer as she evaluated me. "I'm watching you," she whispered and her eyes fell away from me. A dismissal. I backed out of her office and wondered what it was that she knew and I didn't.

Since then, there have been fleeting moments of being in close proximity to Patrick Harrington that I have clung to and rehashed over and over in my mind. The time that he walked into the coffee shop around the corner from the office building as I was paying for my morning cup, I dropped my change and he deftly picked it up and handed it to me. I had blushed with embarrassment for being so clumsy. I could have sworn I felt electricity as our skin touched.

There was also the time that Eloise and I had seen him in the Concorde Room, the First Class lounge at Heathrow's Terminal Five ahead of another trip to New York. Patrick and Eloise had a cordial conversation, which seemed to mask something deeper about the way they truly feel about each other. All the while, I sat on the couch beside her and felt his gaze drift over me, stopping for a nanosecond as our eyes met. My cheeks flushed and Eloise, with her cat like senses, had truncated their conversation. Much to my disappointment he had moved away and settled himself out of view on the other side of the lounge.

The Caldwell Executives have the luxury of travelling first class. Their support crew are lucky enough to fly business class. I was green with envy that Eloise was in such close quarters with Patrick for seven whole hours. She had come through to my cabin to hand me a stack of work and dropped me a few precious scraps of information about him. "Patrick is watching movies and laughing far too loudly for my liking. I think he's had more than one glass of wine with his meal." I relished the intimate glimpse, albeit second-hand, that the fabulous Mr Harrington did not take himself too seriously.

Eloise is teetotal, unwavering as a practising vegan and a compulsive workaholic. She looks fantastic and her looks belie her fifty-five years. She is petite and slim with thick shoulder length chestnut hair worn in a perfectly manicured bob with a very straight fringe (or 'bangs' as she would call them). She could be mistaken for Anna Wintour. Eloise has flawless skin from a strict nutrition plan prohibiting her from ingesting the same toxins as the rest of us mere mortals, she has barely a wrinkle on her face. One exception to Eloise's 'my body is a temple' mantra is regular 'Teosyal' gel fillers around her eyes, lips and across her forehead to maintain a youthful complexion.

Eloise had chosen to talk to me about her desire for a facelift, discussing the merits of the best cosmetic surgeons in Paris, Los Angeles and London. I could do nothing but listen, in awe of the lessons I was learning about plastic surgery. Instead of taking this more drastic step, Eloise had elected to use injections to look younger. I was privy to information about my boss that extended beyond the office.

In the twelve months since I have been working with Eloise, we have grown close - or as close as anyone can be to her. I have earned her trust and become part of her 'inner circle', which is no mean feat. Eloise has a well-earned reputation of being direct, execution focused and fearless. She is exacting, demanding and borderline obsessive. Her expectations of others are as high as the ones she places on herself. The description 'ball breaker' is often used in conjunction with her name.

On the flip side, Eloise had frequently opened up to me during our gruelling schedule of business trips and revealed her softer human aspects. We had reached the stage where we could pass transit time in companionable conversation. She and I had shared intimate details of our lives with each other. We had both lost our fathers in the same year some years earlier, and despite the difference in circumstances, we were able to compare notes on where we were with our grieving processes. We sometimes dined together when travelling and would plan to meet in the hotel gymnasium each morning, utilising treadmills that stood companionably side-by-side.

Flying for Eloise consisted of churning through as much material as possible between takeoff and landing. This normally meant that I too would be working throughout the flight, and often for hours more upon landing, after setting up my mobile office in my hotel room. Time zone differences were always disregarded and I was on duty from the second I met her at the airport to the moment we parted ways on our return to London.

I am snapped back to the present moment as I hear him move; he is unaware that he is being watched. My stomach is churning and I feel a bit queasy, a little shaky and slightly excited all at once. The flutters in my belly move south and I feel ashamed at the racy thoughts that are streaming into my head, unadulterated. *Is he really that dangerous? Why does this thought make him even more attractive to me?*

I move awkwardly towards my desk. Half of me prays that I can get there without being noticed. The other half realises that even if this is true, he will see me when he leaves and will think I am rude for not having greeted him. Both my better nature and my career-mindedness dispel any notion of pretending I have not seen him.

I make it to my desk and sit down with a sigh. My mind is racing and I have no inclination to start any work. I can only concentrate on one thing. Him. My mind flashes with a vivid image, almost as if I am out-of-body, viewing it from above. The papers from my desk are strewn across the floor, and I am lying on my desk, my hands gripping its edges, my jeans and panties pushed around my ankles. Patrick is kneeling on the floor in front of me with his head between my legs.

My cheeks burn, and I blink hard several times to try to clear the salacious images from my mind.

Brought back to consciousness, I hear the music a little louder now that I am closer to his office, and I recognise the melodious voice of Alicia Keyes. *How current*, I think, and then remember that he is only 40.

I have been working for Caldwell, one of Britain's largest high street banks with a very profitable Capital Markets business, for the entirety of my eight-year career. Eloise Little is the Chief Finance Officer and a harsh taskmaster. I have worked hard and landed myself a coveted role as one of her aides. It is common knowledge within the firm that a role as the right hand person to one of the Executives is a sure fire way to accelerate your career. If you can cut it.

In reality, it is the mundane to the sublime. I find myself staying late in the evening to collate and staple papers because Eloise doesn't trust anyone else to come into contact with highly sensitive documents. In other heady moments, I will act on delegated authority and make important decisions for, or more accurately, 'as' Eloise. I am privy to everything that comes through her office, from commercially sensitive financial data to seeing the packages offered to senior staff joining or being 'asked to leave' the bank.

My position does have a few perks, one of which is the ability to look up personal information, including pay data, about anyone in the company. Patrick earns a fortune each year. The bank awarded him more than ten million quid last year. For the rest of the world's population, it's tantamount to winning the lottery annually. Along with the knowledge of his telephone-number-length compensation package, one of the other facts I know about the gorgeous Patrick Florence Harrington is that we share the same birthday. Eleven years apart, but the same date, and the hopeless romantic in me assumes that there is something fated in that.

I sense movement, and from the corner of my eye I see him looking through the privacy frosting strips on his glass office front. I feel the slow creep of a blush again, as blood rushes up my neck and to my face. I keep my head forward but my eyes trained on his office. He is still watching me. I see his lips slowly curl into a small smile.

I take a deep breath and close my eyes. I find myself standing up with a confidence I don't think I possess and walking as purposefully as I can toward his office. He is leaning back in his chair now, tracking my progress. *What do you think you're doing? What are you going to say?* My mind screams.

I stop in the doorway, leaning on the jamb, but keeping most of my body out of view. I inwardly curse myself for not dressing better or applying any makeup before leaving my house that morning. My dry throat reminds me of the hangover I am suffering. I swallow hard a few times and squeak a timid, "Hello."

His icy cool blue eyes are dancing and his face softens into a wide boyish smile. "Hello, Alexandra. What an unexpected pleasure."

My nerves tingle as I sweep my eyes over his lean body and come to rest on his face. I reflect his smile nervously and our eyes lock in such a way that I couldn't tear them away even if I tried.

"What are you doing here on a Sunday?" he asks me.

The words tumble out of my mouth as I tell him about my night out and that I was not expecting to see anyone today, almost as an excuse for my dishevelled appearance. He surveys me and nods imperceptibly. His face gives nothing away but his eyes continue to sparkle.

We fall into easy conversation and I marvel at his ability to make me feel like I actually matter in his world. I am so nervous yet I feel exhilarated at the same time. He asks me why I am so diligent with my work and I feel myself relax a little. This is comfortable ground for me. As long as I don't mention Eloise. Caldwell's CEO, Brad Stone, relies on no other member of his Executive Team the way he does Eloise and she is his most trusted advisor. She had been one of the most vocal in support of his recruitment in front of the Board when he was hired to join the bank years previously. Yet Patrick has made the bank a lot of money and he is a ruthless businessman. They both vie for Brad's attention and it seems that if he is aware of the tension between the two of them, he is not concerned enough to do anything about it. *Perhaps he even fosters this rivalry*, I think to myself.

I hear myself telling Patrick that I want to be promoted and wonder to myself why I am being so candid with him, particularly given that there is no love lost between this man and my boss who holds the keys to my future career.

He looks at me intently. His eyes are boring into mine, and he tells me that if there is anything he can do to help my career he will. I can't believe that I, Alexandra Fisher, am having this conversation with such a powerful and disarmingly good-looking man.

I congratulate him on his promotion and tell him that I'm in awe of his meteoric rise through the company's ranks. I see his mask of calm slip for a second as he processes the compliment.

He pauses and looks at me with such intensity that I feel almost naked. "If you ever want to have dinner with me to discuss your career let me know," he breathes. I am stupefied. *Is the amazing Patrick Harrington asking me on a date?*

I suddenly feel the overwhelming urge to get out from under his gaze. I mumble something about needing to get on with my work and escape from out of his office doorway.

My head and heart pound in unison as I make my way back to the safety of my desk. *Why didn't I take him up on the offer of dinner? Would he really want to have a meal with me?* I'm rattled and cursing myself for throwing away the opportunity presented to me. I'd been dreaming about a date with this amazing man. I had the chance to make it a reality and I blew it.

I decide to take my laptop and the papers I need and work from home. Not ideal to turn around and trek back west to Putney after such a short stay in the office, but it will get me away from the alluring Patrick and spare me the ordeal of a second interaction today. I cannot focus with him in such close proximity, especially knowing that we are alone on the floor.

That night, I replay every moment of our conversation, over and over. I fall into an exhausted sleep next to my faithful yet dull by comparison boyfriend. It turned out to be anything but a normal day.

Harrington

It started out as a normal day. I think to myself, *I will be spending my precious leisure time working. Again.*

I glance at my reflection in my bathroom mirror and smile to myself. I am in great shape and my muscles tingle slightly from the sex I had earlier this morning.

I am still slightly irritated at not finding someone to pick up at my regular hangout, the bar at Mayfair's Nobu Berkeley, last night. But on reflection, I saved myself the hassle of having to eject a hopeful slut from my house in the early hours of the day. I don't do sleepovers. Thankfully, Faezeh was, as usual, more than willing to come over when I called this morning. I rang an Addison Lee taxi to collect her and had them wait, unbeknown to her, as I was not planning to set aside time for cuddles or conversation after I had taken what I wanted. My time is precious and post-coital pleasantries don't feature on my agenda.

I had padded to the door, my jeans barely done up, my checked shirt hanging open following the sound of the doorbell. As soon as she had crossed the threshold of the front door of my house I had her in my arms, urgently kissing her, as I moved her from the hallway toward the kitchen. I did not want her in my bedroom.

I cast my mind back reflecting on the interaction. She is hungry for me as usual. I can tell she is trying hard to resist me, but given the ease with which she agrees to come over and the lengths she is willing to go for me, we both know it's a charade.

I am actually bored of her but I rank sex with her a little higher than masturbation. I stop kissing her long enough so she can take off her coat. She is wearing nothing but white lacy underwear underneath. She doesn't remove her heels. She knows better. I smile at her and she flashes me what she thinks is a dazzling grin. To me she looks unnecessarily eager and I lose respect for her. I prefer a challenge. I know she is thinking she has impressed me with her sheer lingerie when in fact I am feeling rather smug about the disarming effect I have on women. That, and the fact that her lack of clothes means I can get her out of my place quicker. She only needs to throw her coat back on. If only she knew what I was thinking. Thankfully I am well practised at this and my face doesn't betray what is going through my mind.

Faezeh Farahani works at the Financial Times as a reporter covering Capital Markets and the Banking industry generally. She is often at the same events and conferences as I am and we met at a seminar a few years ago where I was on the panel answering questions from investors. Upon meeting her, I had discovered Faezeh had a hotel room at the summit venue. Her glad eyes told me that she was up for anything. Without much persuasion on my part I had ensured we had made use of that hotel room during each break that day. She has watched my career progress at Caldwell and has always written favourably about me in the paper. I know from experience that she is willing to take what little I offer her while volunteering to me whatever I want in return.

Faezeh is foreign, Iranian, which has always had a strange appeal. Maybe it is the passing resemblance to the Kardashian girls. Her hair is a deep brown, and her eyes are crinkled with crow's feet, the giveaway that she is in her mid-forties. Ten years ago she was probably very attractive. She tries hard to make herself look pretty but there is limited raw material to work with. She has large fake breasts, which are her redeeming feature, sitting round and pert on her chest. They allow me to overlook the cellulite on her thighs as I lift her onto my kitchen counter. She lays her body back and obediently opens her legs. I pull at her panties with one hand while deftly unhooking her bra with the other. I absently think that she should spend more money on her lingerie.

I start running the fingers of one hand in tiny circles around her left breast and she moans on cue, her nipple growing hard to my touch. My groin twitches. Not because this woman turns me on, but because of the power I have over her. I shuffle out of my jeans without taking my hand from her body. I am not wearing any boxer shorts and my erection springs free.

With my other hand I none-too-gently push her lips apart and rub her clitoris. She is already wet. "Have you got any naughty stories to tell me?" I ask her.

She has her head back, writhing slowly under my touch, her breasts barely shifting while her back arches. "I can't stop thinking about you, Patrick. I was so happy you called." My erection fades slightly. I don't want to hear this.

"Have you found another woman for us to play with?" I prompt. My sexual appetite is insatiable and when I know I have a woman under my command I will push her to try things she may never have been willing to before. Faezeh has proven that she will go above and beyond what most woman will do just to stay on side with me. This is as much appealing as it is a turn-off.

"There's a woman at work that I think would be interested," she whispers as her breathing quickens. This is more like it, and the thought of two women simultaneously pleasuring me has the blood rushing back to my cock.

"Tell me about her," I order as I continue to work my fingers around her labia, teasing her, feeling her body succumbing to me. I grab roughly at her large breasts, squeezing her nipples, and she lets out a sharp gasp.

"I would do anything for you, Pat," she says in a husky voice. My annoyance returns unbidden. I don't like to be called Pat by anyone and the thought that this woman thinks we are intimate enough to be calling me by anything other than my full name irks me immensely.

I try once more to keep the conversation on the subject at hand. "What does she look like?" I ask as I slide one finger inside her. I feel her pelvic floor clench and her vagina respond. I quickly move a second finger in and push hard into her wetness.

"She is blonde. Young, about 25, I think. She is attractive, just gorgeous. From the stories she has told me I think she's a filthy bitch." Her voice is ragged as her breath catches as she tries to speak while I continue to push my fingers deep inside her. I can see she is trying hard to be seductive, looking up at me from beneath her eyelashes, hoping to please me.

The picture of another blonde pervades my mind. *Why am I thinking about her?* The thrill of infatuation fills my senses and I suddenly want this woman here with me out of my house as soon as possible.

I grab a condom that earlier I had tactically placed close by, and deftly slide it on. Within moments I am pulling her hips toward me and entering her with hard, sharp thrusts.

I can't get the image of Alexandra Fisher out of my head. I look down at Faezeh pushing herself against me, moaning and contorting her face, her hands gripping each side of the kitchen counter. I block her out of my consciousness. I imagine the lithe form of Alex Fisher instead as my body pushes rhythmically towards an orgasm. I feel the tingling sensations build and the wave of pleasure surge through my groin until I am spent. Underneath me, Faezeh is groaning and whimpering. Perhaps she faked it. I don't really care.

I step away from her, pull on my jeans and let her pick up her underwear. The smell of our sex hangs heavy in the air.

"You seem distracted," she says to me after a moment.

I realise I need to throw her a bone in case I need her again. I put on an appreciative stare and say, with meaning I don't feel, "You were amazing as always, Fuzzy." I see her relax and her eyes light up.

I walk over and kiss her lightly on the mouth. I ask about her job, which sets her off chattering. I am barely listening as my mind shifts to the work I have to do today. At the first appropriate opportunity, I tell her I need to head into the office. I see her face drop momentarily but she quickly gathers herself as she realises there will be no breakfast or niceties. I see her face register that I am asking her to leave.

I gesture toward the front door and tell her the taxi is waiting to take her wherever she needs to go. I walk away, towards my bathroom and hear the front door click as she leaves. I probably should have at least shown her out.

Once showered, I am ready to leave. John, my driver, is waiting to take my briefcase and holds the rear car door open for me. John knows to have the passenger seat wound as far forward as it will go, allowing me to sit in the back and extend my long legs. Being 6'3 has both its advantages and disadvantages. While women love tall men, the basis of natural selection, getting comfortable when travelling is nearly impossible.

My iPhone flashes with a text message. I check it and see there are several unread texts. The most recent one is from Faezeh: 'P, it was truly amazing this morning. I feel unreal. I'll be horny all day thanks to you. F xx'

I cannot believe how desperate some women are. It does them no favours. There will be no reply to her until I think she might be of use again. I quickly scan the other messages. Tanja the masseuse reminding me of my appointment that afternoon. Dave, my best friend, asking me if I'm free for a burger tonight.

I leave my phone and start reading emails on my Blackberry as the BMW saloon glides through Knightsbridge towards the city aiming for the tall modern office buildings of Canary Wharf. It is an icy cold February morning in London and the skies are an unending grey. Stopped at traffic lights on the Thames Embankment, warmed by the BMW's heated reclining seat, I reflect on the hustle and bustle of London. Despite the inclement weather there are still plenty of people walking in the street, rugged up against the cold and huddled under their umbrellas, going about their business.

I go back to reading an important email on the impact of recent Financial Services Authority regulation on bankers' remuneration. A topic close to my heart and one the media both in this country and across the Atlantic are all over. 'Fat cat bankers', they love to report.

My eyes soften and I stop seeing the typeface in front of me. Instead I picture the timid smile of Alexandra Fisher in my mind's eye and my heart beats faster. I noticed her on the first day I had moved into my new office. She sits at a desk on my floor, outside the office of Eloise Little. Eloise is not my biggest fan and the feeling is entirely mutual. I was sure Alex knew who I was but I wanted to engage her in conversation to see how she would respond to the attentions of a rich, powerful, successful man.

The first opportunity I had to introduce myself to her was before an Executive Team meeting in New York, my first, soon after my promotion. She had been polite and professional. There was no hint that she might fancy me. No apparent nerves and certainly no flirting. A cold reaction is not something I am used to getting from a beautiful woman and I feel compelled to correct this. I am at odds. *How is it that this young girl has this effect on me while I have had so little effect on her?*

I arrive at my prized corner office and smile to myself. I have almost made it. Having been recently promoted to the Executive Team of the bank, I am one step away from my ultimate goal, becoming CEO of the company I have worked for my whole career. I joined Caldwell as a graduate on their trading training programme. Back then the bank was predominantly a Retail Banking organisation. Now, the Capital Markets business is a dominant profit-making force and it overshadows its poor cousin, the retail division. Through organic growth and acquisition, Caldwell's Investment Bank has grown into one of the world's leading risk management houses and global financiers, rivalling the Wall Street banks in size, revenue and profile. As the company grew, my aspirations grew with it.

I settle into my tall-backed white leather chair and look at the pile of papers my personal assistant has left on my desk. I grab my iPhone and, still in no mood to reply to any of the earlier text messages, I set music playing instead. Soon, I am in the zone, the music relaxing me as I read and mark up papers in readiness for what the coming week has to bring.

I am so engrossed in what I am doing that I am somewhat startled to realise there is now someone else on the floor. My reverie broken, I look up and realise I cannot see who it is through the privacy frosting of my glass fronted office.

When my new office was being set up, not only did I pick the paint colour for the walls and choose the artwork, but I was also very explicit about the placement of the desk. I wanted to be in a position where I can always discreetly check to see who is coming and going. Making opportunities out of seemingly casual encounters. The spectacular view from the forty-second floor out over the docklands and the city of London holds little appeal for me. This job is all about relationships. Tactical relationships. Of which, I am the master.

I lean down to see between the privacy frosting strips and my heart begins to beat a little quicker. It is she. I smile to myself, thinking of the sex I had this morning, sex I enjoyed for the sole reason that I was visualising her body writhing underneath me.

I feel myself growing hard as I watch the exquisite form of Ms Alexandra Fisher moving across the open plan office toward her desk. If she has noticed me, she is pretending she hasn't. I take in her tousled blonde hair, the simple black figure hugging top, showing the curve of her full breasts, her ripped jeans, skinny and hugging her long legs. My eyes trace from her narrow waist, down her slender thighs and see that her jeans disappear into knee high boots. My erection is now pushing uncomfortably against my fly and my heart is beating fast.

I watch her as she sits, folding one long shapely leg underneath her. She extracts her laptop from her desk drawer, docks it into the monitors sitting on her desk and fires it up. I watch her wrists, her fingers, her hands and a movie reel spins through my head of those hands all over my body, pleasuring me. For a few moments, she sits very still and stares straight ahead. Then without warning she is on her feet striding across to my office.

I swivel my seat so the lower half of my body is hidden by my desk and lean back in my chair in an effort to look nonchalant. I will my body's reaction to seeing her to dissipate. Alexandra Fisher is standing in my doorway, but she is not letting me see the full extent of herself. Unlike our interchange in New York, this time her nerves are palpable. I feel myself breaking into a wide smile.

Alexandra takes two full breaths and then utters, "Hello."

"Hello, Alexandra. What an unexpected pleasure."

Later, as John is driving me back across the city, I reflect on our exchange and I am frustrated that I find myself so infatuated by this girl. She told me that she admires my meteoric rise through the company's ranks and I chuckle to myself and think that this girl is completely unaware of the meteoric rise she caused in my pants by being there this morning.

During the short conversation we had, I offered to take her out to dinner and she had blinked at me and retreated as quickly as she could without being rude. *Does she not find me attractive?* I dismiss that thought from my head as quickly as it arrives.

I feel like I am skating on thin ice. Eloise 'the nut cracker' Little, Alexandra's boss, cannot stand me. I do my best to feign a relationship with her but she is a zealot, and I don't like her. I imagine Eloise thinks that I'm trouble, and will no doubt have heard the tales I know people tell. Everyone loves to talk about the enigmatic Patrick Harrington. Just over forty and never been married. Good looking, successful and made very wealthy by a career in trading followed by elevation into management.

I am also fairly certain that Eloise is annoyed that I have never hit on her. She is one of the few women I cannot bring myself to flirt with. I know that her opinion of me will have some bearing on the reaction I witnessed from Alex but I'm still annoyed. *How am I going to fulfil my desires and fantasies if I cannot even entice Alexandra to go out for a meal with me?*

I feel pent up with frustration. I check my diary and see that I have a massage with my regular masseuse Tanja at 5pm, which is forty-five minutes away. I grab my iPhone and text Tanja. "See you soon sweet lady."

Tanja is Croatian born and very good at what she does. The Notting Hill Spa employs her, which is just across Hyde Park from my Knightsbridge house. Tanja is also stunning, with her closely cropped brown hair and sharp angular features. I tingle at the thought of her strong slender hands rubbing me down with fragrant oils, and the finale of the massage which will be that brunette head bobbing up and down as I watch her take me deep into her throat and I climax. Tanja likes to swallow which pleases me immensely. She also has no misconceptions about what our relationship is: purely transactional. We both get what we want. I relax and she gets paid, handsomely, for an hours work.

Today, the massage and 'happy ending' with Tanja doesn't work its usual magic. That night, after a burger with Dave and his saccharine sweet but dull as dishwater girlfriend I think back to my unexpected office encounter. I am thinking obsessively about Alexandra Fisher. Despite two sexual interactions today I feel wholly unsatisfied and entirely frustrated. I am used to getting what I want.

After jerking myself off to images of Alexandra Fisher acting out my fantasies, I fall into an exhausted sleep in my empty super-king bed. It turned out to be anything but a normal day.

Alexandra

Monotonous days pass, and that Sunday encounter with Patrick Harrington at work begins to feel like it was an eternity ago. I feel like a battery hen. I get up in the dark; I spend what little daylight time there is indoors and then leave for home well after dark. I feel blue. The fun of all the Christmas festivities are over and summer is still months away.

February has turned into March and I am busy as always, with Eloise working on the financials for the Caldwell Annual General Meeting and the materials for presenting to shareholders and investors. I run my fingers down the list of presenters, lingering on Patrick Harrington's name.

The mere thought of him starts butterflies fluttering in my stomach and a pulsing of blood to my groin. I try to push him out of my thoughts, as he is in them constantly these days, but nothing seems to work. I feel a little restless with desire and this makes me feel foolish as I have a doting and loyal boyfriend. Joseph Levy. Loving, stable, dependable Joey. But Joey is driving me nuts. I think that my unfathomable crush on such a powerful and attractive man seems to be influencing my views on my current situation.

Joey and I have been together since I was 20. I had never really had a serious boyfriend before this, and my sexual experiences were limited to a few clumsy drunken trysts and short-lived flings. I was so focused on my studies and enjoying the experience of living away from home that I didn't have time for men. I was scared of being intimate with guys and I did not like to let anyone get too close to me.

Joey and I met at Cambridge University where we were both studying History at Clare College. I was on a partial scholarship and, along with a summer job in a local shoe store, to make ends meet I had secretly tutored secondary school kids in what little spare time I had, despite being against the rules of Cambridge University. Joey's youngest brother Gabriel was one of my students.

The Levy family are wealthy. Joey had never wanted for anything growing up and was part of a strong family unit full of love and laughter. A stark contrast to my family situation and upbringing. His parents had sent their four boys, of which Joey was the oldest, to the renowned Perse School in Cambridge. They still live close by, up the River Cam, in Grantchester Village.

During our time at university, Joey and his friends would go to the same events, 'ents' or 'bops' as the students affectionately call them, as my friends and me. From parties to formal dinners we spent a good deal of our social time moving in the same circles. The weeks would be similar. An average evening would start at a drinking society and end up in one of the many nightclubs in the centre of Cambridge. Fifth Avenue on a Tuesday for example, a seedy club, where you had to queue on the stairs only to get in to find a small bar and a dance floor enhanced with disco balls and mirrors creating shadows like the walls of Hiroshima. The big draw cards were the foam parties and 80s nights.

I have fond memories of Wednesday evenings spent at Life, drinking alcopops, listening to an ageing but amenable DJ before moving on to Toxic8. Thursday night was always spent at Fez Club, with its cosy atmosphere helped by its unique layout of many nooks and crannies, making it perfect for intimate 'conversations'.

And then there were the weekends. Clare Cellars, the seventeenth Century crypt, was popular on a Saturday night for break beats and hip-hop, or for a themed party; 'Beach Night' where the girls would turn up in bikinis and little else, or 'Back to School Night' for short uniforms, pigtails and school ties.

I think back now and wonder how I managed to make my grades and keep my jobs in between all the frenetic socialising. I also wonder how many experiences I missed out on, having maintained a level of innocence - or even perhaps ignorance - where men and intimacy were concerned. I had been so cautious at university.

Joey and I were friends for the first two years at Cambridge. Joey had a girlfriend for much of this time, but we would often end an evening comparing our nights out in front of the 'Vans of Life and Death', the two mobile units dispensing kebabs, burgers and chips to drunken students until 3am every morning. In the pre-dawn hours, the heart of Cambridge takes on a ghostly, desolate air, and the market square with its two vans becomes, for better or worse, the animated centre of post-closing-time social life.

It wasn't until my final year that we became an item, much to the delight of Gabriel and the wider Levy clan. It was 'Suicide Sunday': the last Sunday of the summer term and the start of May Week and the term break. We had finished our exams but the results had not been published, so it is traditionally a period of nerves and suspense for students. The day is named as such to mark the celebration that students haven't committed suicide due to the stress of exams.

We were both at the much anticipated 7am Suicide Sunday cocktail party. By lunchtime, Joey was pretty drunk and brimming with Dutch courage. He had been following me around attentively for much of the day, checking on my drink and making sure I was okay. We had ended up, just the two of us, having a curry at the Star of India in the early evening after a full day of drinking. We had laughed and enjoyed each other's company. The next day, as I was on my way out of the college, walking through the porter's lodge, I found that Joey had left an invitation to the opulent Trinity Ball for me in my pigeonhole.

I had accepted the invitation, much to the envy of my friends. At £430 per ticket it was the most expensive of the May Week balls and the one that everyone wanted to attend. It was out of my league based on the ticket price alone and to try to look the part I had to borrow a suitable ball gown from a friend. Thankfully, my job at the shoe store with its generous staff discount allowed me to buy a stunning pair of heels for the occasion that ordinarily I would never have been able to justify to myself.

The ball, held every year since 1866, was notorious for being lavish. It featured a five-course meal served in Trinity Great Hall, free-flowing champagne and an open bar. The night was traditionally concluded with a spectacular fireworks display.

After the pyrotechnics, we had walked arm-in-arm to the river. I remember gathering up the length of my dress, and we had clambered into a punt. The sun was just beginning to come up. My hair, sleek and pinned at the beginning of the evening, was now a dishevelled mess. Joey was happy, jubilant even, and was tender with his touches and looks. We lay together in contented exhaustion, Joey's arms wrapped protectively around me, as we made our way down the River Cam, to enjoy breakfast in the college gardens. As the punt moved downriver, Joey was stroking my hair, my cheek and before I knew what was happening he had turned my face gently towards his and leaned down to kiss me. Softly at first, and then harder, with longing and intensity. I felt a rush of unfamiliar emotion as our lips parted. I felt safe and loved.

The fact is the tie I have to Joseph is as much emotional as it is obligatory. The irony of Joey and I starting our relationship on Suicide Sunday is not lost on me. During my final year of university, my father took his own life in circumstances as shocking as they were tragic.

I still remember the chilly November Tuesday when the ringing of my phone pierced my dreams at around 3am. My mother, hysterical, was trying to tell me between retching sobs that my father was dead. Despite having been estranged from my father for close to a decade, she had the police on her doorstep, asking her to come and identify the body of a man who had been found naked, hanging from a tree, in a forest in Kent. She had called me immediately, distraught, asking for me to come home at once and Joseph had been the one I had turned to. He had taken control, packing a bag for me, commandeering his mother's car and driving me back to London as the sun crept slowly over the horizon. I wept as if my world had ended. He never left my side as the horror of what my father had done was revealed. We have been together ever since, moving down to London together after graduation and moving into a contemporary two bedroom open-plan apartment, in a purpose built building just off the river in Putney, South West London.

Though my hurt and pain are not as raw, I still flinch as I think of how, as the story of my father's death had unfolded, so did a minor media frenzy given the bizarre and sexual nature of his death. It was so bad I contemplated taking my mother's maiden name to escape the taint of the Fisher surname. In the end I didn't have the heart to insult my father in this way, even in death, so put up with the speculative enquiries and frankly inappropriate comments that strangers and acquaintances felt compelled to make.

My father, Eric Fisher, had suffered from depression for as long as I can remember. It had driven a wedge through my parent's marriage and made my childhood memorable for all the wrong reasons. The police had told us that my father had paid two escort girls to meet him in the forest, pose as executioners, and act out a hanging. The women maintain he had insisted that he would be wearing a safety harness.

When they arrived at the designated meeting point in the forest they had found him in a noose, standing on a wooden step. Believing it was all part of an elaborate sex game, they said they left him momentarily to return to their car to get whips, chains and riding crops, the bondage instruments he had requested, before returning to find that he had jumped off the step with no harness on after all.

It transpired that my father had previously and frequently taken girls from a local escort agency in Bexley to the wood on Dartford Heath, in Kent, for sadomasochist games. The escort agency told us that a couple of weeks before he died he had as many as six girls out in the woods and he had paid them to abuse him.

On the night of his death, he had contacted the agency again and sent a text saying he wanted a couple of girls to meet him up on the Heath.

He said in his message 'I want them to pretend they are executioners who are going to kill me.' When the girls got there he was sobbing with the noose already around his neck. They were adamant he was still very much alive and standing on the step when they left him.

Apparently, they had walked away laughing and thought it was all just a weird fantasy, something which they often observed in their line of work. But when they came back they noticed he was swinging and his lips had turned blue. They called an ambulance immediately and tried to free him but it was too late.

My mother had, of course, known about my father's masochist tendencies. For me, it was a complete shock and completely shattered my reality. Not only did I have to deal with the sorrow and grief of losing my father in a sudden and tragic way, but I also had to reconcile his predilection for receiving pain and humiliation with the image I had of him as my father. I was, and remain, haunted that he had been in such a dark place that he thought the only way out was to end his life.

My own sexual experience, and my experience of men more generally, is limited, but it is enough to know that Joey adores me and that compared to other relationships I hold as examples, including my parents and most of my friends, I should count myself lucky. The passion in our relationship has long since ebbed, however, and we behave more as friends and housemates than lovers. Lately, when we do have sex, it is perfunctory and unremarkable. And recently, to make matters worse, I have been pushing thoughts of Patrick Harrington out of my mind when Joey is touching me. I do love Joey, but I wonder if I'm still in love with him.

He and I have been talking a lot recently about my restlessness. I am naturally impatient and want to progress my career and I don't think Joey understands this. He has a good job as a commercial lawyer for Clifford Chance, one of London's 'Magic Circle' law firms. He works hard but is not particularly ambitious and seems happy with what he has achieved. *An easy position to take when you come from a wealthy family and have never had to go without*, I think unkindly.

I push him constantly to try to encourage him to think longer term, to raise his profile at work and build relationships with the senior partners. He is just not interested and shuts me down every time I try to enquire about his work, knowing that it will inevitably lead to an argument. It stops me wanting to talk about my own ambitions, which may explain why I dumped my career aspirations on Patrick Harrington.

I have seen Patrick in the office from a distance but we have not crossed paths again. I think to myself that I must have imagined that there was anything in that exchange and that he certainly didn't mean to ask me out. How absurd.

Then it happens. Due to the plethora of papers on my desk I almost missed the crisp white parchment envelope marked 'Private' with my name written in elegant script using a fountain pen across its front, left for me to find.

With trembling hands, I open it. My breathing quickens as I see the simple white card with 'Patrick F. Harrington' in neat black embossing across the top. I steal a glance around the office before extracting the card that I can see bears the same lovely handwriting as the envelope. I feel light-headed and pray that it is not something related to work.

'Alexandra,

I wanted to let you know that everyone on the forty-second floor appreciates you. I hear excellent things about you and I know that you have a bright future at Caldwell. On a personal note, if you ever wish to have dinner with me to discuss your career, my private email address is PFH2104@gmail.com.'

It is signed with a grand gesture, a large looping P and an H with one vertical flicking out in a flourish.

I realise that I have been holding my breath. Patrick Harrington is asking me out for the second time. The numbers in his email address are the day and month of his birthday. Our birthday. Everything about the card is perfect.

Harrington

Monotonous days pass, and that Sunday encounter with Alexandra Fisher at work begins to feel like it was an eternity ago. I have had no shortage of women to keep me entertained but I am consumed by a longing for Alex, to the point of being fixated on my initial objective of taking her out on a date.

Yesterday, I had an unexpected invitation from a couple I met during my recent Christmas break in Mustique. They were in London briefly, en route to Paris and wanted to catch up.

I have spent the last three Christmases in Mustique, as I have no desire to be with my family in Ireland. Staying in cold, grey London bustling with happy holiday shoppers and tourists holds no appeal. I am used to vacationing on my own and actually, I quite enjoy it. Time for solitude, and when I do want company I can usually find it. There is plenty to do on the island including the usual past times of the wealthy: golf, tennis, diving, and sailing and of course 'being seen'. I enjoy holidaying alongside other successful businessmen, fashion designers and rock stars. Last year I had been in the company of Paul Allen, Tom Ford and Mick Jagger to name but a few. Mr Jagger gives me a run for my money as the god of all things sexual. This swaggering big-

27

lipped rocker frequently tries to get 'satisfaction' with women younger than his daughter. Goddamn.

The beautiful 5-star Cotton House Hotel, the only hotel on the island, is where I stay. Taking a villa on my own would be a tad too reclusive, even for me. The Cotton House hoteliers pride themselves on their discretion and do all they can to create a sense of exclusivity. Their staff remember you by name and will do whatever it takes to ensure you have a wonderful stay. Ideally for me, the hotel is the island's social hub. Villa owners and visitors mingle there as a central meeting point.

Mustique is a tiny island, and every beach, restaurant, activity and bar is only minutes away by a mule, of the mechanical kind: an easy-to-drive, four-seater, souped-up golf cart.

For me the appeal of Mustique lies in its contradictions. It's sophisticated yet natural, Caribbean casual yet Upper East Side elegant, endlessly social yet perfectly private.

It attracts other wealthy people like me. I met the Edelsteins on the 19 of December when Ephraim Edelstein had sent a bottle of Ruinart Blanc de Blancs to my table. They had seen me eating alone for the days preceding and this was his way of introducing himself. From that day on, I spent much of my two and a half week holiday with the Edelsteins, including seeing in the New Year with them at Firefly's Martini Club. They had rented a villa on the island but spent quite a lot of time at Cotton House for the social aspect, and to ensure their children had other kids to play with.

Ephraim Edelstein is one half of the Edelstein brothers, who are well-known jewellery and art dealers from New York. His wife, Lizzy, is a bewitching and gorgeous woman fifteen years his junior. At 36 she is the picture of health, with a tight, fit body despite bearing three children to Ephraim. Her glossy platinum blonde tresses fall in soft waves down her back, with long layers at the front framing her heart-shaped face. Her skin is a healthy golden brown in spite of leaving New York in the midst of its winter.

Unsurprisingly, Lizzy is dripping in diamonds and exotic gemstones. She is always immaculately turned out, be it lounging by the pool in tiny Pucci bikinis and wedges, or donning body hugging Alaïa dresses and sky scrapper Giuseppe Zanotti heels for the regular Tuesday evening cocktail party at Cotton

House. Lizzy is always happy. Appropriate. Animated, witty and engaging she holds her own in conversation, while respecting her husband and giving him the space to assert his power and dominance. I think she might just be the perfect woman and the fact that she is married doesn't deter me in the slightest. It is a challenge and all the more appealing.

In that first week I had worked hard to build up Ephraim's trust while being polite but standoffish toward Liz. It was a well-practised routine that, as always, paid off. On Christmas Eve, Ephraim retired to their villa and left Liz and I alone to our nightcaps. After Eph had turned in for the evening, it didn't take me long to persuade Liz to come back to my bungalow and we were giggling and kissing like high school teenagers from the second we were out of public view.

As our mouths moved in time with each other I raked my fingers through her glorious hair. Liz's lips moved from my face, down my neck, and all I could think was how good it was to have the opportunity to fuck another man's wife.

She had unbuttoned my shirt and pushed down my Vilebrequin swimming shorts, all the while complimenting me on my athletic body. I knew she had been admiring me from behind her oversized designer sunglasses in the previous days.

Liz had lowered herself to her knees, caressing my inner thighs and grazing past my balls and teasing me with each exquisite stroke. My erection, freed from my shorts, was large and throbbing in front of her face. She was panting from the passionate kissing and her unbridled desire for me.

Suddenly she had grabbed my cock roughly and pulled the head of my throbbing penis into her mouth, beginning to suck, slowly at first, with rhythmic movements. Her hands moved to my balls and gently she inserted a finger into the rim of my anus, probing a little and rubbing around the edge. Her mouth alternated between my shaft, my head, my balls, and all the while rubbing with increasing intensity around my perineum. Her wedding and engagement rings glinting as they caught the light as her hands expertly moved around my groin. She was intense, wild and determined.

I looked down at her platinum blonde head moving softly, then fiercely and knew that I was going to have a mind-blowing orgasm. She pulled her head back for a moment to look me in the eye, before spitting on my penis for extra lubrication. Her hands were moving in circles up and down my shaft while her tongue flipped around my head. I was curling my toes and my eyes began to glaze over as the energy built. I felt her take me deep into her throat and I couldn't contain myself. I reached forward to tap her on the head, as I didn't want her to think I expected her to swallow. As she moved her head back in response, I felt the full force of my climax exploding out of me. Liz reacted quickly and took me back into her mouth and sucked me until I was done, swallowing. I was quivering all over.

Afterwards, we were sitting on the couch, having replaced our clothing, smiling at each other. She had told me that she and Ephraim rarely have intercourse but that he demands regular fellatio, which explained why this woman, who married a rich man at a young age, is so good at oral sex. Liz began to tell me more about their marriage and I realised that she was actually quite intoxicated.

She had gone to make a move to my bed and, realising with horror that she was going to lie down, I had grabbed her arm and steered her outside. I could feel her shoulders shaking and I knew then that she was crying. For god's sake, I had thought to myself, irritated. Crying is a major buzz killer. At least the tears came after I did.

"I've never cheated on Eph before. I feel terrible," she had stammered between sobs. "But I'm not sexually satisfied and I find you irresistible." The words were coming out thick and slurred and looking at her wet face ruined my post orgasm high.

I had calmed her down by wrapping my strong arms around her and uttering soothing words. I had walked her some of the way back to her villa, conscious that she might try to kiss me again. I did not want to be seen by her husband or any of their three kids. I watched as she stumbled up the driveway, toward the front door.

It was Christmas the next day, and I did not see the Edelsteins. I was not concerned as being Jewish they were celebrating the eight days of Hanukkah which happened to fall in late December that year. It was several days before I saw Ephraim again. He had walked purposefully toward me. Although not physically threatened by this man, or even that I care, I experienced that fleeting thought - *have I been rumbled?*

Eph greets me warmly and I know that I have once again got away with it. It's not a crime if you don't get caught. He asks about my Christmas and invites me to join him and the family on his yacht for a day trip. I politely decline.

That same afternoon, a note was delivered to me while I lay poolside. Liz had sent me her mobile phone number and her email address, an Edelstein Brothers account. I smiled to myself. I had been thinking about the encounter with Lizzy but had written her off after the emotional display she had put on. This note had piqued my interest and I put her firmly back on my agenda, knowing that I could fuck her when I was in New York and not have to worry too much about intimacy. She was another man's wife, after all, and that was his problem.

I look back on that first encounter and realise that it was not hard to persuade Lizzy to keep cheating on Eph. We connected on Blackberry messenger, after agreeing that email was too dangerous, and engineered a couple of clandestine trysts when I was in New York for business trips in the New Year. We had managed to get through the rest of the holiday without touching each other. I did convince her to send me salacious photos of herself to ensure she whet my appetite. I realised that playing the long game with Liz was a better use of my time and would reap better rewards. In any event, Sophie the Swedish bar girl was more than happy to service me for the rest of my trip.

The last time Liz and I were together in New York, she had been emphatic that we must not continue our affair. She had stopped the continuous thread of messages on BBM and the naked photos had dried up. It was no great shakes to me, other than losing a certain fuck when stateside. Liz had been tearful and childlike. She had made me promise to stay away from her and Ephraim. So I am surprised when I get an email announcing that they are both in town and wish to have dinner with me.

We plan to meet at the Connaught Hotel in Mayfair for a drink before walking up Mount Street to dine at Scott's, my favourite seafood restaurant. I smile as I walk through the large revolving door of the hotel, marvelling at the beauty of the old building, with its sweeping curved frontage. When I enter the Coburg Bar, I find Lizzy waiting on her own, sitting in one of the soft armchairs by the wall. She looks at once both ravishingly beautiful and decidedly nervous. She sees me walk in and moves her head to stare upward at the beautifully ornate ceiling and seems momentarily transfixed by the art deco chandelier. She glances at me and then away again. "Eph has been held up with an art dealer over on Albemarle Street, but he'll join us later at the restaurant," she tells me, her voice husky with obvious desire. Now she is studying the hexagon-patterned carpet. I can tell that she still has feelings for me and is pent up with sexual frustration, to the point where she can barely look me in the eye.

I glance around and spot Mathieu, the bar manager, dressed in the smart old world uniform the waiters are required to wear. He has not seen me. I bring many women to the two bars at the Connaught Hotel for drinks. I offer my hand to Liz and lift her out of her chair. I need to get her out of here, as I don't want Mathieu or one of the other waiters being overly familiar with me and freaking Liz out before I've had what I want.

She follows me through the oak doors and on to the reception desk where I ask for a room. All the while, Liz remains silent. We both know we don't have much time. We tumble into the impeccably decorated suite as soon as I have the door open, neither of us appreciating the finely appointed room with its brocade soft furnishings, expensive lamps and heavy drapes.

Liz is hitching up her skirt and pushing her panties down. I lower my trousers and push her hard onto the crisply made white bed coverings. She lets out a gasp. Buoyed by the knowledge that I have the upper hand, I am feeling dominant and climb onto the large bed, straddling her. I yank her top up and tug her bra down to expose her hard pink nipples. She is giving me a startled and slightly frightened look, which I confess I enjoy. I roll a condom on and gently push just the tip of my penis inside her. Her bra is still on her body with her breasts pushing up over the top of the lacy fabric. Neither of us has uttered a word since leaving the bar.

I am suddenly consumed by disgust for this woman. Willing to be doted on by her loving husband, a decent man and a good father yet also happy to allow me to fuck her at the drop of a hat. Slut.

I wait just a moment, staring into her eyes with as much intensity as I can garner, before thrusting into her with all my might. She cries out, throwing her head back exposing the creamy skin of her neck. I feel myself get rock hard as blood rushes to my cock. I grab her legs and hoist them toward the ceiling while pushing her ankles apart. Her arse is off the bed and her weight is bearing down on her shoulder blades pushing her breasts upwards. I grind my hips into her pelvis, back and forth repeatedly, with as much pressure as I can muster. I am in complete control and relish the power I am feeling over Liz.

I feel sweat beading on my forehead as I keep pushing her legs further apart so I can penetrate deep inside her. I have not warmed her up but if she cares she doesn't show it. She arches her back as I slide all the way out pausing for a microsecond before slamming myself back into her. She is grunting and squealing, her fists gripping the bed coverings, as her orgasm takes hold. I feel myself getting close to ejaculation and pull out. With a flip of my wrist the condom is off and I rub myself until I come all over her face and chest. She looks horrified but says nothing.

Later over dinner, I reflect that my attraction to Lizzy is waning. Of course she is gorgeous and I love the naughtiness of our forbidden endeavours but I know I have conquered this challenge. Besides, I still can't stop thinking about Alexandra Fisher.

Earlier that day, before leaving the office for an external meeting, I had taken a chance while Eloise and Alexandra were busy in Eloise's office, and her PA was away from her desk. I surreptitiously placed an envelope under a pile of papers on Alexandra's workspace, smiling to myself as I noticed close to a dozen pairs of high-heeled shoes lined up neatly under her desk. An assortment, from plain black patent heels by LK Bennett, and stylish, office appropriate Manolo Blahniks, to a more eccentric looking pair by the Belgian designer Dries Van Noten. *Not a bad collection,* I think, *but nothing bedroom worthy.* She is sensible at work but I have a sneaking suspicion there is a wild sexual creature bursting to break out from behind those doe eyes, and I am just the man to set her free.

I notice there are no photos on display. No evidence of a boyfriend or husband. I spy a 'one a day' shoe calendar near her monitor and smile to myself. *I like this girl more and more.*

I had written the card three times, ripping each one up and starting again before finalising the wording. I was careful to ensure it could be interpreted as purely professional if for some reason she took offence to it. I feel good. Everything about the card is perfect.

Alexandra

I am counting the days since the card was left on my desk. I am noticeably preoccupied. Eloise comments several times that I seem distracted. I realise that I am allowing myself to daydream about dinner with Patrick and then, to make matters worse, my romantic heart plays out scenarios of where the dinner might lead... I do like the sound of Alexandra Harrington.

Relations between Joey and I are more strained than ever. He seems to know intuitively that something is up. If I am honest with myself, there has been something missing in our relationship for the better part of the past year. I think back to Christmas time, where the cracks were starting to show to others.

The Levy family always go away in December and it is expected that Joseph and I will join them. Being an only child, and with my mother being on her own, this always puts me in a difficult position. My mother is invited to join us but she never would. Since my father's death, she has shut the world out. The years of being married to him took their toll on her confidence and chipped away at her positive outlook. Now, she is a shell of a woman who doesn't interact with the outside world, other than with me, and even then I have to force the issue. The money she received as the sole beneficiary of my father's life insurance policy had enabled her to be free from the necessity to work. This was just as well given her fragile state. She had paid her mortgage off years before and lived meagrely. I sometimes transferred money into her savings account and this would occur without comment from either of us.

I had decided that I would let Joey go away with his family, to a resort on the Red Sea, in Egypt, without me. His family had been astonished, and I had both Gabriel and Joey's dad on the phone to me trying to persuade me to change my mind. They had been forthright in asking what the problem was. I had been angry that Joe had not smoothed the path for me but then he was too deeply hurt about the decision I had made. I had told his family that my mother needed me. I knew that they didn't buy it as I had left her in the UK on her own over the festive period in previous years. Even while my mother was stuck in a funk, she was clear-sighted enough to encourage me to make the most of the opportunities in my life.

I had spent the break just outside London, staying with my Mum in her semi-detached house, backing onto the railway tracks, out in Epsom, Surrey. It had been a relatively happy time for us both. Eloise was in California, at her house in Malibu, and this afforded me much of the day free from interruption, without emails or calls given the time difference.

My mum and I had had a nice blend of quiet days in her house, drinking tea and listening to the radio. We had also managed several outings into the city, including a visit to the National Portrait Gallery, and a day of shopping before ice-skating at Somerset House. We had laughed and smiled together more over that week than I can ever remember. I think she had realised that it was okay to leave her postcode and that she was entitled to have some joy in her life. I had realised that the space and time apart from Joseph had suited me just fine and I was relishing the breathing space.

So much can happen in a short space of time. Fast-forward several months and the card from Patrick Harrington is being carted around in my handbag. I did not want to leave it at work and I was too scared to put it anywhere in the flat that Joey and I shared.

My heart was aching. I knew that regardless of the card and all it might imply, I was in a relationship. I couldn't possibly accept this dinner date. *Or could I?*

Every fibre in my being wanted to write to the remarkable Patrick Harrington and tell him that I thought he was wonderful and that it would be an absolute pleasure to dine with him. *It was only a dinner and maybe he wasn't even thinking about it as a date, but genuinely as an opportunity to give me some career advice?*

At home that evening, five days after receiving the card, I sit down at my laptop to compose an email in response. I had decided to accept the dinner invitation; it is just dinner after all. I am the one letting my overactive imagination play out what might be possible. I will eat with this man and use it as a chance to get advice from someone I admire who is clearly successful. Nothing more.

I turn the luxurious card over and over in my hand and I smile to myself thinking about the impact of little touches such as personalised stationery. A real statement of certainty, of confidence.

I type out a polite response and stare at it, checking every word, comma and line break. I don't wish to appear too keen or give away any hint that I have been having scandalous thoughts ever since that Sunday encounter. Mischievously, I add a subject line 'From the personalised (electronic) stationery of Alexandra Fisher'. I take a deep breath and hit send.

I walk through to the kitchen, and see Joey lying on the couch watching TV. His dinner dishes are everywhere and he has kicked his shoes and socks off. His suit jacket and tie are piled in a heap next to his discarded shoes. I sigh audibly. I feel like I might explode. Joey's mother has always dutifully taken care of her husband and four boys to the point where Joseph has come to expect the same from me. It's as though he thinks mess gets tidied up as if by magic. It feels like he doesn't respect me, just assuming that I will pick up after him.

I watch him for a while and feel a little repulsed. He is watching the Simpsons. An episode I know he has seen several times. He is not even laughing. He tells me that watching television relaxes him. I find it has the opposite effect on me. His choice of television programmes reminds me of how different he is in every way to the sophisticated Patrick Harrington. I feel as though I am dating someone who is almost childlike, all the while being tantalised by a man.

I turn and walk out. I don't know if he heard me come into the room and he did not acknowledge me if he did. This is how it has been. We both work long hours and then come home and simply exist in the same house. Gone are the days where we would commute to and from work together, eager to spend every possible second together. I always arrive home later than Joe. He used to wait to eat with me in the evenings, or at least save me some food but even this has long since stopped. I see now with clarity that it doesn't bother me. I am surprised that this didn't become something else for us to fight about and instead, it seems we have both accepted it as an inevitable outcome of our growing apart.

I head upstairs to run myself a bath. As I cross the threshold into the bathroom I see used towels on the floor, along with Joe's dirty workout clothes from that morning. Ungraciously, he has left an all-but empty toilet roll still on the holder. I seethe with rage. Nowhere in our flat is there a place where I feel like I can seek sanctuary. The bedroom contains an unmade bed, the kitchen and living areas are strewn with items that shouldn't be there and the bathroom looks like a bombsite.

I am fed up. I stomp back downstairs. This time when I enter the room Joey looks up briefly and then goes back to the stupid yellow cartoons with their annoying voices on the screen. I walk over and grab the remote and switch the TV off. He sits up in surprise and looks at me wide eyed. I am never deliberately confrontational.

"I can't take this any more, Joe." I am shaking, with all my pent up emotions threatening to burst out, yet I feel an eerie sense of calm at the same time.

He stands up and moves to hug me in a conciliatory gesture. I step back. He is surprised. My body language is saying everything I am too afraid to say. I don't trust myself to open my mouth.

He looks hurt and stares at me for a moment before asking me what exactly it is that I can't take. Without any order to my thoughts, a catalogue of the petty little things he has done wrong tumble forth, concluding with the state of the flat and how there is not one inch of space that allows me to feel peaceful or relaxed after a long day at the office.

"I think you're being a drama queen, Alex. I can pick up my things while you have a long soak in the tub and it'll be fine. You'll feel much better afterwards. You work too hard and always come home drained of any energy. That job gets the best of you and there is nothing left over for me."

I am incensed. *How can he make this about what I am not giving him? And blaming my job?* It is more than I can bear.

"Joseph," I yell a little too loudly. "This isn't just about clothes on the floor and an unmade bed. You and I both know it goes deeper than that. We don't act in a loving way towards each other and haven't done so for a long time. I feel lonely and trapped."

I see his brow furrow as he takes in what I have said. The hurt is evident in his eyes.

"Well, maybe I should just move out then." His attitude is flippant.

Surprising myself, and him, I respond, "I think that'd be a good idea."

We spend the rest of the evening on the couch. Not touching, both crying, reflecting on our relationship and how we got to where we are. Neither of us raises the idea of reconciliation or of trying to make it work. It feels odd to be so candid with Joey after all these months of us both skirting around the issues. We talk about how to break the news to the Levy family, which brings on another round of tears. My heart is breaking and I watch Joey in pieces before me. I wish I could take his pain away but at the same time I know we are doing the right thing.

At work the next day, Eloise calls me into her office as soon as she arrives. "What's wrong with you?" she quizzes me unceremoniously. I am constantly impressed at how much this woman can read from faces and body language. She had all of thirty seconds as she passed by my desk to get to her office. I tell her that Joey and I had broken up the night before and that he is in the process of arranging to move out. Her face softens slightly.

"Don't let him hang about, Alexandra." Eloise has always maintained that Joseph was not the man for me. Her opinion is that I should be with someone more motivated, more dynamic, and more charismatic. If only she knew who I was planning to have dinner with.

Then it is back to business as she removes papers from her

bag and starts talking about the things I need to do. I am pleased for the distraction and am relieved that I am out of the spotlight.

Back at my desk, I see that I have a 'C-chat' message. Caldwell-chat or C-chat is Caldwell Bank's internal instant messaging system. It is from Patrick Harrington and it is short and to the point. 'Check your personal email please.'

I quickly close the pop up window and change my status to 'away' as I don't want anyone walking by my screen to see that I am in a chat conversation with the Head of the Investment Bank.

I grab my phone and head to the ladies room. I lock myself into a cubicle. I put the toilet lid down and sit down heavily. With trembling hands, I refresh my email and see that Patrick sent me two messages within an hour of my email to him last night. I had been so immersed in breaking up with Joey that I had not even thought to check my email for a response. I guess Patrick doesn't mess around and doesn't take kindly to waiting.

'Why thank you Ms Fisher, I was delighted to get your email and will make arrangements for us to dine at Shanghai Blues on Friday night at 7pm. Please confirm. PH.'

The next one asks me if I was surprised that he had left the card on my desk. I check the calendar in my phone and see that I am due to catch up with the girls on Friday night. *I will cry off* I think. In any case, I can't bear the thought of the interrogation that will inevitably follow once I announce the news about Joey and me.

I reply in haste, 'See you on Friday. I was surprised to get your card. Thanks, Alex.'

I am buzzing from the interaction and feel a sense of anxious anticipation. Friday is four days away. *Was I too keen to accept the first offer? Should I have played harder to get?*

No, I think. *It is only dinner and in any event, I am not in the right headspace for games.* I write to my best friend Candice to let her know that work will prohibit me from joining the planned girls' night. They all know that I need to be available at Eloise's whim and as a result they are used to me being the last to turn up to social occasions, if I turn up at all.

I return to my inbox and I am amazed to see that Patrick has written back to me already. 'Pleasantly?' is all it says.

'Yes.' I type.

Again, he is right back to me. 'Well, I am glad I did it then. There will be a black BMW saloon car waiting for me outside the building at 6.30pm if you wish to travel to the restaurant with me. PH.'

I smile to myself. I know that I have a major crush and that I am getting myself into a potentially dangerous situation but I feel more alive than I have in a long time.

Harrington

I am counting the days since I left the card on Alexandra's desk. I am noticeably preoccupied. Last week, my PA commented several times that I seem distracted. I realise that I am allowing myself to fantasise about dinner with Alex Fisher and then to make matters worse my imaginative mind plays out scenarios of where the dinner might lead... I do like the thought of having dirty sex with Alexandra Fisher.

I have been refreshing my personal email on my iPhone and iPad constantly waiting to see her name in my inbox. *Why is she taking so long to reply?* I am single-minded about getting this woman to go out with me to the point where this objective is consuming me. I can be obsessive when it comes to bedding woman but this is the worst I have been in a long time. I am used to getting what I want, when I want it.

I grab my iPad and log into Facebook. I have my own account despite the advice of the media team at the bank not to do so. I mollified them by agreeing not to post any photos or comments. They worry that Facebook may be an outlet for unhappy customers or investors to vent but I have my privacy settings so locked down that nobody can find me. I don't use it in the way it was intended, to socially network, and I have no desire to broadcast about my life. Instead, I like to 'friend' women I sleep with who I may wish to sleep with again. It allows me some insight into their lives saving me valuable time. Sometimes what I see puts me off, including inane status updates or terrible photos, and worst of all, evidence of children. Other times, the 'over-sharing' of raunchy photographs raises their position on my priority list a few notches.

I type Alexandra Fisher into the search box. The search returns a number of results but it is easy for me to pick her out. Her profile photo is a close-up headshot, of her smiling into the camera with the wind sweeping a few wayward strands of her blonde hair across her eyes. I click on the Alexandra Fisher I want and her profile page comes up with no restrictions. I can see her timeline and know that I will be able to view her photos. *Foolish*, I think, while at the same time being pleased to have this opportunity to get better aquatinted with the object of my desire.

I double-click on her profile picture to enlarge it. It is a stunning photo. She is laughing, her beautiful face is lit up, her brown eyes are sparkling and she looks relaxed and happy. I then scan through her profile page to see her recent activity. It seems she is a regular user of this social networking site and I follow threads of comments she has made on her friend's walls, along with witty status updates to her own profile. I am reminded that there is an age gap as I scan the banter. More than once she gives me a chuckle with her quick witted, somewhat dry responses to her friends' comments. I click on the 'info' panel and my interest turns to irritation as I note that her status shows she is 'in a relationship'.

I start looking through her photo albums. A trip to Japan with a girlfriend, one Candice Stapleton. While Alex looks lovely, I grow bored of seeing touristy shots of her and her friend in front of temples and shrines. It is the boyfriend I wish to see. My stomach clenches at the thought of competition and I swallow hard as I navigate through more photos. It doesn't take me long to find him.

Joseph Levy. I try to get to his page from the photo 'tag' but his privacy settings are better than hers. I have to be content with no more information than his name. I go through several albums looking intensely at their body language and sizing him up.

He is not much taller than her, with dark hair and a pleasant demeanour. He looks like he is no trouble to anyone. Mundane. There is a photo of them lying side-by-side, together in a hammock, outside a beach hut in Palolem, Goa. She looks amazing in a white bikini, with sun-kissed skin and salt-tousled hair. I note with annoyance that he has a well-defined upper body, with broad shoulders, muscular arms, and a six-pack. He clearly works out regularly. I keep myself fit and I am lean but I don't have the time to devote to sculpting my body to this extent. It has never concerned me until now. He clearly doesn't have a successful career if he has that much time to pump iron. This thought makes me feel slightly better.

I look at photo after photo and all the while my ire grows. I note that he has a tattoo on his left arm. It starts at his shoulder and wraps around his bicep ending near his elbow. I concede with vexation that it is somewhat tasteful, as far as tattoos go, rather than trashy. I am surprised that Alex would choose a guy like this. *Is this her type?* He is the polar opposite of me.

Clearly Joseph adores her from the puppy dog look I see repeatedly directed at her as I flick through the pictures. There are many travel photos of the two of them, on a long boat on the Mekong Delta in Vietnam, cycling in the hills of Tuscany, and smiling happily at the camera from a bar in Obispo, Havana. Alex has carefully captioned all her photos, which allows me to be both voyeuristic and know exactly what I am looking at.

There are other pictures, family dinners, birthdays, and outings with friends. I cannot look at any more of these photos. It is clear they have been together for some time from the pictorial evidence.

I don't want Alex for anything more than pleasure but for some reason the fact that she has a boyfriend has disconcerted me. My quest may be more difficult than I had anticipated. I feel pangs of jealously deep in my stomach, which unnerves me. Spouses, boyfriends, or any attachment has never concerned me in the past but I fear Alex is the steadfastly loyal type. The challenge is immense, which thrills me, but at the same time a small voice that I can't quieten is planting the idea that this woman may be out of my reach. I find it hard to believe that there is any woman out there that is unobtainable.

I go back to the overview of albums and scan the ones that I have not dipped into. My eyes land on one entitled 'Eric Fisher memorials'. I open and scan the collection of photos and read the album description, 'Faces hide as much as they reveal, and things aren't always what they seem. Eric Fisher took his own life tragically on 27 November 2007. Beloved son of Frank and Audrey, husband of Julie and much loved father of Alexandra.' I am curious about the choice of quote but can't glean anything more about the circumstances surrounding her father's death.

I log out of Facebook feeling good about the amount of information I have secretly obtained about Alex Fisher. My mood is mixed though as I think of the smiling pictures of Joseph Levy and the insight into the death of her father.

I refresh my mail again for the umpteenth time. The swirling circle shows me mail is downloading and I feel jubilant when I see her name in my inbox. I knew she would reply to the card although it has been almost a week, which is longer than I had anticipated having to wait.

I look at the subject line 'From the personalised (electronic) stationery of Alexandra Fisher'. She is mocking me. Making reference to the fact that the card I had left for her was on my personalised stationery. Cheeky. A good sign for me as it indicates she is willing to be playful, even flirty.

I open the email.

'Hi,

Thanks for the card you left on my desk last week. I would be delighted to have dinner with you - it would be good to continue the career conversation we started. On the basis I am a mere mortal, while you are clearly busy with your plans for world domination, I will leave it over to you to suggest some dates.

Stay cool,

Alex.'

I can't help but really like this girl. I immediately reply even though her email was only sent an hour or so before. I don't follow the same rules as the rest of the populace when it comes to chasing women. I am so well practised at this that I know they love the attention, and the fact that I am rich and powerful will usually outweigh any issue they feel about the relentlessness of my pursuit. I do check myself quickly knowing that I could get myself into hot water at work with Alex if things go wrong, but this is a risk I am willing to take. I bank on the fact that she won't wish to disclose anything that may ruin her own reputation, which should mean my reputation would also be safe. I guess you could say that I'm a betting man.

I certainly know this to be true from other women from work that I have bedded. One woman in particular gives me regular pleasure. As much for the fact that she is clearly ensnared in my tractor beam as for the fact that she too works for Eloise 'the terrible' Little. Amber Chilworth is the Head of Finance for the Investment Bank. Eloise would die if she knew that I was fucking Amber.

Amber is tall with a curvaceous body. She works hard to keep herself looking good. I often see her gym gear in her office. However, while her body is attractive, her style is not much to my taste. Her wardrobe is a little bland and she doesn't seem to appreciate the value of a good pair of heels. She piles her blonde hair high up on her head and wears plunging necklines and skirts that are short enough to be questionable in the workplace. The look she seems to perpetuate screams 'down to fuck'.

Amber is determined to get ahead, it seems at any price. Before anything had happened between us, I had thought she was the consummate professional; always willing to go the extra mile to ensure my leadership team and I had the best advice and support. I smile to myself as I think about how Amber 'goes the extra mile' for me now.

After our first few sexual encounters, I learned that she was leaving her husband of seven years. They lived in Yorkshire, with Amber staying in London during the week, in a flat in Covent Garden, and returning to spend the weekends in the countryside with her partner.

It remains fascinating to me that while I am only interested in woman for the thrill of the chase and the pleasure they can offer me, I often find that they open up to me as if I am akin to the horse whisperer.

I have a talent that many men don't possess. I can make a woman feel like they are the only girl in the world, without promising anything, giving just enough intimacy and detail about myself to make them fall under my spell. In the odd instance my charms don't work, I move swiftly on to the next object of desire. Otherwise, I collect woman like a philatelist collects stamps, although with substantially less emotional attachment. Sex is purely transactional to me; I have no need for companionship beyond this physical interaction.

I did worry that Amber had deliberately left her husband in the hope that she and I would be more than just fuck buddies. I stayed away from her for a while; only interacting on work matters until I heard that she was banging the head of Foreign Exchange Products. This gave me some reassurance but also made me realise that I preferred her to be servicing me rather than him.

A couple of seductive text messages had her back on side in no time. With Amber, I loved to slip innuendo into a work email or during a face-to-face meeting and watch her respond. It was like a sport and she rarely failed to disappoint me.

I found that she would find time to meet me in the disabled toilets on floor forty-two of the Bank's headquarters despite her office being in the Investment Banking building up the road. She would make the trip between offices to give me head pretty much whenever I wanted it. I was well aware that mine was not the only cock she would be sucking at the Bank. She was a filthy whore, in actual fact, but I for one was willing to make the most of it. There is nothing like fellatio to ease the tension of a stressful day in the office.

I make a call to Shanghai Blues and book a table for 7pm on Friday. They know me well there, as it is one of the many places I frequent in London. I have spent enough money there over the years that they will accommodate me at short notice and I always get a great table. They are discreet too, given the bevy of woman that come through those doors on my arm. I don't mind making some arrangements for myself. It saves my PA knowing my every move.

I am curious about Ms Fisher. Her response is teasing and fun yet with a professional tinge to it. I sense that she is testing me. This is categorically a date in my books, not a mentoring conversation.

I write back to her again and ask her if she was surprised to get my note.

The next day is Monday and I am still checking my personal email obsessively. I am not a patient man. I can see from my office that Alex is in, and that she has been in and out of Eloise's office all morning. I think she must be very good at her job to have lasted the distance with Eloise 'the ice maiden' Little.

I fire up Caldwell's instant messaging system and ping Alex a message instructing her to check her email. I watch as she comes back to her desk and sits down. Within moments she scoops up her phone and leaves her desk. I move over to the round table in my office to join a conference call but I have my iPhone with me in anticipation of hearing from her again.

Alex responds to confirm that she will indeed join me for dinner on Friday. I feel a bit light headed and jubilant. My smile turns to a frown as I try to make sense of the unexpected reaction I am experiencing. This woman is having an unusual effect on me. I shake it off knowing that I will go through the motions like the expert I am with the ultimate goal of getting her naked and willing to do anything to please me.

I smile to myself. I know that I am consumed by infatuation and that I am getting myself into a potentially dangerous situation but I feel more alive than I have in a long time.

Alexandra

I dress very deliberately on Friday morning. I feel a heady mix of anxiety, apprehension and excitement as I survey my wardrobe and select my outfit for the day and the night ahead. I need to look professional for work, but I also want to be attractive for Patrick - without arousing suspicion from either Joseph or Eloise.

Joseph has yet to move out. As Eloise rightly predicted, he is dragging his feet and is not showing any signs of searching for a new place to live. One small consolation is that he has moved into the spare room and we're managing to avoid seeing each other. I have finished work late every night this week, coming home to a dark flat and falling into bed exhausted, only to get up and repeat it all again the next day. Another late finish to round off the week should go unnoticed, and anyway, should Joey care to remember my plans, he will recall that I am due to be out with the girls.

I sigh to myself. I don't need to admit my actual plans and I don't feel that I owe Joseph an explanation, as much for the fact that we have broken up as for the reality that this is simply a work dinner.

My mind is over-analysing as usual. I need to keep the mantra in my head that this is nothing more than a mentoring type conversation, over a meal. I think Patrick likes me but I doubt he is interested in me. I can imagine he has gorgeous women falling all over themselves to be with him. Women more accomplished and experienced than I am. I am flattered that he is giving me some of his valuable time and this alone keeps the pendulum in my head swinging between self-doubt and hope. *But then what am I hoping for?*

I walk into the bathroom to fix my hair and makeup before leaving for work. I scrutinise myself in the mirror. I have lost weight in the last week as the stress of the break-up took hold and my appetite vanished. It was much like the period of time following my father's death. My face is gaunt and my skin is suffering for lack of sunlight. I pinch my cheeks trying to get some colour into them and put my hair up, pulling at the golden wispy strands to try to get them to behave. I then think better of it and pull it down again. Instead, I spray some anti-frizz in and hope that I can tame it again at the end of the day.

I catch myself smiling and realise I am feeling just a little bit like the cat that got the cream. I, the unworldly Alexandra Fisher, am the chosen dinner companion of the debonair Patrick Harrington. The mere thought of sitting across a table from him causes my stomach to tie itself in knots. I attempt a coquettish face and then quickly shake my head at my reflection. I grab my makeup bag, hurriedly jamming it into my handbag before skipping out the door. I don't bid Joseph farewell. I'm not even sure if he is awake.

I have been online, to look at the website for Shanghai Blues. The restaurant looks lovely. I have already decided what I will order, which will take the pressure off me when I am under the intense blue-eyed gaze of Mr Harrington.

My morning commute on the underground passes in a blur and I realise I have been fantasising about the night in front of me instead of my usual routine of getting myself into work mode by reading my Blackberry.

Reality bites as I emerge from the tube station into the freezing winter air. I make my way through the concrete jungle that is Canary Wharf, and into the Caldwell building amongst the trickle of early starters. Now my Blackberry is in hand, my fingers deftly scrolling through the messages that have come in overnight, all the while managing to remain aware enough of my surroundings to negotiate myself through the building barriers and into the elevator - a skill I have perfected from years of practice. I can multitask with one hand and one eye on my Blackberry to the point where it is almost an extension of me. Joseph banned me from using it in the bedroom, as many nights he would be trying to drift off to sleep while hearing the 'tick tick tick' as I tapped the keys responding to an 'urgent' message from Eloise.

The daily round table meeting with Eloise is not scheduled until 9am. I have at least ninety minutes to prepare for her arrival and anticipate her requirements for the day based on what I can see in her email inbox. Or at least fool myself that I could ever be one step in front of this razor-sharp woman.

I walk onto floor forty-two and the lights turn on overhead. Relief floods through me as the electrics confirm that I am the first person on the floor today. Another emotion is present too, I realise, as the memories of that Sunday encounter pervade my mind. *What is it? Desire?*

Alexandra Fisher, you foolish girl, I scold myself inwardly. My body is experiencing a physical reaction, my pulse quickening as I remember how his presence had sent my imagination into overdrive, deluging my mind with images of us having sex on my desk. I feel myself flush deeply and sit down heavily on my chair. *Get a hold of yourself*, I admonish.

Thoughts of naughty sex send images of my father spinning into my mind's view and my excitement is quickly replaced by crashing waves of anger, sadness and confusion. My eyebrows furrow as I struggle to reconcile how my mind and heart are oscillating between thoughts of my father and Patrick Harrington.

Before I know it, Eloise breezes into the office and I realise that I have not used the time I had wisely. I have been lost in my own thoughts. Both my head and my heart are heavy as my mind played through images of my father in happier times, along with the sensationalised newspaper headings, his funeral service and the scene of the inquest into his death.

The inquest was held in May, some six months after the tragic evening of my father's death. My mother and I had attended the Westminster Coroner's Court and listened in numb silence as the Coroner read out the police reports, showed photographs taken at the scene and recorded a verdict of suicide. The verdict did not surprise anyone. The experience however, had served to reopen the wounds of grief in a profound and public way. The only brief respite came when the statement I had written about my father was read and entered into public record.

I was intent on adding a human element to the formal proceedings and, against my mother's wishes I had composed a short tribute to my father, which the Coroner had read to the Court. It spoke about who he was, and acknowledged the illness he had suffered. It had given me some comfort to know that it was not merely a stuffy official occasion and that along with the horrific details of my father's passing the archive would also contain a testament to the fact that Eric Fisher had been loved very dearly.

The day of the inquest had been made all the more surreal by the attendance of the call girls who had been with my father that fateful night. We had known they would be there as the escort agency had been decent enough to forewarn us. I had implored my mother to keep them away from me. I was scared that my latent anger would erupt and I would cause a scene.

One of the women, not much older than me, had come up to us as we all waited in the anteroom for the inquest to begin. I had been blindsided, but instead of rage, I had felt a deep sadness and a surprising sense of solitude. The woman was sobbing and apologised to us repeatedly, and somewhat incoherently, through her tears. I had softened as I realised that she was carrying a burden of guilt that she did not deserve. I found myself consoling her and telling her that we did not blame her for what had happened. My mother stood silently beside me, watching the interchange but unable to utter a word. Her face was hard and expressionless, her eyes vacant.

Thankfully, Eloise was in back-to-back meetings for most of the day and she was leaving the office early to have her hair done. We, her PA and I, knew that the hairdresser was where she was going. The party line in case Brad needed her was, of course, that we would get a message to her in the 'meeting' she was in. Being duplicitous for Eloise was now second nature to me. What was incredible was the fact that the lies we all told were never acknowledged and at times it seemed as if we believed the cover story to be the truth.

My C-chat had popped up earlier in the day with a message

from Patrick. It contained nothing more than a mobile phone number. I was preoccupied and still deeply wrapped up in the thoughts and memories of my father and had entered it into my phone with no thought of replying.

Somewhat thankfully, given my mood, I had not seen Patrick all day. At six o'clock, I had packed my work papers and laptop away and left the floor with murmurings to my colleagues about the girl's night I was about to partake in. While we felt a sense of solidarity together through the intensity of the work we carried out on Eloise's behalf, we typically didn't linger on a Friday, particularly if Eloise had already left the building. We did not go out for drinks as a team or tend to share many personal details with each other either. It was tacitly agreed that being too intimate in such a highly charged setting was dangerous. Nobody wanted to voluntarily give any more of themselves than they already did.

Candice had replied to my email imploring me to turn up to the girls' night, late, once I had finished work, regardless of the time. I had not replied. I knew I was not going to see those friends this night.

For the second time that day, I find myself scrutinising my reflection in a bathroom mirror. I had donned a simple black dress, matched with plain black Kate Spade stilettos. To my eye, the dress was appropriate. It was figure hugging so a little suggestive but not too revealing. To 'jazz up' my outfit I am wearing my prized Akris leopard print shrug. It is a beautiful piece of clothing that I had procured in a sale, paying a fraction of the usually hefty price tag. It is my pride and joy. I perk up a little as I smooth my dress and remove blonde hairs that had attached themselves to my clothing during the day. This was a continual nuisance; my hair seemed to be falling out at an alarming rate and the unattached strands were very noticeable, especially on dark clothing.

I reapply my makeup. I had never been very interested in trying to improve my looks with cosmetics. In any event I preferred to look natural. A quick swish of pressed powder and a fresh application of eyeliner and mascara, finished with lip-gloss and I am done. I look at my watch. That had taken all of ten minutes. I am ready to head downstairs to the car, and the enormity of what I am about to do hits me like a ton of bricks.

I find the black BMW saloon with ease, open the rear door and climb in without saying a word. The driver glances at me in the rear view mirror as I slide across the back seat to sit behind him.

"Hello Alex, my name is John."

Why am I not surprised that Patrick Harrington's driver is *a) expecting me and b) knows my name?* Never mind the fact that he is, it seems, comfortable enough to address me as Alex rather than Alexandra.

"Good evening, sir," I say politely.

I know that all the Executives have allocated drivers. Eloise has been through a number of chauffeurs in the year I have been with her, given that most people can't live up to her exacting standards. Curious about the man that gets to drive Patrick around, I think about the glimpse I got of him as I slid across the backseat. This man has a big round belly, straining against his clothing. *Evidence of a sedentary lifestyle*, I think harshly.

I watch the digital clock on the dashboard tick through the minutes as if they were hours. My mouth is dry, the butterflies in my stomach are going crazy and my legs feel like dead weights. Then all of a sudden the fantastic Mr Harrington is folding his long, lean body beside me onto the seat and simultaneously closing the car door.

As if by intuition, the driver has already started the ignition and was pulling away from the curb.

"You didn't send me your mobile number on instant messenger and you didn't text me, Alexandra," he states without so much as a hello.

My mind flashed with the thought that I was having dinner with the male equivalent of Eloise.

"How was your day, Mr Harrington?"

I want to avoid the confrontation he had created but as soon as the question was out of my mouth I wince inwardly at its formality. *Just be yourself*, I repeat in my head over and over as I will my heartbeat to slow down by lengthening my breathing. My regular yoga practise was coming in useful.

His eyes are everywhere. My face, my body, and my legs and back to my face, the movements almost imperceptible. He breathes out the breath he seemed to be holding and smiles.

"Please, call me Patrick," he says, his voice like honey.

"Of course, as long as you call me Alex," I retort.

His face breaks into a wide smile and he laughs.

"Well, okay then, Alex. Are you looking forward to having dinner with me this evening?"

He turns his body toward me, so the car door is at his back, and inches a little closer to me. I check myself and note that I have my legs together, slanted in his direction, and I am leaning forward ever so slightly.

I need to play it cool. I press my shoulders back into the soft leather of the car seat and square my knees toward the front of the car. At least my breathing had slowed down.

"It will be good to talk about our careers, Patrick." I turn my head and look him square in the eye as I spoke. I hope my body language and tone doesn't give away any hint of the other things I would like to talk to Patrick about. I try to read the situation. There is definitely some sexual tension building and it is wreaking havoc with my self-control.

"Alex. We can talk about work for as long as you like, but I'd also like to take this opportunity to get to know you, okay?"

I nod and look down at my hands. I feel like I have been told off. The car ride from Canary Wharf to the West End of London passes by in a blur. Patrick fires questions at me, all banal getting-to-know-you questions, which I answer with as much detail as I can manage. I am struggling and the evening has barely started.

I am trying to read into everything he says, analysing his words and mine. I am overcome with fear about what I am getting myself into and it is paralysing my tongue and making it hard for me to appear calm and confident.

The longer I sit close to this man, the more anxious I become. The BMW arrives in front of Shanghai Blues and John is quickly out of the car and coming round the vehicle to open the door for Patrick. I have to wait for Patrick to move as my door is blocked by a constant stream of London traffic.

Instead of turning to the open door, Patrick grabs my hands.

"Alex, please relax. I won't bite. Let's have a fun evening."

I stare at him. He is still holding my hands and I realise he is waiting for me to respond.

"We will have a wonderful time, I'm really looking forward to getting to know you, Patrick."

I force a smile. I feel like an actress reading her lines.

Satisfied, he drops my hands and manoeuvres himself out

of the car, very deftly for a man of his height. The opening of the door and the movement of his body send a rush of cold air towards me, carrying the heady smell of Patrick's aftershave. I take a deep breath in and savour his scent. It does nothing to quieten the judgmental voice in my head. I realise I am feeling guilty about Joey every time I acknowledge to myself that I am attracted to Patrick.

I get out of the car as gracefully as I can, trying to keep my legs together, pulling at the hem of my dress as my winter coat falls open, in an attempt to protect my modesty. All the while, Mr Harrington has his eyes on me. I stand up straight, position my handbag, and take a deep breath. I have many pairs of high-heeled shoes and love to wear them, but for all the practice I get I don't seem to have truly mastered how to glide elegantly in them.

I had been given the nickname 'Bambi' by Eloise's PA. She told me that I often looked like a newborn foal as I was tottering around the office on impossibly high heels. To my relief and slight dismay, Patrick puts his arm lightly around my back as we walk into the restaurant. I cover the ten metres or so from the car into the restaurant without incident, a minor victory given the state I had gotten myself into.

The restaurant, situated in a Grade II listed building called Holborn Hall, is walking distance from popular Covent Garden and buzzy Soho. I look around, taking in the entrance, the ceiling, and the furnishings. Sophisticated and fashionable, while still being discreet. It is a stunning space, opulently adorned like an Oriental Palace. Clever lighting makes it feel intimate and inviting, private and spacious all at once.

Once they have taken our coats, we are escorted immediately to a large square table in the very corner of the room, away from the other diners. The chairs are arranged so we are sitting beside each other, rather than across the table from each other. I wonder if Patrick has deliberately asked for this. Our knees graze as we both make ourselves comfortable. This sets off my already rattled nerves.

Without being asked, we are presented with chilled champagne flutes, and a freshly opened bottle of Krug is held out for Patrick's approval. He smiles and the waiter pours a few centimetres into his glass. Patrick picks it up as if he is going to taste it and then changes his mind. He holds the flute out to me.

I feel the familiar creep of embarrassment burning up my neck to my cheeks. I know nothing about wine. I take the proffered glass and hold it to my nose. I swirl the bubbly liquid around before taking the glass to my lips. I thank heavens for the Levy family and all that spending time with them has taught me. I have watched Joseph's father complete this task at many fine-dining establishments. My heart aches as his face flashes into my head.

I look up at the waiter and indicate that the champagne is acceptable. I hardly taste it and would have motioned my approval in any event to avoid any further embarrassment. The waiter moves to fill Patrick's and then my glass and is gone in but a moment. This restaurant has impeccable service.

"Here's to our health and continued success."

Patrick is holding up his flute and the fizz is dancing in the top of the glass. I pick my glass up to clink with his. I can do nothing more than smile.

As soon as the glass is to my lips, I inhale the heady aroma and take a long pull of the champagne, experiencing the pleasure as the icy cold bubbles hit my tongue and slide down my throat.

Before I know it, the flute is empty. My glass is promptly refilled and I make a mental note that I am drinking too quickly in an attempt to assuage my nerves. Patrick is making polite conversation, in the safe territory of work matters to which we are both privy. I am holding my own in the exchange, my sentences getting longer with each sip of the exquisite champagne.

After I have drained my second glass, I feel myself starting to relax and enjoy the buzz as the alcohol starts to numb my senses.

Patrick gestures toward my menu. I pick it up and stare at it, and realise the words are swimming in front of my eyes. Evidently, two glasses of Krug on an empty stomach reacts quickly. I focus intently on the list of dishes even though my brain is not registering what it is seeing. When the waiter comes I order as planned, remembering what I chose from the menu on the website. I congratulate myself on my forethought, knowing that had I not checked beforehand I would have been confounded by the extensive list of dim sum and some of the more unusual offerings from shark-fin soup, barbecued 'pi-pa' duck and the Shanghai Devil.

Somewhere in the depths of my brain, a warning bell sounds as I hear myself asking Patrick why he asked me out to dinner.

No more wine until there is something in your belly to soak it up, I think to myself.

His eyes are on me and I realise I am enjoying the look he is giving me. I am reading it as curiosity tinged with desire. My pulse quickens as I blink slowly, push my lips together seductively and return the intensity of his gaze.

"I want to kiss you, Alexandra. May I?" he breathes, leaning forward into my personal space. Again my nostrils fill with the deliciously potent smell of his cologne. I feel the hairs on the back of my neck stand up and my nipples harden. My body is tense, waiting for the imminent kiss.

I nod without even thinking, my body reacting quicker than my brain. It seems my base instincts are stronger, primal, overriding any sensible thoughts my mind might come up with. His hands reach forward; one grasps my closest shoulder drawing my body nearer to him, the other rests on the back of my neck easing my head toward his. Before I know it, his mouth is on mine and his tongue gently pushes into my slightly parted lips. I start to return the kiss.

I move my hand onto his knee under the table and as I lean closer to him, I slide my palm up the inside of his thigh, bouncing my fingers like I am playing the piano. I bring my hand to rest in the crevice where his leg ends and his torso begins. As soon as I am touching his body, his kiss becomes more urgent. I pull my face back, leaving my hand where it is and grin at him. I see surprise flicker briefly in his eyes as he gently strokes my cheek and slowly lets me go.

As if the kiss never happened, Patrick resumes conversation. We chat easily, covering further standard 'getting to know you' ground. Our taste in music, where we had travelled, and the degrees we had studied and why we had chosen our career paths. I feel like I am gaining insight into this man, yet at the same time I am acutely aware that he is not really giving much away.

The starters arrive as if by magic, and with them a bottle of French white wine. I gather from the attentive sommelier that it is an expensive Burgundy. Our champagne flutes are gone, replaced with wide, shallow white wine glasses. These are filled with a mere centimetre of the fabulous wine under Patrick's instruction. I learn that he likes his white wine to be arctic cold.

As we begin to eat Patrick, admonishes me. "I'm surprised you would kiss me, Alex. Your muscled tattooed boyfriend wouldn't like that would he?"

Through my wine haze, I hear the words but it takes a while for my brain to process them. *How does he know about Joey? And how can he possibly know what he looks like?*

My bewilderment must be evident on my face. I can not hide my confusion. Patrick tries again.

"I have a few confessions to make, Alex. First, I guess I have to tell you that I have wanted to ask you out since the first moment I laid eyes on you. I don't know what I want... but I do know that for months I have wanted to have the chance to sit this close to you for an evening and get to know you."

I feel like I am standing in the warmth of the blazing sun as he speaks. Again, while I am basking in his attention, I can't shake the niggling feeling that this is a well-practised routine for this man. I ignore it and smile timidly at him, waiting for him to continue.

"Second, I have to tell you off for not being more cautious with the privacy settings on your Facebook account."

The words crash into my head as I realise that he has been cyber-stalking me and that is how he knows about Joey. He has been looking at my photos. I feel at once flattered and exposed. I rack my drink-addled brain trying to think of what else my Facebook page might betray about me.

In an attempt to buy some time, I pick up my wine glass and feel the silky, rich wine as it slides down my throat. I am flummoxed. I can't believe that Patrick Harrington has seen intimate details of my life without my permission - yet I only have myself to blame. I should have been more careful to ensure my online presence was adequately protected. It dawns on me that Patrick Harrington has taken the time to Face-stalk me. I guess that fact outweighs the creepiness of it. He is not just anyone after all.

"I don't have a boyfriend, and frankly I don't wish to discuss this with you," I say churlishly. As soon as the words are out of my mouth I wish I could take them back and replace them with something more considered. There is an awkward moment as our dinner plates are cleared and silence ensues.

Patrick takes control, and relieves the tension by telling me how good the desserts are there. He suggests we order and take them upstairs to the more relaxed atmosphere of the restaurant's lounge.

The rest of the evening passes in a blink. The strains of a harp, slowly ascending in volume, punctuate my consciousness. Through half-open eyes, I reach for my phone to silence the noise and see that it is 6am on Saturday morning. My alarm is still set for work. I have a thumping headache and a queasy stomach and it takes me a moment to recall where I have been and what I was doing the night before. I feel incredibly nauseous but also incredibly grateful for the fact that I do not have to face going into the office today.

My mind flashes with snippets of my date with Patrick Harrington. Our conversation over dinner, moving upstairs to sit in the mezzanine lounge with its private banquets to eat dessert and enjoy a night cap. Kissing and touching each other, him putting me into a black cab as I pleaded with him... *What was I saying to him? What did I want?*

I scrunch my eyes shut, willing the images and partial recollections to stop streaming into my head. I feel the chill of reality biting, I can't piece together the evening and can feel myself starting to panic. Good god, why was I pleading with him? What had I done?

I know I had barely touched my food but had been quite happy to empty my wine glass. A glass that seemed to refill itself magically. I had lost my inhibitions, that much I can remember. I can't recall the taxi journey home, or how I got into the apartment. I gingerly open my eyes, bracing myself this time against the bright sunlight streaming though my blinds and see my handbag where I had unceremoniously dumped it, the contents strewn across the carpet.

I lift my duvet and see that I have managed to get out of my clothes, but had fallen into bed with my lingerie and stockings still on. I lean over without getting out of bed, and grab for my wallet, one of the many items littering my bedroom floor. I know that I did not have enough cash on me for the cab fare home so I am hoping to figure out some details since my memory is giving me nothing. A taxi receipt is sticking out of my purse. I pluck it out and laugh bleakly to myself as I see that I had paid by credit card. I am surprised I had remembered my PIN. I must have been in a right state. The paper stub doesn't rouse any memory of my journey or arrival home last night.

Next, I pick up my phone again from the bedside table. I marvel at the fact that in my drunken stupor I had the presence of mind to place it where I habitually do. I have no messages, and thankfully I did not send any, or make any calls while so severely under the influence.

I feel physically and emotionally ill. *Did I see or speak to Joey when I got home?* I am scared to leave the safety of my bed. I will myself to go back to sleep to try to recover. I want to weep for letting myself get so drunk and disorderly in the company of such a powerful man. I fervently wish I could remember more of the evening.

I am going to head out and visit my mother today, I think, *when I am well enough to leave my bed, and the quiet safety of my house.*

I am unsure of what to think of last night, and what to do next. Maybe there is nothing to do. That's it. A first (and probably last) date with the object of my infatuation.

Harrington

I dress very deliberately on Friday morning. I feel a heady mix of anxiety, apprehension and excitement as I survey my wardrobe and select my outfit for the day and the night ahead. I want to be immaculate for Alexandra so I select my favourite shirt, tie and cufflink combination, and set them against a deep blue suit.

I have that happy Friday feeling as I arrive in the office. I sweep past the bank of desks where Alex sits on my way to my office. This is not the most direct route from the elevator to my corner suite but I am hoping to catch a glimpse of what she is wearing for our date.

She is not at her desk. I glance into Eloise's office as I pass and she is not in there either. I do hope she is in the office today and not unwell. I am so determined in my pursuit that it would not suit me one bit to reschedule.

I am already regretting that I am going to Dublin tomorrow for my brother's birthday. Not something I would normally do but in a moment of weakness I allowed my darling mother to convince me that it was a good idea. I had been thinking that if tonight goes well that I could move swiftly on to date number two. I am anticipating at least three dates with Alex before I can get her into bed and lord knows I am not a patient man.

My PA, Barbra, follows me into my office and is already rattling through my day, asking if I want anything changed, what I want for lunch and pointing at neat piles on my conference table of the papers I need for each meeting I have today. She is the model of efficiency. Deliberately, I selected an older, matronly, overweight secretary when I was choosing an assistant years ago. As I moved up through the company echelons, she moved with me.

This is one relationship where I am smart enough to know that it must remain platonic. Instead, I have cultivated a lasting work friendship appealing to her maternal instincts, which ensures I get completely looked after. Of course I flirt with her a little, as it would be unfair for her to miss out on the pleasure of engaging my playful side.

I am in back-to-back, wall-to-wall meetings, which would ordinarily displease me. I need headspace between my appointments to remain on top of my game. Today, my schedule will ensure that I am sufficiently distracted while the time passes until I find myself sitting in the back seat of the BMW with Alex. My groin twitches a little in response to the thought.

My lunch is brought in to me on a silver tray courtesy of the Michelin star chef that has his kitchen on the other side of the forty-second floor. He and his staff are on hand to cater important internal and external meetings as well as provide for every whim of the Executives. I look at my tuna salad with a side of chopped melon and think how low maintenance I am, usually eating something from the day's menu.

I know for a fact that this is a stark contrast to Eloise 'know it all' Little who is notorious for having the kitchen staff running in circles. If the carrots on her salad are grated, she will want them sliced. If the cherry tomatoes are too dry they need to be removed. Eloise will even try to dictate what the whole Executive Team eats at our regular meetings or off-sites. I am very considerate of what I put in my body and know the health and aesthetic value of eating well but Eloise is evangelical and frankly quite scary when it comes to nutrition. I think she needs to lighten up, and not just about food.

I am certain that Alex will not have informed her menacing boss about who she is dining with this evening. That thought makes me feel good. I will take any opportunity I can get to be one up on Eloise 'the iceberg' Little.

I realise it has been more than a week since I have asked Amber Chilworth to make her way up the Colonnade to indulge me. I have been quite distracted from my stock and trade harlots on the basis that I have become obsessive about Alex Fisher. I have a lot riding on this evening. The conquest begins in earnest.

That is not to say I have taken a vow of chastity. Last night I had the surreal experience of being seduced from very unlikely quarters. I had come home earlier than usual to find my house-keeper, Violetta, still in the house finishing up her duties. Along with her was Maria, the woman who runs the cleaning company Violetta works for.

Maria and I have known each other for years, conversing about my house cleaning needs through regular text messages. The other convenient benefit that Maria can provide is a discreet 'escort' service. Maria is a saint of sorts, finding work for Eastern European women who wish to live and work in London. Some of them are prepared to do backbreaking work for not much more than £10 an hour. Others prefer to work on their backs for multiples of that.

I have on occasion, out of laziness or when I have been short on time, asked Maria to send me one of her girls. The upside of a hooker over picking up a girl in a bar is that a hooker wants to hightail it once the business transaction is complete. Men pay prostitutes to leave. In addition, they are professionals. The small talk is often better and the sex is usually amazing, given how practised these pros are.

Maria is a good-looking woman in her late forties. Her petite frame contradicts her ability to command respect from her cohort of girls and her demanding clients. Much to my approval, Maria always wears impossibly high heels to try to elevate her stature. She must be five foot nothing without her shoes on.

Bulgarian in origin, she speaks perfect English with only the slightest accent. Although I enjoy text flirting with her, I had never really thought of her as a prospect - she served her purpose for me by ensuring her girls were attentive to my every need. I have to say, even if it makes me sound like the disgraced former head of the International Monetary Fund, Dominique Strauss-Kahn, I do enjoy a good dusting from the maid.

In their native tongue Maria had dismissed Violetta, who left muttering something deferential in her broken English as she backed out the front door. Once she was gone, it felt like all the air in the room had been sucked out. The sexual tension was palpable. It was so hot and thick I felt like I was wearing it or like I could spread it on a bun.

I was overcome with desire, and felt my body responding to the seductive stare Maria was giving me. *I'm going to make her work for this*, I thought to myself. I was horny, and in the mood for a kinky encounter, but I liked the thought of this Madame trying to tame me. I knew her girls must report back to her and clearly she had decided, given that the opportunity had presented itself, to find out about Patrick Harrington's sexual prowess herself.

"I wasn't expecting to see you, Patrick," she purred, gazing at me through her well-lacquered lashes.

I remained silent, returning her intense gaze, knowing that my enticing blue eyes were having the desired effect. Maria moved closer to me so we were standing barely a foot apart. Her hand moved to my tie, her fingers flicking behind the silk fabric. I could hear her breathing.

With a sharp pull she had me bending down so our faces were on the verge of touching.

"You will do as you are told," she commanded.

Her eyes still trained on mine, she stepped away and shook her arms out of the blazer she was wearing, letting it fall to the floor. Underneath, she was wearing a sheer blouse and no bra. Her small, pert breasts were in soft focus, her nipples clearly erect.

I broke into a smile as I wondered if she was wearing any knickers.

"I don't want to hear you speak. Do you understand me? I'm the one in control here."

Her tone brooked no argument. *This was going to be wild*, I thought to myself. I had been through a phase of trying out bondage and discipline but being submissive had never appealed to me. I did not need to be the Dominant either as it all seemed too contrived. Ordinarily, I was the one who had the power and thus was in command. Tonight, I would allow Maria to think she could dominate me, if only for the craic.

I nodded and tried to look sufficiently diffident. Maria unzipped her pencil skirt and let that drop to the floor too. She stepped over it, while unbuttoning her blouse. She was wearing panties, along with suspenders to hold up her micro-fishnet black stockings. The black suspenders were soft elastic, a combination of narrow and wide straps that ran together creating a cage effect pattern, caressing her tiny waist and hips.

Underneath, she wore a pretty, small translucent thong, revealing her Brazilian 'landing strip' wax job. I smiled as I felt the familiar sensation of the beginnings of an erection. I liked a woman who kept herself tidy. Her lack of bra coupled with this underwear was screaming 'naughty'.

She walked away from me, beckoning me to follow her, her undone blouse moving as she walked, revealing her naked flesh. She strode with purpose, certain that I would be right behind her. As she stepped down the carpeted stairs expertly on her stilettos, I caught a glimpse of the sole of one of her shoes, the telltale red of a pair of Christian Louboutins. That man made sexy shoes an art form. I also noticed that her stockings had a visible seam running up the back of her calves. Her stems looked incredible. I was now rock hard.

Maria was not touching the banister as she descended the stairs. Instead, she was pushing both hands into her hair, winding her tresses up on top of her head, exposing the milky white skin of her neck. I swallowed hard. This woman clearly knew what she was doing.

She was headed toward the basement floor, at the base of the stairs she made her way across my den, the early evening providing little illumination through the skylights as she crossed the room to the door leading to the sunken garden. I walked closely behind her, admiring the curve of her peachy arse, with the dental floss thin G-string splitting the creamy skin of her butt cheeks.

Expertly, Maria unlocked the tri-folding doors and peeled them open. She was strong for her size. The water feature that adorned the back garden wall, dropping water more than 10 metres through soft lighting set against a living wall, provided a surreal ambience. *I haven't fucked anyone down here before*, I thought to myself, and wondered why I hadn't contemplated it before now. Then I thought about the hi-tech recording equipment I had installed in the house, covering most rooms I might fuck a woman in and realised that none of the cameras would capture this view. I was disappointed I wouldn't be recording this evening for prosperity. I contemplated asking Maria if we could film our antics. If a girl says yes to being taped, she usually doesn't say no to anything else.

Maria stopped and demanded that I did so too, barking instructions not to move. I acquiesced. This was hot. Being told what to do in my own home. *Funny*, I reflected, *on another day with another woman I wouldn't even countenance this.* I wasn't going to push my luck by asking about the cameras and realised that not only would it alter the dynamic she had worked so hard to build, it would also mean I had to trust her with the revelation that I had a mixing desk and so much recording equipment that the setup wouldn't look out of place at the BBC. That needed to remain my little secret.

Maria was suddenly up in my face, no mean feat for a woman of her pint size, her arms wound round my neck pulling me close, her eyelashes batting as she planted tiny kisses on my nose, my throat, my neck. She was being gentle. My mind was reeling trying to figure out how this was going to play out.

Maria ran her hands under my suit jacket down my torso leaving goose bumps in her wake. She lowered herself to a squatting position and set about removing my shoes and socks. Slowly, she circled around me until she was standing behind me. I felt her hands reach around and start to undo my trousers. Her hands deftly worked the hooks and fly despite the fact that she couldn't see them. Once my pants were around my ankles she gave me a rough shove in the small of my back, bidding me to step away from my clothes.

I was naked from the waist down, still in my shirt, jacket and necktie. As soon as my skin was exposed, the cool March air bit me around my legs and groin, but it did nothing to dull my raging erection. My arms hung at my side, I was not moving unless instructed, my senses were exhilarated.

As I felt the cold air singeing my skin and the hairs on my legs stand up, I watched Maria who was wearing very little. The only tell-tale sign that she was feeling the chill were her erect nipples, pushing through the fabric of her blouse as she moved.

Next, she was unbuttoning my shirt, loosening my tie, but not removing either. With her hands on my ribs she walked me backward until the back of my legs hit the wrought iron chair, part of the outdoor furniture I kept in this garden but never really used. The deck on the level above us caught all the sun.

Her hands moved up to my shoulders forcing me to sit down. Her breasts were in my face once my naked arse hit the cold of the iron seat. I restrained myself from tearing at her blouse. The cold, the sounds, the petite nearly naked form of Maria before me; all of it was combining to heighten my arousal. It was a heady mix and I was enjoying every second.

Her hands were pulling at my tie to remove it. I couldn't fathom what she was planning to do, but was relishing the suspense. The chill of the seat against my skin led me to lift myself from the chair.

Maria pushed me harshly back down. "Sit still," she ordered.

I watched her push her G-string to the side and start to rub her clitoris. She was not more than a foot from me and I desperately wanted to touch her, run my hands over her body and help her with the task she was undertaking.

Suitably chastised though, I watched her enjoying herself and thought that I might explode. Then she wrapped my tie around her neck and knotted it, turning her body around so her peachy arse and those exquisite suspenders holding up those sexy stockings were my new view. Bending forward, with her hands on either side of her butt cheeks pulling them apart, she showed me her wet pussy. I was burning with desire even in the chilly night air.

Carefully on her stilettos, still bent forward, she backed up toward me, flicking my tie to land on her back. Her hands were reaching back to find my hard cock. She sat herself down so just the tip of me was inside her and bent forward to put her hands on the ground. She was agile, flexible and just the right height for this.

She began to slide herself up and down my length, pushing down harder and harder, building rhythm and causing me to pant and grip the arms of the chair I was sitting in. I saw her bring one hand up off the ground to find her clitoris and I felt myself grinning. She was not just here for my pleasure. Watching her rub herself, seeing her arse bobbing in front of me, and her tight wet pussy wrapped around my huge dick sent me over the edge. I grabbed at my tie and pulled her head back, restricting her breathing. I could only imagine this is what she had wanted.

I could feel her orgasm take hold as her vaginal muscles clenched and unclenched around my cock. I threw my head back and let out a guttural sound as my own orgasm pulsated through my body and I came hard inside her.

The memory of the sex with Maria brings a smile to my lips as I make my way out of the office building at 6.30pm sharp, looking for John and the car. He is waiting, as always, and I can see that Alexandra is already in the back seat. *Good girl*, I think. My smile broadens.

I slide myself into the back seat beside her and take a good look at her. I feel the mix of tension and excitement that comes with being with someone new. She is wearing her coat so I cannot see how she has dressed for me yet.

During the car ride to the restaurant I continue to watch Alex. We are chatting, or at least I am. I contemplate her and feel like I have trapped a mouse. Once we arrive at our destination, and John is out of earshot, I take a moment to try to persuade her to relax, before we get out of the car.

I stand in the cool evening air and watch her try to get out of the saloon as elegantly as she can. I approve of the plain black stilettos she is wearing. They could be more exciting but they are certainly sexier than any of the pairs I saw under her desk at work.

Once we are inside the restaurant and she has a glass of champagne in front of her, she seems to relax. She is wearing a black dress that clings in all the right places. Over her shoulders is an odd animal print garment that I instantly dislike. I compliment her on her dress and chose not to comment on the thing that looks like a spotted hyena holding onto her neck for dear life. I pride myself on my sense of style and I take an interest in fashion trends for both men and women.

I have admired Alex's figure from afar for some time and am pleased I have the opportunity of examining it up close. I know this is one doll I am going to enjoy dressing. *She needs it*, I think, based on her choice of leopard pattern accessory. I feel like taking her to Sloane Street for a shopping extravaganza tomorrow and lament my Ireland jaunt. My Mam can persuade me to do things I don't want to. She is the only woman in the world with this ability. Being the youngest of her children I have always been her favourite and we have a close bond.

I manoeuvre Alex through the standard first date conversation without saying too much about myself. She is also reticent but I am not concerned. I am very interested in this girl, but if I don't know her favourite colour by the end of the evening it won't be a problem.

I have asked for my usual table, with the chairs sat next to each other rather than across the table. This affords me greater opportunity to touch my dining companion and establish a ruse of intimacy. Once Alex has her second glass of champagne, and I think her inhibitions are suitably loosened, I try one of my favourite lines on her.

"I want to kiss you, Alexandra. May I?" I am almost whispering but leaning in towards her so my intention is clear.

Her eyes widen like a deer in headlights and she nods. I place my hands on her body. I am struck by how good this feels despite us still having all our clothes on. I use a little pressure on her shoulder to close the distance between us, and a hand behind her neck to bring her lips to mine. Our kiss is soft and tender at first. I don't want to frighten her.

I am starting to feel the sweet sensation of arousal as the blood in my body moves south. I am caught off guard as I feel Alex run her hand up my thigh drumming her fingers against my leg as she goes, stopping to rest when she reaches the enlarging form in my trousers. I start to kiss her hard. I am so turned on by this girl and the unexpected reaction my kiss generates from her. I can sense a deeply potent sexuality to this creature, made even more appealing by the sense that she herself seems totally unaware of it.

She pulls away from me, even though my hands are gripping her tightly, and smiles right into my face as if she knows what I have been thinking. I let her go, sit back in my chair and resume conversation. I love that she touched me liked she did. Whether she realises it or not she has unlocked the door just a crack, and I fully intend to push it wide open.

On arrival I had ordered my favourite wine, which had been

decanted while we had our aperitifs, a bottle of Montrachet Domaine de BaronThenard from Maison Remoissenet Pere et Fils. The colour of the wine as it is poured is a pale straw colour. The initial nose embodies bergamot, lemon and fresh marzipan. With time and air, I knew there would be notes of fresh mushroom and earth, blending perfectly. The palate is balanced and crisp with incredible complexity. Delicious. Money well spent.

I watch during the meal as Alexandra slugs the expensive Burgundy like it is water. I am partly amused and partly annoyed. Fine wine is something I will need to coach her on if we are going to spend more time together. I guess I should have expected this, given her age and from hearing scraps of detail about her upbringing.

I tell her about my family, and find myself saying more than I usually would to a woman on a first date. I don't know what it is about Alexandra but I am acutely aware that I need to watch myself, as I don't do attachment, yet she seems to be getting under my skin. She asks intellectually curious questions. Not probing or nosey but interested, like she genuinely wants to get to know me. I find most women are like broken records, talking incessantly about themselves. Boring.

I tell her about my siblings, about my parents and more about the mother I adore than I think I have ever told a woman. Any mention of Mam usually sends a woman into amateur psychoanalysis thinking that my relationship with her is unhealthy and explains my inability to commit. Either that or they assume they require her stamp of approval, and expect to be introduced. The reality is that there is not a woman on the planet that could hold a candle to my Mam, and when any date starts in with the therapist babble I have already mentally checked out. I may fuck her but I won't bother seeing her again.

Alex is fun and easy to be around. I find myself relaxing enough to be enjoying myself. Impressive for a first date as I am usually plotting like a master tactician rather than having fun. Fun is something I can emulate, as a form of social camouflage, and I recognise it but it is rare to feel like I am part of it. I reflect again that this girl is probably more of a woman than I gave her credit for. Her wisdom, reason and good sense extends beyond her years.

I notice that she is hardly eating but her glass is being refilled more often than mine. I do like a drink - I am Irish after all - however, I always exercise a level of self-restraint. I cannot bear to lose my memory or become sloppy. I smile warmly at my dinner companion and suggest we move upstairs to the restaurant's mezzanine level to have our desserts. *She is my dessert*, I think. I plan to steal more than one kiss this evening and certainly hope she will be willing to put her hands on me again.

I speak quietly, instructing the waiter that we plan to move. I order a second bottle of wine, a decent - but cheap by comparison to the Montrachet - Sauvignon Blanc from the Marlborough region of New Zealand. Alex had mentioned that she likes New World wine so I thought that was an easy point to score with her.

Once upstairs, the wine seems to evaporate as we sit close together on the banquet seating. Alex is showing the effects of the wine; her cheeks are flushed red and her eyes are wide and a little glazed. To her credit, she is not slurring and is in no danger of losing the plot as the conversation dances through a variety of topics, from current events to Caldwell history to our current surrounds. It seems she is a regular drinker. This fact can only help me with my crusade as I think about how her inhibitions demonstrably loosened after a few drinks this evening.

Alex is sitting beside me and her thighs, enveloped in tight black fabric, are right there teasing me. I want another kiss so I place one hand down her back and one on her leg and wait for her to respond. And respond she does. I see her eyes light up and her lips pout slightly, and then she is almost on top of me. Her mouth is on mine kissing me, her hands are in my hair. She is almost in a frenzy. I like this side of her and I use my hands to explore the body I have been coveting all evening.

Without warning, she retracts and stands up abruptly, a little unsteady on her heels. I am surprised and wait for her next move. I am at a loss to explain this sudden turn, but do not wish to scare her away.

"I need to go home." She says and raises her hands to cover her face.

"Of course, Alex, darling, I'll get you a taxi." I stand too, and help her to make her way down the stairs to reception and the cloakroom. In moments we are in our coats and standing outside the restaurant. I have a tab at Shanghai Blues and they know I am good for it so we are not stopped from departing in haste.

The cold of the night seems to have frozen her tongue. Alex is standing beside me looking a bit worse for wear and decidedly forlorn.

"Are you okay?" I ask gently and she nods almost imperceptibly.

I hail a black cab and realise I have no idea where she lives once I have approached the window to instruct the cabbie. I turn back to ask and realise Alex is right there, standing close behind me.

"Patrick, take me home with you," she says with certainty.

I have a split second to make a decision. I take her hands and tell her that I will see her again and that it's best if we go our separate ways. I almost don't recognise myself as I'm saying the words.

"Please. Please. I really need this." She is pleading now, through her words, in her eyes, her body leaning forward hopefully.

I ignore her, with all the will power I possess. "Where do you live?"

She pushes past me, bundles herself into the taxi and slams the door unceremoniously. I watch as the car pulls away from the curb. I don't know how the evening ended like this.

I wake up the next morning and luxuriate in my bed. A fleeting thought passes through my mind like a comet. I could have been waking up next to Alexandra Fisher.

I am unsure of what to think of last night, and what to do next. Maybe there is nothing to do. That was it. A first (and probably last) date with the object of my infatuation.

Alexandra

I am staring at the ceiling but my eyes are not actually seeing it. As I think back over my evening with Patrick Harrington, I feel an odd mixture of regret and arousal. I lie there reflecting on our time together. The regret wins out and I feel decidedly anxious.

I allow myself to smile a little as I think about the passionate kissing and his hands touching my body. I push the duvet back and clumsily manoeuvre myself out from under the cover, my stomach knotted and my head aching.

I get up and make my way to the bathroom. I am still angry at myself but know that worrying is pointless. I hear Candice and my other friends reminding me that I am prone to allowing feelings of guilt to overwhelm me, to the point of making decisions led by this emotion. Always doing what I 'should' do rather than what I want to do all in an effort to avoid feeling guilty.

I feel a pang of love for Candice and immediately feel bad for letting her down last night. I will have to 'fess up to Candy soon as it won't be long before she knows that all is not as I am portraying it. She can read me like a book. I feel like laughing as I realise there it is again, that all-consuming feeling of guilt. I also realise I need her advice. Candy changes men like she changes her underwear and I swear Nelly Furtado wrote her track 'Maneater' especially for her. The melody dances through my mind: 'She's a Man-eater, make you work hard, make you spend hard, make you want all of her love...' I make a mental note to call her before the weekend is over for a chat and to make a date to catch up.

I cannot influence what will happen next with Patrick, and I will decide how I will react once I know if there is anything to react to. Given how sick I feel I know I will become anxious and tearful if I let my mind run away.

I practice saying my usual morning mantra in the mirror: "You are good enough. Everything you need is within you now," and feel slightly better. The face that is reflected back at me looks tired and a little sheepish. I had such high expectations for my night out with the spectacular Patrick Harrington and it didn't pan out at all how I had envisaged it in my mind. I was experiencing an anti-climax based on what I had anticipated, heightened all the more by my dehydration and aching head.

After a long, hot shower, a cup of herbal tea and some pain-killers I feel slightly more human. I call my Mum and tell her I am on my way and that I will stay the night. I do not have any plans and could do with both the company and the escape from the flat. I have managed to avoid Joey. I leave a short note on the kitchen counter as a courtesy and make my way to the train station to head out to Surrey.

On board the train, I check my personal email. He hasn't written to me. I unlock my phone and stare at his contact record. *Should I send him a message and thank him for taking me to dinner?* I probably should but I don't trust myself at the moment. I will do it tomorrow when I am feeling better and hopefully less fragile.

The journey is agonising. My senses jar at every screech, bump and lurch, never mind the changing odours assaulting my nose. I have yet to eat anything, I am holding out for my mother's home cooking. I am grateful I've waited to eat, as I don't think I could keep anything down. I add motion sickness to my catalogue of ailments.

I send Candice a text to see how the girls' night went. Typing the letters as the train sways and rolls along makes me feel queasy so I keep it brief and throw my phone back in my bag, turning to focus on the horizon outside, and the London landscape whizzing by. I keep watching as the terraced houses give way to lush green countryside. The dull grey sky mirrors my mood and I try resolutely to block out the music coming from the headphones of the guy sitting beside me. I feel like he is too close, in my personal space. I can still smell the burger he was finishing when I boarded the train. I feel crowded in by all the people in the carriage. There is a child behind me who seems to alternate between screaming at the top of his lungs and kicking my chair with vigour. I feel like I am in my own personal hell.

I am relieved to reach the sanctuary of my mother's house. I drop my bag at the door and flop onto her sofa. It feels like home and I instantly feel myself relax, comforted by the familiar surrounds. She appears from the kitchen, holding a tea towel. I see her eyebrows lift as she takes in the state of me. She hasn't even said anything yet and I feel like bursting into tears. I want a hug or even a peck on the cheek but we have never been very tactile in my family so I stay where I am.

I take a deep breath to hold the tears back and force a bright smile. I can see she wants to ask me how I am but knows better than to do so. "Dinner will be ready about 5pm, sweetie. After hearing your voice on the phone I thought you might need an early night. Perhaps we could watch a movie this afternoon? I've rented 'The Life of David Gale' with Kate Winslet and Kevin Spacey on LoveFilm. Get it started and I will join you in a moment."

My mum loves Kate Winslet. She and I have watched 'Titanic' more times than I care to count. She retreats to the kitchen without waiting for me to respond. I stay horizontal on the couch. In a few minutes she is back in the room and turning the TV on. She lifts my legs and sits down under them so I can still have the length of the couch. I watch her squinting at the remote control as she tries to figure out which buttons do what. I put my hand out and she passes it over without protest.

I realise, as the opening credits roll, that I have seen this movie before. It looks at the morality of the death penalty in Texas. Kevin Spacey is a college professor and long-time activist against capital punishment who finds himself on death row after being sentenced for murder. I recall it being melodramatic and a bit ludicrous but a tearjerker none the less. I will be able to cry unashamedly, releasing all my pent up emotions from last night and if my mother asks I will blame the scenes on the screen.

The floodgates open much sooner than I expect, as I watch Spacey addressing a lecture hall full of college students. His words touch my core as I think about Patrick Harrington, Joey, my father and my own recent desires.

"According to Lacan, fantasies have to be unrealistic. The moment you get what you see you don't want it any more. In order to continue to exist, desire must have its objects perpetually absent. It's not the it that you want; it's the fantasy of it. Desire supports crazy fantasies."

I am dumb founded as I listen. I feel like he is speaking directly to me as I think about all the absurd scenarios I have been running over and over in my head. He continues to the attentive lecture hall, "According to Pascal, we are only truly happy when daydreaming about future happiness. Therefore, 'the hunt is sweeter than the kill.' Also, and therefore, be careful what you wish for; not because you'll get it, but because you're bound not to want it once you do."

I sit up on one elbow, eyes and ears transfixed. It is like clouds parting to reveal the sun as the situation I find myself in becomes clear to me. This is exactly what drives Patrick Harrington. It's the thrill of the chase and once he catches me, *then what?* I lay back down letting my body sink deeply into the comforting sofa cushions. My emotions are bubbling up, threatening to overflow as each sentence is delivered. I am feeling overwrought.

"As Lacan says, leading by your wants will never make you truly happy. Therefore, to be fully human, you have to strive to live by your ideals and ideas, and not to measure your life in terms of what desires you have gained but by those small moments of integrity, compassion, rationality and self-sacrifice. The only way we can measure the significance of our own lives, therefore, is by valuing the lives of others."

The tears are sliding down my face and dropping off my chin, pooling on my clavicle. I focus on trying to stifle my sobs. I am struggling to understand the significance of my own life as I think about the pain and suffering I have endured. I hate myself for fantasising about a man that can only bring me more hurt, and feel the all-too-familiar guilt washing over me, as though I have betrayed Joey and the sanctity of our relationship for being able to move into a state of frenzied desire so quickly after our break-up. The whole notion of fantasy is sickening to me as I think about my father's fetishes and what he liked to do. This ponderous film is plunging me into self-examination and I don't like it. I feel neurotic and highly agitated but other than the tears that are silently rolling down my face, I manage to outwardly contain my angst.

My mother acts oblivious to my crying and quietly watches the screen. I slow my breathing down and try to restore myself to calm. By the time the movie ends I am calm, but I also feel hollow. My mother gets up, turns the TV off and disappears into the kitchen to finish preparing our meal. I realise my mouth is watering as the aromas of the roast cooking with onion and garlic waft through to me. My mother's roast chicken has such a reassuring smell to me, it's a smell that takes me back to happier times in my childhood and signals that everything will be alright.

We sit in companionable silence at my mother's tiny kitchen table and I devour the plate of food she has put in front of me. I can feel her watching me but I avoid making eye contact or starting a conversation. We sit together eating, the sound of our cutlery scraping against the crockery the only noise in the kitchen. I know my mother senses that all is not well with me but she is also not one to push me, as she knows I will clam up.

"Joey and I broke up, Mum," I say looking down at my empty plate.

I dare not look up, as I do not want to see the pity in her eyes. I see the tears dropping onto the china in front of me and my shoulders start to shake. I know I am crying about what I have lost as much as I am crying with remorse for my actions last night.

We have a short conversation. My mum is as brutally honest as Eloise was on hearing the news. She tells me that I am better off without Joey and that while she will always love him, she never thought he was the man I would spend my life with. It is so typical that people see fit to tell you what they really think of your relationship once you have broken up. I scoff at her words and instantly regret it. I see the hurt look and the pain in my mother's eyes. I can't help it that I don't believe in the fairytale 'happily ever after' *and who can blame me when I grew up in the shadows of my parents' failing marriage?*

"Is there someone else?" she ventures. I feel as if her eyes can see into my soul. I nod meekly.

"Alexandra. I know you. I know you feel guilty but there is

no reason to. You need to prioritise your own happiness. If you don't, you will always be second at best. I say please yourself. At least that way you're pleasing someone."

I laugh at this. I admire her for this insight given how unhappy her life has been. She is right but the words are easy to say, harder live by. I decide I need to confide in someone and I know my mother is as safe as a vault. But then given her solitary lifestyle, *who would she tell?*

I skip over the details of the break-up with Joey and instead find my energy picking up as I animatedly describe Patrick, the note he left on my desk, the excitement I felt at being asked out, and going to dinner with him.

I can see her scrutinising me and trying not to let her face betray the concern I know she is feeling for me. I wonder to myself if she wants to take back the advice she gave me earlier. My mother has never met Eloise but she knows enough about her and me to know how much my relationship with her means to me, and how dedicated I am to my job.

"I think you should always trust your gut instinct, Alex. Ever since you were a little girl you've had an uncanny ability to read people and situations quickly. I remember a time, you can't have been more than five, when you spotted a bully in the playground and where the other children were frightened, and you weren't. I was ready to intervene but before I had even got to my feet you'd plucked up the courage to approach him and I watched with pride and disbelief as you won that boy over with your kindness." She is smiling as she remembers and I feel a little embarrassed.

"You are diplomatic, loyal and caring. Sometimes to a fault. Remember, as I said earlier, you're responsible for your own happiness. You'll be the best judge of what's right for you. Not Eloise, or Patrick or Joey. This is your life and you must live it how you choose."

I want to cry again at these words. I need to trust my instincts and take responsibility for my own happiness. I smile at my mum. I feel completely drained, the effects of the night before and the emotional roller coaster of the day catching up with me. I excuse myself and head upstairs to the spare room. It is all made up, ready for me. The duvet pulled straight, no crinkles to be seen. I know everything is freshly laundered from the cosy flannel sheets to the floral Laura Ashley quilt cover with matching feather pillows all stacked neatly, standing to attention. I almost don't want to get into bed for fear of disturbing what my mum has so meticulously put together. There are two fluffy white towels and a face cloth sitting on the chest of drawers, alongside a glass jug with iced water and lemon, condensation dripping onto the coaster underneath it.

I curse myself as I realise I have left my bag downstairs by the door. I have no energy to make the trip down and back up the stairs to fetch my things so decide to sleep in my underwear. I don't need an alarm and I can skip brushing my teeth for one night. My head hits the pillow and I drift off as I hear the train tracks thundering from the back garden with the noise of an approaching train. The house shakes a little as it passes and then silence descends again.

After a dreamless sleep, I get up in the morning. Well, just; it is close to noon by the time I pad downstairs in my mother's bathrobe. I am famished and parched. My mother is at the kitchen table knitting. I put my hands on her shoulders and squeeze them as I pass her. The radio is on Classical FM and I feel uplifted as the lively notes of Bizet's Carmen fill the room.

My mother is smiling at me. I know she will be relieved to see that my dour mood has shifted and that there is more colour in my cheeks. I know that I looked like the walking dead yesterday and she would have been worried. She waves at me to take a seat and gets up to put the kettle on, lighting the Aga. As she prepares eggs and toast I get up to retrieve my bag. I take my phone out and my heart skips a beat as I see that Patrick Harrington has sent me a text message.

I open it and see that it was sent yesterday. It is a photo of him in a black cab. The message reads 'On my way to the airport. I enjoyed myself last night. Do let me know that you got home safely. P x.'

I am elated. And a bit shocked. I am pleased that he got in touch with me, and that he signed off with a kiss. But then I haven't replied and I know he doesn't like to wait; his expectation is a quick response. His message pierces my memory as I recall that he was going to Dublin for the night to celebrate his brother's birthday. I curse myself again for leaving my bag downstairs and for being too lazy to retrieve it last night. But then, I think to myself with satisfaction, *forcing an impatient man to wait may just work in my favour.*

I compose a response. 'I got home safely. Thank you for a lovely evening.' I do not add my initial or a kiss. I think this is safe. I hit send. Within moments my phone is flashing with his name and the familiar chirrup sound accompanies the incoming message. My mother smiles and looks at me knowingly as she places a heaped plate of food in front of me. I blush.

'Did you like my photo? I fly back soon. What are your plans for the afternoon? I want to see you again, and not in the office on Monday. You name a place and I'll be there. P x.'

Wow. My mind doesn't know how to respond but my body is definitely reacting. My heart is hammering and my mouth has gone dry. My legs are bouncing up and down on the chair, my feet tapping the floor. I feel my back straighten as I try to process the fact that the breathtaking Patrick Harrington is asking me out again, even after my drunken display of neediness. I am fraught with terror at the thought of seeing him again when I don't remember everything that was said and done on Friday night. I also know I'm not going to pass on the offer so I will have to face my fears.

While shovelling egg into my mouth with one hand, I rack my brains for an acceptable venue and am searching the Top Table app with my other hand, checking reviews to see if each venue is suitable for taking a man of the world, THE Patrick Harrington, there. All I can find on the app are restaurants and I don't want to presume that we are eating together. I realise that wherever we go will be a far cry from the places he is used to. I reply sending him the address and postcode for the Boathouse, a pub around the corner from my flat. I know he lives in Knightsbridge so I am surprised that he is willing to come to Putney to see me, but I won't argue.

'I'll be there at 4pm as long as you don't mind me coming straight from the airport. You still haven't commented on the photo Alex.' This time there is no sign off or kiss. I guess I have annoyed him. I was so focused on where to meet him that I had ignored his question. I take a second look at the picture and smile to myself. It's a self-taken headshot. He looks a little awkward given he is trying to frame himself and take the picture but he looks incredible. No signs of the night before showing on his face I notice. Fresh worry pushes into my brain as I wonder how much drunker than him I was. I am sure he doesn't have blanks in his memory.

'You look great! Ax.' I hit send without pausing, as I know I will erase the kiss if I think too long about it. I am grinning like a Cheshire cat. I glance up and see my mother smiling. "Go take a shower and get moving, Alex," she encourages me.

I get to the Boathouse and scan the Sunday drinkers. I can't see him so I make my way upstairs. It is a clear bright day, and the clocks have recently gone forward proclaiming the end of winter. It is still cool out but the collective mood of the city is lifting, safe in the knowledge that the winter is over for another year. I see him and take a deep breath. I had forgotten how devilishly handsome he looks in casual clothing.

He is wearing a shiny black quilted jacket with fleece sleeves. *Probably Moncler*, I think to myself as I approach. I love clothes and consequently shopping. My fashion knowledge has been buoyed by the Vogue magazine that gets delivered to my house each month and by a year of working for the ever-style-conscious Eloise Little. Patrick stands up; he has yet to see me. He shrugs out of his coat and flips it round to hang it on the chair. He has only beaten me here by moments, I realise as I look at my watch. It is not yet four o'clock.

I pull up a seat as he sits down. He is back on his feet immediately, moving out from the table to help me with my chair, ever the gentleman. As soon as I am close, that masculine scent he wears is pervading the air, making me dizzy with desire. We both sit down and our gazes lock. *I am smitten*, I think helplessly. Yesterday's self-recrimination is largely forgotten.

"Interesting neighbourhood, Alex." His eyes are twinkling, he is smiling at me and I can't help but simper back at him. I feel a sense of excitement that not even my fears about the events of Friday night can quell.

A waitress is with us and she purrs as she engages Patrick, asking what he would like as he scans the wine list. He orders a bottle of Cloudy Bay Sauvignon Blanc and a large bottle of sparkling water. She ignores me, her full focus on the good-looking man in front of her. I want to laugh at her brazenness but instead I am watching his reaction. He is charming and pleasant causing her to giggle and bat her eyelids. This must be a regular occurrence for the dashing Mr Harrington.

When she is gone, he turns that charm on me. "I can't stop thinking about you, Alex. I couldn't wait to see you again and I wanted to make sure we were okay after Friday night."

I smile at him and then look down at my hands. The intensity of his look is too much. *He couldn't wait to see me? And he used the word 'we'.* I can feel his eyes on me. *What can I say when I know I departed in haste but I am unsure why?* I know that I was begging him for something before I got in the taxi but I have no idea what I was saying.

"I'm sorry I didn't take you up on your request to accompany me home but I didn't think it was right. I know I have a reputation as a ladies' man but I respect you, Alex. I didn't want you to think you were anything but special."

My heart sinks like a lead balloon. I can't believe my ears. I was pleading with him to take me home and he refused. But then it's because he wants more than sex. I decide to make light of it and try to move the situation swiftly on. I am mortified but try not to show it.

"I guess I really enjoyed that divine wine you ordered. Perhaps a little too much. I'm really pleased you asked to see me today and I promise not to overdo it this time." I manage a weak smile and hope my response is enough. *Enough for what I ask myself?*

We finish the bottle of wine and chat companionably as the last of the sunlight disappears from the sky, its pastel hues melting into the ripples of the Thames. He tells me about his trip home to Ireland and I listen attentively as he tells me all about his brother's birthday party and how he had a wonderful time catching up with his family. His eyes sparkle as he talks about his mother and we laugh as he describes the claptrap car that his sister arrived at the airport to collect him in.

I really like this man. I can't quite reconcile why he is interested in me but I am revelling in the fact that I am here on a second date. The same waitress has been back, trying to divert Patrick's attention away from me; unsuccessfully, I note with pleasure.

Patrick walks me to the High Street where he has a cab waiting to take him home. I had wondered where his overnight bag was. He must spend a fortune to have cars waiting on him. He insists on walking me to my flat but I am worried about running into Joey, and I don't think it is right that Patrick gets to see where I live. It is bad enough we are on the street together so dangerously close to my apartment.

He reluctantly realises he will not convince me when I refuse him for the third time, telling him it is a short walk. He makes me promise to text him once I am safely inside my flat. I nod and grin. There is no mention of a follow up date or of even seeing each other at work tomorrow. *He is a formidable man*, I think as he gets into the car after planting a chaste kiss on my cheek. I was hoping for more but then I guess if this is going to go anywhere I need to play it cool. Particularly after my last performance. As the door to the flat clicks behind me I fire off a quick 'Home safe.' to ensure that I comply with Mr Harrington's orders. 'Pleased' flashes up seconds later.

I feel really happy. I think of my mother's words and smile, all the way to my eyes. There are certain things I know I can't change, but I can change how I think about them. And I can enjoy myself in the moment. Immensely.

Harrington

I am staring at the ceiling but my eyes are not actually seeing it. As I think back over my evening with Alexandra Fisher, I feel an odd mixture of regret and arousal. I lie there reflecting on our time together. The arousal wins out and I feel decidedly frisky.

I smile to myself as I think about the passionate kissing and her hands touching my body. I push the duvet back and clumsily manoeuvre myself out of my boxers and start to touch myself as the images of Alexandra Fisher stream unbidden into my mind.

I need to get up and get moving. I have a flight to catch. I can't stop smiling as the black cab takes me to Paddington to catch the Heathrow Express. I snap a 'selfie' with my iPhone and decide to tease Alex by sending her the photo. I won't accept that our first date and the way it clumsily ended meant that this pursuit was over.

By the time I have boarded my flight she has still not replied. I know she fancies me so I can only imagine that she is embarrassed about the night before. I have been thinking about it and I decide that I need to see her again. I know if I do, I can smooth over the way our first date ended.

I disembark in Dublin and my dear old mother is waiting at

the airport. Every time I see her I think how she has aged. I come back to Ireland very rarely as I find my family very much like hard work. I have been so much more successful than all of them put together. There is always expectations of loans and hand outs as well as snide remarks from those who can hardly contain their jealously. It is more than I can bear to be in these situations, where I have to bite my tongue. It goes against my better judgement but I would never do anything to upset Mam, as much as I would like to tell my brothers where to get off. "The love of family is one of life's greatest blessings," my mother often says. If only she knew, I thought bleakly.

"Paddy, my love, you look so happy," she beams at me. I am surprised, as I know I usually have to force myself to keep a smile in place whenever I am here. I didn't realise that this might be apparent to my family, and I had thought I definitely had my mother fooled. I should know better. It seems that Ms Fisher has had a lasting effect on me. I cringe a little at the affectionate name my mother has used, reminding me of my childhood.

"If it's a woman you should marry her," she trills. I am jolted at the thought that not only can my darling mother can read my thoughts, but also that she would even think to mention marriage to me.

Again, as if reading my thoughts, she changes tack. "We're all so happy you came over for Danny's birthday. You know it means the world to me, to all of us. So good of you to find time in your busy schedule."

I look at the diminutive, ageing woman beside me, and wonder if that last comment is a barb. It certainly felt like it, but then I am always more sensitive when it comes to my mother. I seek her approval like Jason and the Argonauts sought the Golden Fleece.

Siobhan, my fifty-year old sister, is waiting in the car and starts the engine as we approach. I am ashamed and the embarrassment of getting into a banged up old Volkswagen Golf burns my cheeks. I am quickly reminded why I don't like coming here. Humble roots are one thing but this is a joke. I much prefer the London jet-set life I have worked so hard to cultivate.

My sister nods in my general direction as she pulls away. Siobhan suffers from anxiety attacks and depression. She is surly and uncommunicative, and has been unable to hold down a job for most of her adult life. Like others in my family, she relies on the steady drip feed of money I send to Ireland each month. My mother holds the purse strings and allocates the money according to where she thinks it is needed. This, at least, prevents them all approaching me for separate handouts. I would be leaking money if my family had anything to do with it. I don't know what I will do to manage this situation when my mother dies. I shudder at that thought and dismiss it quickly.

I check my phone again. I have a handful of text messages but nothing from Alex. I sigh and feel myself slipping deep into thought as I contemplate how to grease the wheels to help this situation. It feels like we are stuck. I know she will be unsure of how to proceed after her request to come home with me. If she even remembers.

My sister is grunting something. I don't hear her and ask her to repeat herself. "You staying with Danny, I say." Her eyes are on the road. I look at the side of her face and at her limp, unwashed brown hair falling on pale white skin.

I raise my eyebrows at the Irish-ness of it all. I shake my head and wait for the inevitable intervention from my mother. Why change habits of a lifetime. I know she will see Siobhan off my back. It is a deliberate attempt to goad me into revealing that I am staying in five star accommodation at the Merrion as I always do on my infrequent trips home. I book the garden suite and sometimes, though not this time, Mam will join me as it has a second bedroom and lots of space.

Why not enjoy my hard earned money? There is plenty of it after all. Staying in my own suite at the Merrion gives me the option of trawling for women and it saves the indignity of being woken at 5am by my over-excited nieces and nephews jumping on me. And if I was to have a woman naked in my bed I couldn't countenance any interruptions. Probably the biggest draw card other than privacy is the en suite. I certainly don't take kindly to having to share a bathroom.

"You know Paddy makes his own plans. You leave him be now."

My sister makes a noise like she is hissing but says nothing in response to my mother. She knows better than to get into a tussle when I am the subject, as she knows she will come off second best. She still took the opportunity to show her disapproval, I notice, and I think that she clearly fails to acknowledge the truth that I could cut the money tree down at any time.

Siobhan drops me off and I am pleased to be rid of the negative energy that surrounds her and seems to suck the life force out of me. I know the doormen at the hotel well, they know who I am and how well I tip so they remain professionally nonchalant as I climb out of the beat up car.

I feel at home at once upon entering the ornate white and black marble lobby and feel the relief, as I often do, that having money brings. I know money can't buy happiness but try being happy without it.

I decide to leave my phone in the room as I head out to Danny's party. I am driving myself crazy. Every time it lights up with a message I hope beyond hope it is her. Instead, I get the usual hopefuls checking where I might be going out this Saturday night. Get a life, I think to myself. I will contact you if I want something, not the other way round.

I steel myself knowing it is going to be a long night amongst company not of my choosing. At least I look good, I think as I glance down at my tailor made white shirt that fits my lean frame perfectly, tucked into dark denim True Religion jeans, and finished off with a tan belt with a large buckle. The leather matches my hand made shoes and the belt's centre feature never fails to draw a woman's eyes to my groin, like a promise.

The best part of my evening is being sat next to my beloved mother. We spend much of the meal with our heads together laughing at private jokes and regaling each other with new anecdotes. At 86, my mother's mind is still sharp as a steel trap even if her body is steadily giving up on her. Six children and a hard life have taken their toll.

When it comes time to mingle and the restaurant fills with more of Danny's party revellers, I bide my time. After what seems like an age, I make my way over to the birthday boy and slip him an envelope. I thank him for having me and start to say my goodbyes. "You're taking the mick, Paddy. It's not even midnight, boy." Danny is already worse the wear for liquor and is speaking loudly despite my standing right next to him. He continues oblivious to the filthy look I am giving him. "Mamma says she is still here so how can you leave Paddy-o!" He is making fun of me, and of Mam, and I can't tolerate it. I had put my treasured mother in a taxi close to an hour ago and he hadn't even noticed she was gone.

I decide to walk away as I am fuming. I leave the restaurant amid sounds of raucous laughter and general celebration and make my way back to the hotel, which feels like an oasis after the madness I've endured. I have the fleeting temptation to head out and pick up a woman but after seeing all of the drunk woman at my brother's party I am not feeling very enamoured of the Irish, of either gender. My family, with the exception of my precious mother, make me ashamed of my heritage. They are certainly not poster children for the nation.

I take the elevator down to the eighteenth century wine cellars and as I walk into the oak-panelled bar I realise I can't stomach another drink. I really am furious. And these people wonder why I don't visit more often. If my mother didn't live here I wouldn't come at all, that is for certain.

I turn and push the button to call the elevator back. I look at my reflection in the lift doors. I'm a good-looking man and thankfully I don't have that same peculiarity of features as my relatives. Weak chins, dark eyes with bags, and dark mouths with thin lips that slope downwards like chevrons, failing to cover up their bitterness and rancour.

This thought gives me momentarily relief from the inner turmoil caused by my trip home. I am happy to get into my suite, only to feel my annoyance levels ascend again when I check my phone and there is still no message from Alexandra Fisher. I start to unlock my Blackberry and then decide it is too sad to be alone in a hotel room reading work emails on a Saturday night.

In the morning, following her usual Sunday morning church service, my mother arrives at the hotel to have breakfast with me. I am already in the restaurant with the Sunday morning papers, my Blackberry and coffee. This trip has barely been a reprieve from work. After a good night's sleep I have a little more perspective about the infuriating interactions with my siblings yesterday. Having said that, I can't wait for the flight back to London and normalcy.

"Patrick my dear son, I don't know what it is about you but you look different somehow. We don't talk about women but I do hope that you're happy. I think someone is making you smile. Try and allow yourself that joy, Paddy. Let them in a little. My marriage to your father was a disaster to be sure. But that doesn't mean you have to shun relationships." She is holding my hand on the table as she speaks earnestly to me. Her blue eyes as piercing and enchanting as my own. She is right; we never talk about my love life. I usually find it very uncomfortable and right now I feel no different.

After eggs and pastries, my sister arrives to take my mother home. I hug my mother tightly, bending down to put my chin on her shoulder. Her fragile form is evident in my arms. I squeeze her and tell her I love her. I feel myself welling up with emotion and concern. I worry that each time I say goodbye it may be the last time I see my precious Mam.

"Go for it Paddy. A chuisle mo chroí," she whispers in my ear, the Gaelic expression meaning 'Pulse of my heart.' I ignore my sister and I don't see them out, as I do not wish to lay eyes on that dilapidated vehicle again. That would be enough to send me back into a tailspin.

I arrive at the airport and make my way to the lounge. Another thing that annoys me about travelling back to Dublin is the airport doesn't have the same amenities I am used to. Along with frequent fliers, anyone can enter the lounge on paying the requisite fee. This means that instead of the usual high-class clientele, I am forced to share space with the average traveller, marvelling loudly about the luxury of the facilities. They haven't lived, I think to myself.

Thankfully, my PA knows not to book me on Aer Lingus or Ryan Air. I am on a British Airways flight. This means I will get treated like I deserve to be treated, even on this short haul hop. As a member of Caldwell's Executive team I am now a British Airways Premier Card holder. While being a gold card member of the BA Executive Club had its perks, this is the exclusive loyalty card that every frequent traveller wants. This card is only available by invitation and the British Airways Board determines membership. A high honour indeed.

The benefits include being handled with kid gloves from the moment you arrive at the airport, through to the lounge, at the gate, in-flight and then disembarking and being whisked to the front of the immigration queue once at your destination. I love other travellers looking at me trying to determine who I am and why I am being treated like a superstar. The airline ensures that your every whim is catered for. They will bump someone off a flight to ensure you get a seat if requested, and they will even hold up an aircraft if a late arriving flight means you may miss your connection.

I board the London-bound aircraft and take my seat in 1A. I put the black Premier Card back in my wallet, alongside my Centurion American Express. Another card that ensures I can live the good life. While I pay an annual membership fee, I have access to pretty much anything I need, with a first rate dedicated concierge service and travel agent ready to help me twenty-four hours a day.

The card itself is made of anodized titanium, with the information and numbers etched in carbon fibre. It never fails to impress the ladies, even if they are unaware of the high bar that Amex set for invitation to their elite society. Sometimes, judging by the woman, I will not use the card, preferring to pay in cash or choosing to dine at an establishment that runs a tab for me. I am acutely aware that some women are bewitched by my wealth and lose sight of the fact that their sole purpose should be pleasing me, instead betraying themselves as the gold diggers they are.

My phone pings with the familiar iPhone tri-tone signalling a text message. I fish my phone from my jacket pocket and am delighted to see that Alex Fisher has finally deigned to reply to me. I decide to ask her out. I figure I can head straight from the airport to her neighbourhood, as long as she doesn't live outside central London. I figure this is a safe bet; anyone that works for Eloise 'the brow beater' Little works all the hours that god gives. I am sure she will be within a reasonable tube journey to Canary Wharf and not an express train into the countryside.

Alex accepts my invitation and gives me an address of a pub in Putney, South West London. Perfect, I think. I never check baggage, regardless of how far I fly for or for how long. There is always a laundry service or I can buy what I need at my destination. Waiting at a luggage carousel is a waste of my precious time. I can be off the flight, into a cab and sharing a drink with object of my affection in a few hours' time. Just how I like it. The frustration of my family and Alex's lack of responses are forgotten as I smile to myself. This is date two. I will woo her and ensure this day ends without incident, thus ensuring a smooth transition to date three and my bedroom.

The taxi drops me on the south side of Putney Bridge and I

walk onto Putney Wharf to the riverfront and find the Boathouse. Not my kind of place, I observe, as I study the outside. It has two floors and a rowing boat affixed to the façade. Interesting choice, Ms Fisher.

I scan the interior as I walk in, looking for Alex and checking out the clientele. There are plenty of Sunday afternoon drinkers already ensconced downstairs at the wooden tables with their mismatching chairs. I decide to make my way upstairs and find a table under the exposed steel beams, close to the floor to ceiling windows that overlook the flowing Thames River. I cannot see Alex anywhere. I pull a chair out with my back to the view, ever the gentleman, giving the lady the best seat.

I take my puffa jacket off and hang it on the back of my chair and sit down. No sooner has my arse touched the seat and she is in front of me. She looks divine in a trench coat and scarf. Skinny jeans are just evident and she is wearing ankle boots with a good size heel. I approve, Ms Fisher. I am on my feet and pulling back a chair for her as she removes her coat to reveal a tight-fitting top. Her figure is exquisite.

She puts her woollen hat down on the table and I notice her hair is a little messy. Instinctively, an image of her with bed hair flashes into my mind. I touch her arm as she sits and I get an electric shock from static. How poignant, I am hoping she will attribute romance to the reaction rather than science.

"Interesting neighbourhood, Alex," I say in a mocking tone but with gentle eyes and a smile on my lips. Our eyes lock and I realise just how attracted to this girl I am.

A waitress is upon us with menus and the offer of drinks. She is petite with long dark hair and very large breasts, I notice, without looking too hard. As if seeing Alex up close again wasn't enough, my cock twitches in my pants as the waitress flaps around me, clearly flustered by my good looks as I order us a bottle of wine and a bottle of sparkling water. I try to keep the smug feeling from reaching my eyes or playing out in my body language. I would bang this girl for sure but I quickly remind myself of why I am here, to progress with the conquest I have started. A conquest that has consumed me since the moment I laid eyes on this woman. Aside from the obvious smoking hot body and beautiful face, I am drawn to her wisdom and kindness as well as her innocence and naivety. This girl is the real deal.

I decide that a full Patrick Harrington charm offensive is required and want to appeal to her vanity while also assuring her that my intentions are honourable, that I care about her. "I can't stop thinking about you, Alex. I couldn't wait to see you again and I wanted to make sure we were okay after Friday night."

I decide to address the issue of how our Friday night ended head on. "I'm sorry I didn't take you up on your request to accompany me home but I didn't think it was right. I know I have a reputation as a ladies' man but I respect you, Alex. I didn't want you to think you were anything but special."

I hear myself talking and think how delightfully smooth I am. I watch her face and see that I am getting the desired reaction. I was right to tackle this, as it is clear that she would not have brought it up and it is certainly what has been holding her back from feeling comfortable to engage with me freely. I feel rash now for worrying about the lack of text messages from her. I condemn myself; an infrequent and therefore unfamiliar moment of self-doubt.

I see her opening up like a flower in front of me, basking in my attention. She is clearly enthralled by me. We chat amiably and I am again surprised at just how much I am enjoying myself in this girl's company. She makes me laugh; telling me snippets of what it is like to work for Eloise. I note that she has impeccable judgement. At no point do I feel like she is giving away details that I would frown on as an Executive myself. She has a way with words, which is high praise coming from me, and she is very easy to be around.

I ask her old she is. A question that has been bugging me. I have tried to work it out from our conversations and from what I had gleaned about her from Facebook. "How old do you think I am?" she asks teasingly. A question no man, not even one as silver-tongued as me, ever wishes to have to answer. It is on a par with 'does my bum look big in this?'

"Do you know how old I am?" I throw the question back to her. She tips her head to the side as she pretends to examine me and she starts laughing. "You don't play fair, but then I guess I put you in an awkward position. Let's swap drivers' licences." She is pleased with the inventive solution she is proposing and without waiting for me to agree she is fishing her purse from her bag on the floor.

I flip my wallet open and flick my licence across the table to her. She places hers gently in front of me. I pick it up and am drawn to her photograph rather than looking at her date of birth. She is a natural beauty that is for sure, and very photogenic. Photos for licences and passports are notoriously bad but not this one of Alex. She looks lovely with the hint of a smile playing at her lips and her eyes locked into the camera lens, as if the Alex Fisher in the photograph is staring right back at me as I scrutinise her.

I look at her date of birth and feel my head pulling back as if to get a better look. I can't believe it. We have the same birthday. I start chuckling and look up to see her face and she looks worried at the sound of my laughter. "We share the same birthday, Alex. But then with the kind of access you have to Caldwell's data you probably knew that already?" I say in a friendly tone, not wanting her to feel uncomfortable.

I can see the beginnings of a blush as she retorts, "We'll have to compare notes on our birthday celebrations, Patrick Florence." Her smile is warm and the blush has gone. Bold, I think to myself, and I like her all the more for it. I dare not tell her that my father, among his many sins, had wanted Florence as my first name. My mother's good sense had won out and the compromise of having it as my middle name was struck. How different my life might have been if I had endured the indignity of living with a feminine sounding first name.

"Perhaps we might share a celebration...?" I raise an eyebrow and look at her. She slides my licence back to me and doesn't answer. She is not easy to read but I can see she is enjoying herself and I like the fact that she keeps me working for her affection. I take one last look at her driving licence to work out her age, the whole point of this exercise, and causally flip the plastic card back to her.

Alex excuses herself to go to the ladies' room. Within moments, the brunette waitress is buzzing around our table, topping up our wine glasses and making eyes at me. She has the look of a minx about her and I am tempted. In a split second I decide that there is no harm in seeing if I can get her number and in the interests of time I ask her directly.

"Perhaps you'd like to go out sometime?" Before my sentence is even finished she is slipping me a note with her name and phone number on it. I slip it into my wallet and try not to break into a wide smile. The Harrington pull strikes again.

"What about your friend?" she asks, almost petulantly, using her head to gesture to the empty seat, all the while looking at me with unashamed lust.

"I'm sure she won't mind. She might even like to join us," I venture. This causes my new friend to widen both her brown eyes and her smile. We both register that Alex is making her way back to the table. The waitress tops up our water glasses and asks me if we would like anything else as if our interchange has not taken place. Not the first time she has pounced on another woman's man, I think, and I deplore her ethics, even if they suit me down to the ground. What a slut.

"Just the check," I say dismissively, without even looking at her. Alex is sitting down, the trusting look from her doe eyes stabs at my heart. I am exhilarated by the naughtiness of my interaction with the hopeful waitress but it is tinged with another emotion. Is it guilt? Could my ever-perceptive mother be right and this girl is different from all the rest? Never, I think. No chance.

We fall back into easy conversation about the work week ahead as we finish our wine. I insist on walking Alex back to her flat as the light from the sun has long since gone. She insists that it is moments away, a short walk around the corner. I am persistent with my offer as I wish to see where she lives and I wonder fleetingly if she may ask me inside after Friday's pleading. Perhaps it will only take me two dates after all. My cock stirs again at this thought.

We leave the pub and walk along the riverside and back to the bridge and the high street. Alex is holding my arm companionably. I like the feel of her touch. I am looking for the car I have waiting to take me home after realising that Alex is stubbornly not going to let me walk her home, or do anything else for that matter. I am frustrated, but realise pleasantly so, as the dance plays out. Of course she is going to make me wait. What she doesn't realise is that she is creating a monster in me. I win at all costs and the longer this plays out, the worse it will be for her as the stakes increase like a high-roller poker game. I see her in my mind's eye, at my house, and I know exactly what I will do to her, while my cameras roll.

Date three it is, Ms Fisher. But I am not going to play all my cards just yet. I give her a chaste kiss on the cheek. I am about to move away when she takes hold of my arm and kisses me on the lips and moves back again all in a fluid motion. I retreat into the cab and feel the forces of desire running straight into my groin. I return her smile and wave as the car pulls away from the curb.

I feel really happy. I think of my mother's words and smile, all the way to my eyes. There are certain things I know I can't change, but I can influence how this girl thinks about them. And I can enjoy myself in the moment. Immensely.

Alexandra

I am awake before my alarm goes off on Monday morning and I spring out of bed. For a change, I'm feeling like I can't get to work quickly enough. Of course I love my job and the kudos it commands, but all I can think about is seeing Patrick Harrington. I reflect on how easy it was to be in his company yesterday and while I have alarm bells ringing and red flags popping up in my mind about the wisdom of spending more time with him, I push them all aside and practically dance my way to the bathroom to get ready for the day ahead. I feel like singing.

Not even a terse exchange with Joey alters my mood. He and I have not seen each other and as such have managed to avoid rehashing the break-up. I know he has been going out drink-ing with his buddies a lot as I hear him come home late, bang-ing around trying to sort himself out in the wee hours. The spare room smells of unwashed clothes and most days he doesn't bother opening the curtains. I feel awful that he seems to be coping by drowning his sorrows but I can't take on his issues. Any sympathy I might feel is jettisoned by my annoyance at the snail's pace he is moving at trying to find a new place to live. I address the issue of our living arrangements without preamble.

I haven't seen him in days, but I see fit to poke the open wound with my words in the hope that it might get him riled up enough to take action.

I am still smiling as I get to my desk regardless of the fact that it is Monday morning and there is a full week of work ahead of me. My phone beeps as I put my bag down. A text message. I shrug my coat off and go and hang it in the closet. Despite being the end of March it is still chilly out. My phone beeps again impatiently. I sit down and unlock it to see I have a message from Patrick. Instinctively I swivel in my chair to see if he is in his office. He is. My heart starts hammering.

"You look smug, Alex. Good weekend, was it?" Eloise's PA is staring at me across the desks and I realise how risky this whole business is. "Yes, fine thanks. Yours?" I enquire without addressing her comment about my self-satisfied look. I am looking at her over my computer screen now so she can only see my eyes. My heart is about to burst out of my chest at the reminder that I am skating on perilously thin ice. She is smirking at me. "Not sure it was as good as yours, Ms Fisher. Same old, same old, in fact."

I smile politely and look down to end the conversation. I realise that having Patrick Harrington in my phone under his actual name is a bad plan. Both Eloise and her PA are like bloodhounds on the scent as soon as something doesn't smell right, and I do not wish to share this piece of gossip with them. *The whole thing would turn into a circus*, I think with a heavy heart. *What am I getting myself into?*

I adjust his contact entry so his name reads as Rich Banks. I smile at my own wit; it could be a real person and should any prying eyes see this name flash up on my phone they will be none the wiser to the true identity of this 'friend'.

'Fancy meeting up after work tonight? Maybe not Putney this time. PH.'

Oh my god. Date number three. Friday and our first date was only three days ago. He doesn't mess about. I can't tell if the reference to Putney is to show that he was annoyed that he had to come south of the river and out of Zone One to see me. He has not signed the message with a kiss this time. I flick the silent switch on and put my phone down like it's hot. I need to breathe, and to stop analysing every word this man says and sends. My head is starting to ache and I haven't even started work yet.

I begin to read Eloise's email, her inbox overflowing from the weekend traffic, and I try to get myself into the right headspace to work. Before long I see my phone's screen light up out of the corner of my eye. I am glad I thought to turn the ringer off. Eloise's PA would be all over me if she could hear each message sound as it hit my phone. Worse still if she could see my reaction. I can barely disguise my pleasure as I read the second message.

'Got a better offer? I doubt it. P x' I shake my head at the cheek of the man but he is making me smile. And a kiss this time. He is messing with my head that is for sure.

'Depends what you're offering...' I ping back without signing off. I fear this is going to turn into a conversation if I'm not careful. I am smiling like a clown at my screen, though my eyes are not focussing, I am in the middle distance instead. The very thought of him is consuming me, my work is forgotten.

'I think you know what I can offer. I want you... To spend the evening with me...' Wow this is starting to get saucy pretty quickly. I can't wipe the inane grin from my face as I revel in his attention even though those warning bells are clanging loudly again in the recesses of my mind. *This is how he does it*, I think. A well-practised seduction routine. The image of Kevin Spacey registers in my brain; I see the scene from the movie and hear that lecture once more. This is the chase, the hunt. I feel like prey.

I am at loggerheads in my own mind. I want to remain just out of reach and ensure he gets as much of a thrill out of this pursuit as possible. It is the only way he will respect me. I know I desperately want this man's approval. My smile quickly turns to a frown and my heart sinks. How can I ever be good enough? He must be used to fabulous woman, with good looks, sophistication, and experience. I want to see him this evening, I know that an alien invasion wouldn't stop me accepting this invitation, but I feel wholly inadequate. I look down at my stock standard corporate attire. Straight black trousers and a neatly tailored jacket. Expensive clothes bought in the end-of-season sales but nothing amazing. I knew I would probably see Patrick today but I hadn't planned on being close enough to be scrutinised by a man that knows more than the average male about style and women's clothing.

Yesterday, over our bottle of wine he had mentioned that he likes fashion, with a particular penchant for shoes. We had laughed about the collection that I kept under my desk and he mentioned that the knee-high boots I had worn into the office that Sunday were outrageous. I had naively thought at the time that fashion was common ground and something we could discuss and enjoy together. Now, these snippets only serve to heighten my concerns about the way I look and how I dress.

'You know you want to.' Another message from 'Rich Banks'. I guess I am thinking too much and taking too long to respond. I look at the screen on my phone and stare in disbelief at the text exchange. This man could have any woman he wanted and he was pursuing me.

'Of course I do!' I hit send without stopping to even breathe for fear of being too afraid to send anything at all. I wish that I could be quick-witted or provocative but it doesn't come naturally when I know the recipient is the phenomenal Patrick Harrington. I am feeling vulnerable and will myself to exude confidence instead. *That's what he likely finds attractive in a woman* I think. *Self-assurance.*

'The only way to get rid of temptation is to yield to it.' I add my favourite Oscar Wilde quotation as a follow up. I shrug, thinking it would have looked better to send it as one message but alas, I am trying to please an impatient man and my brain is being starved of oxygen from holding my breath.

I set my phone down and promise myself not to look it at again until later in the day when I am eating my lunch. I will get no work done otherwise, and either Eloise or her PA will notice that my phone appears to be glued to my hand if I continue this text banter. Plus, that should give him something to think about. He may be impatient, and I may be insecure but I think about the words my best friend Candice repeats like a mantra. Treat 'em mean, keep 'em keen. At the end of the day, the rules of engagement with any courtship are the same. In this case, I am going head to head with a well-practised tactician and I need to use my common sense and not let my heart rule.

The morning passes in the usual blur of meetings, making calls and responding to the never-ending stream of Eloise's emails. I realise that it is after two o'clock and I am famished. I know from past experience that the main cafeteria has precious little fresh food left by this time. The salad bar, my only port of call amongst the convenience food on offer, will be well picked over. The coffee bars on various floors throughout the building stock a meagre selection of boxed sandwiches along with muffins and cakes. Nothing I would fancy eating.

I check Eloise's diary and see that she will be in her current meeting until three. I have time to slip away before I may be needed. I grab my phone and wallet and head towards the elevator bank. A rare outing into the subterranean malls of Canary Wharf during the day. I stop short, trying to decide if I need my coat, and then think better of it. I can reach the sushi bar at the other end of the underground shopping complex through the labyrinth of passages and thereby stay indoors for the whole time I am out. Out of the office but not outside. Still breathing recycled air.

I look at my phone as the elevator descends. I have six new text messages since the exchange earlier this morning with the Head of the Investment Bank. Five of the six messages are from Patrick. I can't decide if the nauseous feeling in my stomach is a physical reaction to seeing this or is merely hunger. I start to read what he has sent me.

'I can resist anything but temptation.' He is paraphrasing Oscar Wilde back at me. Nice touch.

'I'm looking forward to getting you alone.'

'Daydreaming about hanging out with you later.'

'What are you wearing under that jacket Ms Fisher?'

'I see that EL has you running on her hamster wheel. I will allow you to focus on your work for now, it'll be all pleasure later...'

This was starting to amount to sexting. My body was experiencing another reaction, this time carnal. I am startled out of my fantasy world as the lift doors open and other bank workers board to make their way with me down to lower levels. The curse of working on floor forty-two is that it takes forever just to get to the ground floor. I am shocked to realise how lost in the moment I was. A sound bite of Patrick telling me he respects me replays in my ears. I am beginning to wonder if those sugary reassuring words were all part of his master plan and whether he says the same thing to all the other women he is trying to seduce. I can see clearly that he is hoping to convert this situation from 'the hunt' to 'the kill' but I feel almost powerless to stop it. I feel like I would be shouting into a hurricane.

I wander absently through the subsurface maze of shops and cafes, my hunger forgotten as I try and make sense of the text messages from Patrick. This powerful, irresistibly good-looking man who sits on the Executive Team of my employer is lavishing his attention on me, and it is clear what he wants. I am startled as a hand grabs me on the arm, and I almost step out of my heels as my body is torn between the abrupt jolt and the forward momentum. I spin around to see the tall and imposing form of Patrick Harrington before me.

"Where are you off to, Ms Fisher? Eloise will be missing you." His eyes are alight with mischief.

I feel the now familiar sensation wash through my body at being close to this man. My eyes are trained on his tie. I slowly lift them towards his face, tracing them over his Adams apple and along his chin, which is showing the beginning signs of stubble and I wonder to myself what it would feel like to have that stubble graze my face as we kiss. My lustful musings vanish as I reach his eyes and I realise he is waiting for me to answer. Neither of us can take our eyes off each other. The longing is palpable.

"I just stepped out to grab some lunch. What brings you out into the bowels of the mall, Patrick?" His blue eyes are gleaming and I feel utterly powerless.

His hand is still on my arm. With gentle force he steers me toward the Prêt A Manger sandwich store under the escalators to our right and aims me toward a table. I sit down, the relief of taking the weight off my feet welcome. I don't think I could have endured this conversation on my heels in the middle of the shopping complex, with the weekday shoppers surging around us like a river coursing past rocks mid-stream. Now, sitting at the table with this man I am feeling very much like a fly caught in a spider's web.

"Alex, you're driving me crazy. You sit just outside my office and you're ignoring me. I know you've read my messages and I sense that you can feel the same chemistry I can, so why aren't you replying to me?" His plea is direct and earnest.

I feel silly now for making him wait. While at the same time, I am battling with that same mixture of flattery and concern I felt when Patrick revealed he had trolled me on Facebook. This was pretty full on. He had followed me and I was being told off because I wasn't responsive enough. And all because he can see me from his glass office.

Part of me wants to get up and walk away from this overpowering zealot, and go back to my simple life with Joey. The other part of me, the louder inner voice, is disagreeing and encouraging me to see this through irrespective of the outcome. I have barely dipped my toe in the water.

I smile back at this man and try to match his confidence. A knot of alternative timelines stretch out in front of me as I consider the possibilities. The hairs on my forearms rise as if charged by a strong power source. *That is exactly what you are* I think as I stare back at the determined face of Patrick Harrington. The blood pulses in my temple while simultaneously taps are opened to my groin.

"Coffee?" I offer, trying to buy myself time as I get back to my feet on shaking legs. Without waiting for an answer, I join the queue at the counter and pay the usual king's ransom for two large cappuccinos and slowly make my way back to the table. Patrick is watching me walk back holding the hot cardboard cups. I am taking short steps to ensure I don't spill any of the hot liquid or drop the coffees as I advance, feeling very much like a strong magnet is pulling me forward.

I am now wishing I had stayed put. I haven't got any closer to deciding how to answer this man and I was about to drink caffeine on an empty stomach. *Just what my nerves need*, I think sarcastically as I place his cup down in front of him and he continues to gaze at me. I take the lid off my cup before speaking.

"I'd be delighted to go out with you this evening, Patrick. However, I am conscious that we work together, so I am trying to ensure that we can get to know each other better away from the prying eyes of our colleagues. I don't want to be the subject of gossip and I most certainly am not trying to drive you crazy." Although I have to say I am secretly pleased by this description.

I slowly and very deliberately skim my finger through the froth around the rim of my coffee cup and then put it into my mouth and start to suck, ever so slowly in a bid to be seductive. I watch as Patrick bites his lip as a mirroring response, and his blue eyes gleam. I do not drop my gaze.

The start of a knowing smile plays at the edge of his exquisite lips. A smile that his eyes pick up. Eyes that are silently questioning, responding, a non-spoken conversation of such intensity it is practically telepathy.

I take a long pull of the hot coffee in front of me to try and break the spell of sexual suspense. I can't help smiling at our unspoken outpouring of desire mingled with lust. I am feeling exhilarated that I am being daring enough to behave like a minx, and that I am getting the desired reaction. Caution be damned.

"John will be waiting downstairs at 6pm," he says after a deep sigh and what feels like an eternity. He is looking over my head, avoiding eye contact. He gets up from the table, walks past me and out of the store, leaving his untouched coffee sitting on the table and a dizzy girl in his wake. I am staring straight ahead without seeing anything and feeling a bit shocked at myself for the blatant display of enthusiasm. So much for trying to treat 'em mean.

I get into the back of the BMW just before six o'clock and this time Patrick has beaten me there. He leans forward and kisses me quickly on the lips as soon as my door is shut. My heart leaps with joy thinking of the further physical contact this kiss promises. *Am I ready for this I wonder?*

John drops us on Charing Cross Road, near Leicester Square and I walk quickly, clip clopping in my heels to keep up with Patrick as he leads me into St Martin's Court and up to the door of J Sheekey. He turns and plants another quick kiss on my lips before swinging the door wide to let me in.

I quickly realise we are once again in an establishment where the worldly Patrick Harrington is well known by the staff. We are escorted away from the main restaurant and through to the oyster and champagne bar, the less formal eatery with seating around an elegant horseshoe-shaped bar.

We are seated at the two bar stools at the far end of the counter, the most discreet seats. As I sit down I watch as chefs prepare dishes in front of me. The place setting is simple yet elegant with white paper placemats that double as the menu, framed with gleaming silver cutlery, including all the accoutrements required to eat seafood. I unfurl the white linen napkin with J Sheekey in soft embroidery on the front and drop it into my lap. Patrick has his back to the empty seat next to him. He has positioned his stool so his can fit his long legs under the bar while simultaneously sitting as close to me as possible.

He puts a hand on my thigh. It seems we have progressed to

being more tactile and I get that tingling sensation flooding my system again as I assess the probability that I will soon be having sex with this man, maybe this very evening.

Champagne is poured for us and a niggle starts in the depths of my mind. I did not hear him order this so, like at Shanghai Blues, they just know to serve it on arrival. *Just how many women have sat on this stool and quaffed expensive wine and dined on oysters with this man before me?*

"I'd like to take you on a date, where we have plenty of time and no concerns about work the next day. Are you free on Friday night, Alex?" It is almost not a question as I look at his expectant eyes. After the scene in the shopping mall earlier I don't feel like I can play games with this man, or even refuse him.

I take my jacket off and hang it on the backrest of the bar-stool. I see his eyes appraising me as I extract my bare arms and my skin is revealed. His eyes drop to my chest and I lengthen my breathing so my lungs inflate, pushing my breasts out as I inhale. He had been wondering what I was wearing under my jacket. Now I was showing him. His eyes are hungry and I feel empowered. I raise my hand and touch his chin to bring his eyes back to my face and lean in toward him. His lips are on my lips instantly and his tongue is seeking mine. Initially the kiss is controlled, investigative, but quickly it becomes more frenetic. His hand moves from my thigh up to the hem of my top. His fingers are pushing the fabric up so he can slip his hand underneath. My nipples are responding before his hand reaches my bra.

As we continue to kiss, I open my eyes and scan quickly to check to see if anyone is watching us. There is a chef near us with his head down, focused intently on the knife and chopping board in front of him. The other diners are oblivious to us. The very fact that they might notice us heightens my arousal. His hand is all the way under my top, exposing my stomach as the fabric stretches to allow him to caress me. His fingers are circling my nipple through the lace of my bra and it grows hard to his touch. Time no longer has meaning.

His hand drops as if satisfied. Next he is pulling me gently forward by the band of my trousers so my pelvis tilts toward him and my bottom drops off the stool. I am standing now, almost leaning right on him. I put my hands on his shoulders to stabilise myself. The kissing stops as his lips graze my cheek and come to rest near my ear. As he unzips my trousers he whispers that he wants me. His breathing is ragged as he plunges his fingers into my knickers to find my clitoris. I take a deep breath as he teases me with his fingers. I tuck my bottom in and drop my sacrum so my sex is pushing out to meet his probing digits. I am wet and aching. I desperately want this man inside me. I decide to tell him and whisper the words one by one into his ear, dragging the moment out for as long as I can.

As soon as the last word is off my lips, he removes his hands from my panties in a flash, and he is staring at me intently. "Shall we skip dinner and go straight to dessert, my darling?" His voice is thick with longing.

I shake my head slowly and deliberately as I fasten my trousers and shuffle back onto the stool. I move myself as far away from him as the close quarters will allow. I smooth my top down.

"Okay, let's order then," he says almost petulantly.

We sip our champagne and survey each other. Patrick orders for us, a dozen oysters followed by a portion of their fish pie to share. The energy between us has dropped down the Richter scale. We are still exchanging lustful glances but we are managing to keep our hands to ourselves. I break the silence by asking him about the imminent AGM and quizzing him on the presentation I know he will make to investors and shareholders. He responds well to being asked about himself, and the conversation is flowing easily amid laughter as he regales me with descriptions of the anti-establishment anti-capitalist protestors he knows will be there. He is in good humour as he jokes about being thrilled that he was promoted to a position where he gets the opportunity to go head to head with them.

I am pleased with myself for resisting the urge to take this playboy up on his offer of skipping straight to the action. I decide in that moment that I will make him wait a bit longer. I know Candice would be proud of me. There will be nothing more than kissing happening between us this evening. Four more days of anticipation and tension will only make the inevitable much more pleasurable.

As I hear myself laughing again I reflect on how much fun I am having and how much I enjoy this man's company. I really like him, despite the struggle between my inner voices, the lustful one, and the sensible one that I am mostly ignoring.

The conversation takes a serious turn as he asks me about my parents. I tell him that my father is dead and he admits that he had found some articles online when he had googled me. He was quick to justify himself, saying that he hadn't realised what he would find and that he would let me open up to him in my own time. Almost as a quid pro quo, he gave me a run through his family history, being frank and uncomplimentary about his father while speaking about his mother in glowing terms. I was beginning to form a picture of the woman that gave birth to this man and to appreciate the esteem he held her in. A stark contrast to the scraps of information he let slip about his father. I was thankful for his honesty, even if I felt like the trade was uneven.

Patrick seems to have intuited that I will not be taking him home or accompanying him back to his house this night. I guess he can read body language as well as I can. He asks for the bill and then passes me his American Express card, leaning forward to whisper his PIN number in my ear before disappearing to the gents. The waiter returns quickly with the card machine and makes to leave again when he sees that Patrick is not there. I wave the Amex I am clutching and he nods and proceeds to process the transaction. I find it surprising that Patrick has trusted me with the code to his card when we barely know each other. I guess he pretty much knows where I live, and he obviously knows where I work, so a safe bet while having the desired effect of making me feel like he has faith in me.

I glance at the iPhone and Blackberry he has left sitting upon the bar, his constant companions, and wonder if that PIN number I just memorised might come in handy for accessing those devices. I contemplate unlocking his iPhone but think better of it. All in good time. I move myself so my body position doesn't betray my thoughts in time to see Patrick coming back around the bar to our stools.

As we make our way from the restaurant through the lanes, emerging onto William IV Street where John and the car are waiting, he tells me he has taken the liberty of ordering an Addison Lee taxi to take me back to Putney. I just need to give the driver the exact address. I see a black people carrier sitting behind the BMW. Patrick kisses me deeply before putting me into the waiting car, reminding me that we have a date for Friday. As if it is not burnt into my memory already.

I am lost in my thoughts as the car takes me home, not noticing the beauty of St Martin-in-the-Fields, the majesty of the lions in Trafalgar Square or the splendour of Westminster Cathedral and the Houses of Parliament. The London cityscape is not penetrating my consciousness. Patrick Harrington consumes my thoughts, my feelings and my soul.

Harrington

I am awake before my alarm goes off on Monday morning and I spring out of bed. For a change, I'm feeling like I can't get to work quickly enough. Of course I love my job and the kudos it commands but all I can think about is seeing Alexandra Fisher. I reflect on how easy it was to be in her company yesterday and while I have alarm bells ringing and red flags popping up in my mind about the wisdom of spending more time with her I push them all aside and practically dance my way to the bathroom to get ready for the day ahead. I feel like singing.

Not even the plethora of emails that I barely make a dent in on the car ride to the office can alter my good mood. I guess this is what a love-sick teenager feels like, but without the benefit of a steely resolve that will ensure I protect myself at all costs. It is a heady feeling but I can never imagine losing myself to it. I am not an addict seeking a fix. As I saunter into my office, I greet my assistant warmly, walking up behind her and clasping her shoulders and planting a big smacking kiss on her cheek. *Why should she miss out on a bit of Patrick Harrington loving, just because her vital statistics render her out of the range of my usual objects of affection?*

I have clocked that Alexandra is yet to make it into the office and wonder if sharing a bottle of wine with me yesterday afternoon might have precipitated a continuation of drinking into the evening with friends, or worse yet with her ex, the iron-pumping Joey.

This thought penetrates my mind like a pin popping a balloon and I feel my shoulders tense and my mood deflate. *What kind of self-respecting man goes by the cutesy shortened version of his name?* He clearly isn't smart enough to reach the lofty heights that I have and that alone makes me more of a man than he will ever be. I have to move quickly, and get on with this mission. I don't like the feeling of being on an emotional roller coaster, when I am usually so in control. I feel somewhat appeased as I see Alex sweep onto the floor and glide with feline grace, slim hips carrying her confidently between the office furniture towards her desk. I reach for my phone and fire her a message. I want to see her again, and tonight.

I am watching her as she takes her coat off, revealing ever professional slim-line black trousers enveloping her long legs, flowing upwards from black shoes, the heel suggestively high, the shine like new. My eyes travel back upwards from the shoes taking in her black-clad legs, up to her well-tailored black jacket. I cannot see what is underneath it from this angle, but I would very much like to find out.

My eyes continue their journey along the line of her shoulder, up to the bare skin of her neck. Alex has her hair pulled back and I look at how her neck curves and disappears behind her delicate ear. I want to run the tip of my tongue up the gentle curve, pausing en route to tug at that ear lobe, while caressing her shining hair gently at first and then with more force as I seize that ponytail to pull her head back so I can... already my cock is twitching, hardening, the possibilities alive in my mind.

I watch her swivel strategically after seeing my name on her phone, checking to see if I am in my office. I lean back quickly so she can't see that I have been eyeballing her, my face obscured. As I see her form move back to face her computer screen I resume my former position, where I can continue to examine her from an inconspicuous distance.

She has both hands on her phone so I lob another message in and smile to myself. This is going to be fun. Nothing like a bit of sexy banter by text message to start the day, and perhaps if it gets raunchy enough I might even convince her to go to the bathroom and send me a naughty photo of herself.

My phone flashes up with 'Alex&ra', my personal abbreviation of her name. On our first date, she had mentioned in passing that her family and friends combine her names and call her Alfie as a term of endearment. I much prefer my spin on it.

I read her text message. She has not accepted my offer, and is instead questioning me. *Daring move*, I think, smiling at the fact that she is completely unaware that she is playing chess with a Grand Master.

I reply with an innuendo-laden message. Smiling, I stretch my arms out and bring them to rest behind my head. My phone vibrates as a reply comes in almost immediately. This is more like it. Confirmation that she wants to go out tonight. Then her name is on my screen again. 'The only way to get rid of temptation is to yield to it.' Good girl. My trousers stir again at the certainty that I am reeling her in just like a pro-fisherman. I write straight back quoting Oscar Wilde myself.

My PA walks in to set up a conference call for me and I delay rolling my leather chair over to my conference table for as long as I can, as I won't be able to see Alex once I do. I follow up with another message telling her I can't wait to get her on her own. *This should elicit a flirty response*, I think, and I watch her through the glass frosting, excited to see what she will come back with.

My heightened anticipation plummets into annoyance in a heartbeat as I see her discard her phone and set about getting on with work. God damn Eloise 'the ringmaster' Little. *How can her priorities be more important to Alex than I am?* I will need to remonstrate with Alex as soon as I can. *I am never second best, and certainly not to this old woman.*

The conference call is with senior members of Caldwell's legal team and some of my direct reports. The subject matter is highly confidential. We are to discuss how to protect the Bank's name given some sudden and unwanted curiosity about our dealings with the Bank of England over setting interest rates during the Global Financial Crisis. I have heard the same thing over and over and am, quite frankly, bored of it.

There is a culture here that fails to punish people in a meaningful way for a lack of integrity. I, as well as numerous people who work for me, have capitalised on this, and so too has the bank. We were encouraged to make money and rewarded with bonuses and promotions for doing so. We were not expected to worry about ethical details. I am well aware of the potential reputation damage this may incur but the financial gain was well worth the risk, as it always is. As with everything in life, fortune favours the brave.

I am distracted, re-reading this morning's text message exchange with the lovely Alexandra Fisher. Her revelation through the prose of Oscar Wilde that she is indeed tempted spurs me on to send her a few more teasing messages. My morning passes with more calls and then the arrival of Amber Chilworth to discuss the recent quarter's numbers for the Investment Bank. She is doing everything within her power to try and flirt with me. She has even been so bold as to mention the disabled toilet. But today, the offer from this tart holds no appeal. I look her over and feel repulsed by her cheap shirt, which needs one more button fastened in order to be anywhere near appropriate for this environment. Her skirt is her usual trademark two inches too short. I see now with clarity how wide her thighs are and think to myself that she can work out all she likes but she will always be pear-shaped. I am feeling tense again. I want to check my phone to see if Alex has replied, but I don't want an audience when I do so. It seems that along with consuming my thoughts this girl is also causing me to evaluate things I have previously missed or been prepared to overlook, including Amber's chunky legs. I hear Amber droning on and I interrupt her with a dismissal. I watch her face register surprise and she stands and puts a hand on her hip. "Patrick, we're far from being done." Her tone is suggestive. Instead of exciting me, all her stance serves to do is highlight the issue of her well-upholstered thighs.

I point to the door and tell her I will get my PA to email her. I stand up from my meeting table, walk over to my desk and sit decisively in my chair, ignoring the stupid harlot. I put my hands on my keyboard and start typing to reinforce the message that our meeting is over. I can almost hear the cogs in her peanut brain turning as she struggles to figure out how to get me back on side.

"Get out, Amber." I decide not to waste any more time sharing my air with this loose woman. I hear my office door click as she retreats and immediately grab my phone. Nothing.

I look out at the open plan in time to see Alex stand up from her desk, grabbing her wallet. I have no idea what is next in my busy day but given the fact that I have summarily dismissed Chilworth before her allotted time was up, I figure I have a small window in which to play and I will follow Ms Fisher to wherever it is that she is heading.

I see her disappear through the double doors leading to the elevator lobby. I duck left and skirt the perimeter of the forty-second floor, walking past Brad Stone's office, and the Chairman's corner suite, and through an unmarked door. I press to call for the service elevator, the quickest way to descend from level forty-two to the ground floor. I disembark and hurry around to the main foyer watching the flow of people coming and going from the building. I spot her walking purposefully toward to the passage that joins our building with the underground warren of shops and cafes. I follow her, hanging back a safe distance so she is completely unaware of my presence. My height allowing me to track her as she moves into the stream of daytime shoppers. *Who are all these people and why aren't they working?*

As we walk past Boots, HSBC, and the Mont Blanc store and still onwards I start to worry about where it is she is going. Alex continues to walk and I move a bit quicker so I am now walking right behind her. I am so close I can smell her shampoo, notes of passion fruit and honey.

The light changes above our heads as the mall opens out into an atrium and the circular shopping floors above us are revealed. As my eyes adjust I grab Alex's arm to stop her. She has gone far enough. I feel her body tense as I bring her to an abrupt stop. She turns her head to determine who it is that has stopped her in her tracks. I see the look of astonishment cross her face as she realises it is me. I waste no time in telling her she is driving me crazy and that I do not understand her reticence to reply to my messages. She remains stunned and silent. In moments I have her seated at a table in a nearby sandwich store. She is glaring at me, which makes my pulse race. I like a bit of fire.

She stands, offering me coffee, and strides away to order some as if she is dancing to her own tune and not mine. I will let her think that, even though we both know it is not true. She hasn't bought herself much time as I watch her carefully walking back with two cups, her arms locked, outstretched in front of her.

Her eyes have softened a little and she removes the plastic lid from her coffee cup. She tells me that her intention is not to drive me crazy but rather ensure that our watchful colleagues are not noticing her behaviour. Of course she will join me this evening. I feel foolish for doubting my legendary charm.

I take in her exquisite face. Her makeup is simple but immaculate: reddish purple lipstick and matching nail polish. Her fingers move very deliberately toward the frothy milk topping her drink and like a snake being charmed my eyes follow her long nails as I imagine what they would feel like raking down my back as we fucked. Alex scoops a bit of foam with her fingertip and slowly brings it to her mouth, the colour of her lips and nails identical in their hue. I am buzzing as the sexual tension builds. *This is more like it, Ms Fisher.*

I am devouring this girl with my eyes, and all I can think about is getting her naked. I drink in her gorgeous neck, requiring no adornment, a close neighbour to her pert young bosom where but for one measly button I would be powerless to get my eyes to retreat. Instead I enjoy the change in contours, the swell in the material of her top and the challenge to her well-tailored suit jacket.

I need to get a hold of myself. I have to get back to work. I tear my eyes away and without looking at her face I tell her to be in my waiting car for 6pm. I get up and leave her, my coffee untouched.

Just before six o'clock I leave my office and head once again for the service elevator. Alex is not at her desk but I can see her screen is still on and her overstuffed handbag is slumped amongst the shoes lined up under her desk. I have no doubt she is coming after the seductive scene with the coffee foam earlier.

I am chatting companionably with John when the car door opens and my senses are engulfed by the seductive scent of jasmine and violet before I see her sleek body and smiling face framed by hair tousled by the wind that blows mercilessly through the buildings. Before she is even settled, I instinctively lean forward and steal a kiss.

We arrive on Charing Cross Road and there are people everywhere. I never fail to be impressed by the constant flow of human traffic in this city, a stark contrast to my childhood on a remote farm in County Cork.

We are out of the car and I am guiding Alex through the lanes to the large mirrored door marking the entrance to J Sheekey.

All I have been thinking about in the car is tasting those lips again. Before I swing the door wide and usher Alex through I stop and bend down for another kiss, which she accepts without hesitation.

The headwaiter clocks me as soon as we enter and I tip my head in acknowledgement. Nothing more is required for the wheels of their service machine to start turning for me. I steer Alex past reception and through to the oyster bar. I know we have the last two stools at the end of the bar, where the granite top meets the wall. I also know from experience that this is the most discreet position possible, while still allowing us to enjoy watching the chefs preparing food in front of us. Champagne is being poured as we settle ourselves and I watch Alex taking it all in. The wood panelling with glamorous people shot and framed in black and white hanging on the walls, the silverware, the linen and of course, the silently ordered flute of Louis Roederer being placed before her. I see her brow furrow and realise that instead of being impressed, the usual reaction I get, she is wary. I need to turn this around before she thinks too hard about this.

"I want to take you out again, Alex, on a night where neither of us has to think about work the next day. Go out with me on Friday?"

I am expectant, demanding. It is more of a statement than a question with only the slightest inflection. Without taking her eyes from me Alex begins to unbutton her jacket and shrug it from her shoulders, revealing a figure hugging camisole and bare arms. I knew I wanted to see her take that jacket off and the wait was worth it. She is simply stunning, without even trying. She takes a deep breath in, the air inflating her lungs with the unintended consequence of pushing her pert breasts out and up like an offering to me. Her hand is on my chin and I flick my eyes from her body back to her face and realise this consequence was not unintended at all.

Alex leans in toward me and I close the distance quickly. Our kisses are fast, brutal, wanting it all right now. I kiss her throat and then that neck that I had fantasised about only a few hours previously, while pushing my hand under her top. I hear her gasp as I nibble her soft flesh, my hand finding her breast, pinching her nipple, making her groan with desire. I'm in a frenzy, I want her sex. I need to touch her soft folds.

My hands are on the band of her trousers, urging her closer to me, pulling her off the stool. I stop kissing her long enough to whisper in her ear that I want her. I cannot help myself. I feel a heady mix of power along with my inhibitions slipping away. This feeling is so addictive I feel like a drug user chasing that elusive first time high.

I unzip her trousers, keeping her close to me and to the wood panelled bar so the waiters and chefs cannot see what is happening right in front them. I push my fingers urgently inside her panties, seeking her clitoris.

Alex is tilting her hips up toward me to allow me greater access and better probing space in our close confines. Her breath is ragged as she leans in to whisper in my ear. She tells me one painstakingly slow word at a time "I. Want. You. Inside. Me."

I cannot take this anymore; these words tip me over the edge. All I want to do is ravage this fine young thing, all thoughts of food and drink forgotten. The blood is pushing hard into my groin and my penis is engorged, wanting to be freed from my pants and ideally thrusting deeply inside this whimsical creature in front of me. My mind is racing, trying to think where I can take her. The bathrooms in the basement are probably our best bet. I tell her we should skip straight to dessert and I know my eyes are full of lust and longing.

She straightens herself and zips up her trousers. For a second my racing heart is thrilled as I think she is about to take me up on my offer. But the air shifts and the mood changes infinitesimally, but enough for me to know that I will not be getting back inside those knickers any time this evening. I feel let down and have to take a deep breath to stop myself from telling her she is a cock tease. At least I know I make her wet and crazy with desire. *Next time, Ms Fisher, you will be begging me as you realise that these silly games are all a precursor to the best sex you will ever have.* Once I have shown her how skilled I am she will be completely under my power and control.

I order for both of us to reassert my dominance, and she seems contrite enough to know that she has pushed me to a potentially dangerous place. Amazingly, in no time at all we are laughing and chatting like old friends. I find all of this quite disconcerting. One minute this woman is completely under my spell, and then the next she has the ability to retract but without me losing interest in her. I am having a genuinely good time in her company. I think of my mother, who can read me well enough to handle my idiosyncrasies and not wind me up by being too familiar or expecting me to be predictable. Lord knows I am anything but. She is the only woman in the world that has this ability, or so I thought. I feel slightly wrong footed as I realise that Alexandra Fisher is getting under my skin, and more than just because I want to fuck her senseless.

I shake my head to dismiss these foreign thoughts and shift my focus to Friday night. I will take exactly what I want from her and she will be powerless to stop me. I decide while she is downstairs in the bathroom after we have finished our mains that I will wrap this evening up. I text John to let him know I will be ready soon and I order Alex an Addison Lee taxi to take her back to Putney. I have to maintain my gentlemanly persona and while it is clear that we want each other, I also know she is battling with herself and is clearly thinking she needs to play the situation right. What she doesn't recognise is that while she might think she is playing the game on even terms, the reality is I am the supreme coach so she will never win.

I am lost in my thoughts as the car takes me home, not noticing the beauty of St Martin-in-the-Fields, the majesty of the lions in Trafalgar Square or the splendour of Westminster Cathedral and the Houses of Parliament. The London cityscape is not penetrating my consciousness. Alexandra Fisher consumes my thoughts, my feelings and my soul.

Alexandra

After a confusing Monday night, I am grateful for the arrival of Tuesday and try to go through the usual motions, without letting myself be distracted by the ever-present thoughts of Patrick Harrington. He is all I can think about and the memories and images cause me to break into a smile, along with having moments of being so deep in thought, scenario-running, that I lose myself. Not good.

Tuesday is welcome for two reasons. For one, I have my regular therapy session with Melissa. Since I lost my father I have been in counselling for grief at first and then, as the fog started to clear, I needed help with my tendency to people please and seek approval. I had to try living some sort of life after it felt like my father's death had smashed it into a million tiny little pieces.

Following my hour with Melissa, I have a much needed and overdue dinner date with Candice. I can't wait to get her view on the fast-paced lust-ridden romance that seems to be playing out in my life. I am as powerless to change its course as the captain of the Titanic was that fateful night in April 1912. I shake my head to drop the imagery of a sinking ship, as I certainly don't want to think such negative thoughts in relation to affairs of my heart. While I know Patrick is a dark horse with a colourful background, I do think that he sees something different in me. We seem to have really connected.

I decide that I won't tell Melissa too much as I can't bear to hear the parallels I know she will draw with my father. The feeling in me that nothing was ever good enough, that I was inadequate and that I must be the brightest, shiniest version of myself to even register on his radar. With my father, as a young kid I would consistently over-achieve to try to penetrate his consciousness in the vain hope that I would impress him. I didn't understand his depression at that age. Not that I profess to really get it now either, but at least I can recognise my own destructive behaviour and its triggers and am consequently more self-aware.

I realise that being sparse with the truth with Melissa makes the whole thing much less effective, but I am in no mood to hear reason and I certainly don't want to hear anything that might confirm the musings of my sensible inner voice. Instead, I decide to focus on the break-up with Joey and rake through those ashes. There will be the inevitable spotlight on my issues with guilt, the gift that keeps on giving, but I actually could do with some reminders of how best to manage how I am feeling about Joe. I continue to avoid him, and he me. It is ridiculous that with the means he has, and his parents' willingness to stump up cash, he has failed to find a suitable place to live. I need to address this with him once and for all but all my energy is being drawn to the ubiquitous Patrick Harrington like a moth to a flame.

I leave Melissa's office on Broadgate Circle as the home time bell rings out across the city and merge quickly into the endless stream of bodies moving away from their various places of work and into Liverpool Street station. I head for the other side of the concourse passing under the flashing train indicator boards and weaving my way through the crowds to find the escalators to take me up to Bishopsgate.

Candice works in the Square Mile close to Melissa's office so we had agreed to meet up after I had had my head read. She had taken the liberty of booking the fabulous SushiSamba at the top of Heron Tower. God alone knows how she managed it but that girl always got what she wanted, including last minute reservations at London's hippest restaurants and clubs. I was excited as I had yet to take in the view from the tower and was looking forward to trying the fusion of Japanese, Peruvian and Brazilian cooking.

I check my phone and find that she is already at the bar on level thirty-eight waiting for me, gin and tonic in hand, so I head straight to the small lift lobby that you could almost miss, only being granted access when I confirm that I am the missing guest for the Stapleton party. I board the glass elevator and smile to myself, thinking of Willy Wonka. I am transfixed as the steel cage is sucked up the side of the building, the glass frontage showing me an ever expanding view over London with its twinkling lights and contrasting skyline. Candy certainly knows where things are at. *She is some girl*, I think to myself, and am overcome with good feeling toward my darling friend as I emerge from the elevator and walk around the corner to reception, dragging my eyes away from the stunning view. I find Candy standing outside by a large tree painted orange that dominates the small terrace. She is smoking while trying to brace herself against the winds that are whipping around the building. I wave and watch her from the doorway trying to decide whether to venture out or to watch her until she has finished her fag. I figure she can wait five more minutes so I check my coat and go and sit at the bar and order myself a Tanqueray Ten and tonic.

"Fish face!" Candice's voice rings out. I smile in spite of myself at this less than flattering moniker. I turn on my stool and see Candy has her drink in hand and is being escorted through to the restaurant. Instead of walking over to fetch me she has decided to call attention to us both by hollering across the lobby.

"Nice to see you, Stapleton," I say as I hug her warmly, breathing in her lingering cigarette smoke.

"So you broke Joey's heart. You go girl. Do tell all. Who is the new guy then?" I marvel at her ability to cut straight to the chase and wonder how much she has heard through the grapevine versus making educated guesses. I know the question about Patrick is speculative. There is no way she can know anything about him or our dates.

I take a deep breath and give her the full story, hardly pausing as I run through the Sunday at work, the turmoil with Joseph and the string of dates in quick succession with Patrick. I see her taking it all in and know she is desperate to impart her advice.

"'Bout time you ditched Joe. This new chap sounds like a stalker, Lexi. Tread carefully there," she says with absolute seriousness. I had wanted to show her our recent marathon text exchange to get her view but realise that it's a bad idea. She sees my face drop and is quick to pounce.

"Please don't tell me you're in love with him already, sweetie?" her tone softens but her eyes are steely. I say nothing but know that my feelings are written all over my face for this friend who knows me all too well.

"This guy collects women. You must be able to see that. I bet he has a jar of hearts. I know you can't help how you feel but get as much as you can out of this and then run a mile. Give whatever you have to, but do not give him your heart. I mean it, he is trouble with a capital T. Henceforth I shall call him 'Non-Com' as there is no way he will ever make a commitment, and we both know you're not a good time girl, Al." Her words crash into me like waves against the seashore. Relentless and continual. And true.

"He is having me over to his place for dinner on Friday night," I manage. I don't want to respond to everything she has said even though I know how astute she is and how accurately she has read the situation from her viewpoint on the sidelines. We talk of nothing else as we devour corn tamales, ceviche, sashimi and samba rolls. I know she doesn't mind, as it is rare that I have this much to discuss. Normally it's a cursory mention of Joey and a few anecdotes about life working for Eloise and then we talk about the antics that Candice has been up to so this is a unusual role reversal for us.

I kiss Candy goodbye as we head off to different tube stations to make our respective journeys home. I feel much lighter for having shared everything with her but also a bit wary. I know how I feel, and while I know she cares for me I can't bear to hear that she thinks that I am just another one of Patrick's girls. I have to be more than that. Her expression 'jar of hearts' keeps flipping itself over in my mind. I will be a little more economic with the truth next time I see her, I resolve. We have scheduled a night out on Saturday so she can hear all about my Friday night. I know she wants to know if he is a good shag or not. She has such a one-track mind.

I had packed my bag, putting a change of clothes, small toiletries and two matching lingerie sets in a large handbag on Thursday night. The bag was chosen deliberately so as not to arouse suspicion in the office. Patrick has not directly asked me to stay over but from our increasingly sexual text exchange it is clear that we both know what will happen on Friday night. And Saturday morning. I was bold enough to tell him I like morning sex, which elicited the response, "So we're having sex then!" *Not so urbane*, I think to myself.

It is all I can do to get through the rest of the work week. I have been caught out a few times daydreaming and not listening and Eloise can ferret out the truth using a few well-placed questions. I must be more careful. I have been dodging bullets, blaming the break-up with Joey as the reason behind my distraction but I know this excuse won't wash for too much longer.

I feel like I am about to open a door and not knowing what's behind it is killing me. I can't get this man out of my head and neither do I want to. I get the sense that he feels as preoccupied by me as I am by him. I know that I am different I repeat to myself. I don't think this is just about sex; it can't be, with all this effort he is putting in. I will do all I can to catch this man who has infiltrated my heart.

I walk away from Knightsbridge tube station Friday evening after work, hearing my heart hammering in my ears, and I force myself to take in a lungful of air to try and calm myself down. I am pleased with myself for turning down his offer of a car from Canary Wharf, as that would only have added to my stress levels. I remind myself that we get on really well and that he is besotted with me. I check the map app on my phone to orientate myself and walk down Brompton Road, past Harrods, crossing the road to take the back streets to find Montpellier Walk and his address. As I look at the map, I realise Eloise's house is only a stone's throw away on Cadogan Square.

I ring the doorbell with my heart in my mouth. I have a bottle of Krug with me. It cost me a small fortune but I didn't want to turn up empty handed and I know he likes champagne. The intercom buzzes without me uttering a word. I guess there must be a camera. I push the door open and step inside, shutting the door behind me, which feels hugely symbolic. I put my bag and the wine down and take off my coat. I look down at the wooden floors and wonder if I should take my shoes off.

"Alexandra Fisher." Patrick's dulcet tones reach my ears but he is not visible.

"Take your shoes off please, I have a surprise for you." I blush at the thought that Patrick can read my mind and bend over to remove my heels. I am not wearing any tights, as the weather has been mild for March. I've had my eyebrows threaded and had a pedicure for the occasion and, for the first time in my life, I had made an appointment for a bikini wax at Candice's insistence. I'm groomed and ready for whatever this evening may bring.

I pick up the wine and pad toward where I think Patrick's voice came from. The hallway opens up, with a choice to turn left into a sitting room following the wooden floorboards or to head upstairs stepping onto plush carpet. I make the left and see that the sitting room has been interior designed to the nth degree, from the long low creamy sofa, the smoked glass coffee table to the gunmetal grey bucket seats. Over the mantel, dominating the wall, is a large photograph of a naked woman inside the mouth of a crocodile. I recognise it as Helmut Newton's famous work, 'A Scene from Pina Bausch's Ballet'. My eyes scan down from the large print to the table in front of me. Sat next to the walnut and nickel chessboard, the sole coffee table book is titled ' La Petite Mort'. My amateur French extends far enough to translate that as 'the little death'. The sepia photo on the cover makes me raise my recently sculpted eyebrows and wonder what the book might be about. I file that away as something to google.

I pass through the sitting room and into a dining room dominated by a circular white marble table, already dressed as if a dinner party is about to take place. Golden plates, colourful glassware and cutlery set up symmetrically. Seems he likes the show home look.

I carry on through to the kitchen where Patrick is standing leaning on the black granite counter top watching me. His eyes sweep over me from head to toe. I force a wide smile by way of greeting. He stands up and takes the champagne I am offering out of my hand. I can see he is impressed. He smiles his thanks and opens one of the kitchen cabinets, which hides an American style double fridge where he puts the bottle away. I think he is enjoying toying with me.

He takes my hand and leads me through the French doors out onto the garden balcony, where an outdoor table is set. There are fairy lights, which create an ethereal glow against the backdrop of the garden walls and the early evening night sky. A patio heater keeps any chill at bay. Sitting on the chair closest to me is a white carrier bag.

"For you, Alexandra, I hope you don't mind but I took the liberty of getting you a gift I know we will both enjoy." He is speaking slowly, deliberately all the while staring at me. I look at the bag and back at him and I am flummoxed. I can't hide my surprise and I am momentarily frozen to the spot.

"Go on, open the box, Alex!" he says with the excitement of a kid at Christmas.

With shaking hands I remove a shoebox from the bag emblazoned with 'Sergio Rossi' in gold lettering. My heart skips a beat. These must have cost a fortune. I am soon to have this confirmed as my eye catches the price sticker on the front of the box alongside the model name 'Mesh' and the size, European 38 that he has, of course, got exactly right. My mind scrambles. *Did I tell him this?* I glance up at him, the question unspoken.

"You have more shoes than I care to count under your desk, Alex. It wasn't hard. I didn't want to take the chance that you wouldn't be appropriately dressed for tonight, my darling."

I'm slightly confused by this last statement as I proceed to extract one of the elegant designer Italian shoes from the tissue in the box. They are exquisite. I sit down and proceed to put them on. Peacock blue silk straps with studs in a mesh pattern befitting the shoe's name, atop a platform toe leading up to an ankle strap to assist with keeping the foot in place while tottering on the 5 inch heels.

I stand up and beam at Patrick. Unsurprisingly, they fit perfectly. I know now with certainty that this man is in love with me and I feel myself relax a little amid all the excitement. Patrick picks up a remote from the table and points it back inside. With the touch of a few buttons he sets music playing, Lana del Ray's voice plays off the garden walls, and a spotlight comes on over the table. The lighting is still soft, but not dim; *you clearly like to see everything,* I think. I feel any resistance I might have melt away as he takes me in his arms and starts slow dancing with me.

"I'm going to pleasure you until you don't know your own name, Alexandra," he whispers to me. I move to look at him, a quiet acquiesce, and he kisses me deeply. He manoeuvres me to the table and lays me down gently, right under the spot light, without disturbing the two place settings at the end of the table. He pushes gently on my shoulder to encourage me to lie on my back while pulling my legs to ensure my hips are aligned with the outer edge of the tabletop. I know what's coming, and I am so aroused at the thought of it I can feel I am already wet.

Patrick removes my panties and gets down on his knees. He starts with the tiniest of licks with merely the tip of his tongue, dipping into the grove between my inner and outer lips. He keeps at it, working delicately, as I feel my breath deepen and I can't help but jut my hips towards him. My skin is standing to attention in hypersensitive goose bumps.

He is teasing me to the point of anger. I think I can't stand it anymore and then he presses the full length of his flat tongue across me. I unashamedly push and grind against it. I can hear him click open a tube which I can only imagine is lubricant. I am in the throes of rapture so my brain doesn't stop to figure out what he is up to. Before I know it, he switches a lubricated palm in place of his tongue and I hear him panting. I guess he is saving some stamina. He parries back with laps, with the whole of his tongue running over my clitoris, exposed by his fingers holding my lips open. He alternates between a series of vertical and diagonal strokes with the tiniest of vibrations. *I think I might have died and gone to heaven right here in his backyard.*

At last, he moves down. One thumb takes over my clitoris, the other is rubbing around my perineum, and almost like clockwork every few seconds his tongue darts inside me. He does not change the stroke, pace or rhythm. He doesn't need to. I am in a frenzy and my breathing is coming in staccato bursts. I clamp my legs together tightly as my orgasm takes hold and I feel myself squirt with a force I didn't know I possessed. I hear a guttural sound echo off the garden walls and it takes me a second to realise that it was me, in a base and primal state, which had made it.

Patrick slowly extracts himself and stands up, wiping his chin, his eyes sparkling with mischief and his smile triumphant. He hands me my panties and strolls inside promising to return with champagne flutes and something to nibble on. I hear the laughter in his voice as he walks away. I lie there for a moment, spent. I wait for the waters to calm before sitting up. I leave my panties hanging from his chair and dutifully take a seat opposite, smiling all the while.

I have entered unchartered territory and I feel both a little out of my depth and exhilarated. I think of the warnings Candice bestowed on me, and the turmoil that has been raging within me due to this man. And decide to ignore it all. This evening is all about pleasure; thinking can come later and consequences be damned.

Harrington

After a confusing Monday night, I am grateful for the arrival of Tuesday and try to go through the usual motions, without letting myself be distracted by the ever-present thoughts of Alexandra Fisher. She is all I can think about and the memories and images cause me to break into a smile, along with having moments of being so deep in thought, scenario-running, that I lose myself. Not good.

Tuesday is my standing reservation with Silvy. A mature, curvaceous, well-educated German courtesan, who is based right around the corner from my place. I like going to her flat as it is less personal than having her in my space, and it means that she only knows what I choose tell her about myself. She can't glean information by snooping around my house like I have caught other women doing. Stupid bitches that think they can figure me out by checking my Internet history or reading my mail. It would take a genius to understand me.

I found Silvy online. She is an independent escort, another bonus, as I don't have an agency thinking they can push girls on me. In any case I have Maria, whom I trust, for that. Silvy is 51 years old, 5'7" with short, light hair and fair skin and brown eyes.

She keeps herself in good shape maintaining a 25-inch waist and has round full 36C breasts. She 'enjoys providing a passionate, sensuous girlfriend experience to successful gentlemen, who are looking for an intimate and completely pampering hour, dinner date, or a night, at your place or mine.' For £400 an hour. She must be putting in some hours, I think, given she has an apartment in One Hyde Park. Granted her flat is tiny and it's on the wrong side of the building so misses out on the expansive park views, but still.

What sold me more than her sexy website photographs and her description was her passing resemblance to my mother when she was a similar age. Silvy likes me. I get all the benefits of a loving, doting wife who has a voracious sexual appetite and then I get to close the door and walk the few streets back to my place and not have to deal with the vagaries of female nature.

Not that I would ever admit it to her, or to anyone else for that matter, but Silvy has taught me some amazing tricks. Tricks that I have used to great effect with many of my lovers, certainly the lovers that actually warrant the time and effort it requires to bring a woman to a frenzy and a mind-blowing orgasm. I can't say too many women have fallen into that category. My mind drifts to the sexy Alex Fisher and I know exactly what I am going to do with that piece of arse this Friday night.

I reach Silvy's internal apartment door having buzzed and taken the elevator to her floor. The front door is already expectantly ajar. I knock firmly and enter without waiting or indeed expecting a reply. I find Silvy standing at the large picture window, curtains open, watching the view over the traffic of Knightsbridge below. She is wearing a string of Chanel pearls and a pair of thigh-high patent leather stiletto boots. Nothing else. Her bottom is full but toned; her neck is slender under that power bob of a hairstyle. She doesn't turn or speak but a deft waft of her wrist instructs me to close the gap. I stand behind her and she pushes her ass backwards, testing, no, measuring the degree of my arousal. She locates my left hand and draws it forward to place it conclusively on her left breast. I knead the flesh; tweak at the hardening nipple and then run my hand down across the stomach of a much younger woman.

Silvy inclines her head and offers me her neck in a vampire-like gesture. I accept and with soft bites, licks and kisses work my way from her shoulder to the top of her ear. Her right hand finds my bulge and starts to caress my hardened cock. With the assurance of a safe breaker and still without turning around, she is inside the defences of my trousers and is pulling my cock free. The foreplay is quickly dispensed with; she knows I like to pack as much fucking into my hour as I can.

"Fuck me now, hard," she commands.

I register that it is freezing cold in her flat and that she must have turned the temperature down on purpose. She's the naked one but it seems to have no effect on her. I quickly remove my shoes and clothing and hoist her up, pressing her back against the window and wrapping those booted legs around me. She is only small and she adjusts slightly to allow me to better enter her. Her pussy is wet.

The traffic is far below and over the distant drone I can hear my balls slapping against her as I thrust into her as deeply as I can. Her hands grip hard on my shoulders as I fuck her for all I'm worth. I feel my orgasm approaching and the extra hardness is not missed as Silvy's moans change in tone, more animalistic, more wild.

I come with a regretfully small number of spasms, my hips twitching like my body has been shocked with a bolt of electricity. I withdraw and Silvy leads me away from the window and into her bedroom. I still have around forty minutes to play with.

"I want you to fist me," she says, as she lays her body down upon her bed. This is a first. She widens her legs so I can put my fingers inside her. Two, three and then four. My hand is squeezed so tightly inside I fear any movement may hurt her, but she takes over and works her hips back and forth, effectively fucking my hand. I take my share of the load and start to piston, my elbow firing a small circular motion like the wheel of an old locomotive. On and on, I pound into her. She continues to moan with pleasure even as I start to tire.

I take my hand out of Silvy's gaping pussy and she smiles at me. My fingers are covered in her juice and I feed them in turn into her mouth. Filthy, dirty whore.

After a leisurely fuck doggy-style to blow my second load all over her back, I take a speedy shower and say my farewells. I leave the cash, in fifties, on her bedside table and see myself out. Task-focused. Execution-oriented. That's me.

I emerge from the latticed amorphous steel structure and skip across Knightsbridge and make the short walk to Zuma on Raphael Street where I know Dave will be waiting for me at the bar. He knows about my regular Tuesday night 'therapy' sessions so when we spot each other he matches my broad grin as I walk towards him.

I glance around to see if any of the gold-digging women hanging out in here are worth talking to and quickly assess that nobody takes my fancy. I note the adoring gazes as I pass by the hopefuls and smile to myself. I take the empty chair, saved for me, next to Dave and slap his shoulder as I sit down. Dave is the Head of Risk Management for Caldwell and we joined the company at the same time, as wide-eyed graduates with grand aspirations. This man knows more about my work and leisure pursuits than anyone else I know. Thankfully he also has a predisposition for making easy money and bedding as many women as he possibly can, so it would be mutually assured destruction if either of us were to disclose what we know about the other. Dave's tail chasing has calmed down a bit since hitting forty. *That's as much to do with middle aged spread and the receding hairline* I think. It's harder to pull when all you're offering is cash; not impossible, but it certainly narrows the field. Not an issue I have to worry about thankfully.

Dave has a 25-year-old girlfriend at the moment. Pretty, sure, but thick as two short planks. How he spends time with her I'll never know. She reminds me why I loathe intimate relationships. She is forever nagging Dave and is a soggy wet blanket. She rarely lets Dave go out carousing with me these days. I miss our boys' nights out but the truth is I do just as well picking up women when I'm on my own. A falcon hunts better solo.

The barman pours me a Hendricks and tonic with a sliver of cucumber. I start to tell Dave about my hour with Silvy but decide against it. The contrast between her and Alex is obvious and in terms of my mental real estate, Ms Fisher has the larger portfolio. I see two blondes sidle closer to Dave, both of them eyeing me. They have tried hard with their appearances, but youth is not on their side and their necks betray what dyed roots and layers of makeup try to deny. I shake my head slowly while looking directly at them and with a huff they move on.

Instead, I decide to tell Dave about Alexandra Fisher. I can

barely contain my excitement. I see the look on his face changing as I talk animatedly, telling him how I am having her over to
dinner at my house this Friday night.

"Harry, Harry, Harrington... I can't believe what I'm hearing.
I think this girl might be 'the one' the way you're talking, but
then I know you better, man. Please explain yourself before I
think you've lost the plot!" he is laughing at me, which makes me
realise how my enthusiastic descriptions must be revealing more
than I had hoped.

"Dave, you know me. She reminds me of my big toe. I'll bang
her on every piece of furniture in my house." I joke to try and
cover up my earlier admissions. He eyes me suspiciously.

"Dude, I know you'll pound her till she can hardly walk but
I also think you quite like this one. Certainly more than you've
done any woman in a long time. Just watch yourself. Don't let
her con you into changing, as we both know ultimately you
won't. And you'll resent her. And she works for Eloise 'the stick-
ler' Little for Christ's sake. This is way more serious than that
other Finance bimbo you were fucking. I've never seen you like
this, Harry," he concludes.

We pass the rest of the evening laughing and drinking while
I steer the conversation through a safe course. I am not in the
mood to discuss Alex and I, and I am sick to the back teeth of
talking about the simmering situation at work. I am actually
pleased when we part company at the end of the evening.

I spend Thursday evening making sure everything is in place.
I move a couple of bottles of Ruinart from my wine fridge to
the main fridge. I order food from La Bottega, the Italian Deli in
South Kensington, and leave instructions for my housekeeper,
Violetta, to collect and refrigerate it. I check the angle of the
spotlights and do a test run with the cameras, and in particular the one that surveys the garden to make sure I can review
the footage once Ms Fisher is gone. My sheets will be changed
during the day and everything, including my many mirrors, will
be spotless. Everything is set.

I am ecstatic when I hear my front door bell sound on Friday
evening. I drink Alexandra in as I watch her through the intercom camera standing awkwardly on my stoop. I buzz her in and
wait for her in the kitchen. This is going to be some night.

I tell her to take her shoes off. I didn't really get a decent look at what she has on her feet on the door camera but I am sure they are office appropriate and not suitable for what I have in mind. I like my ladies to leave their shoes on during our relations. But if I have my way I choose the heels, like I have done for Alexandra this evening. The higher the better and they need to be scream-ing sex. The right pair of heels with a woman's foot angled at the right pitch makes me bedrock hard.

Alex makes her way further into my house and meets me in the kitchen. I am leaning on the counter in a bid to look non-chalant; I don't want her to sense how adrenalised I am. I get her out onto the garden mezzanine and have her open the gift I have procured for her, sexy Sergio Rossi stilettos. She immedi-ately tries them on which pleases me. What she doesn't realise is that they won't be leaving her feet until I am thoroughly done with her.

I use the remotes to trigger both the stereo and the spotlight, the latter triggering the camera to start recording. I slow dance with her for a little bit to try to reassure her that there is romance in the air. I hold her close and move her by degrees until I have her right where I want her. I am already hard as I kiss her deeply and tell her I am going to redefine 'pleasure' for her. I lift her up and lay her down on the table. I get a flash of Silvy lying down on her bed ready for me to fist her and shake it away quickly. I remove Alex's panties and start the slow, concentrated job of working her into hysteria expertly with my tongue, my fingers and my palm. I can see that she is manic and her orgasm is build-ing. I am relentless and precise, continuous and unwavering. My face is buried deep between her legs when she finally relents and, surprising me, she squirts into my mouth and all down my chin.

I am going to break this filly. She won't know what innocent is when I'm done with her and she will be beholden to me while I give her nothing more than I care to confer. Another fallen woman. *Patrick Harrington, you legend,* I think to myself. I see her smiling, rapturous face and I almost feel sorry for her. *I bought her the shoes,* I reflect, *and they weren't cheap.* She can show them off to her friends even if she won't care to admit what she traded for them. That's some consolation.

Afterwards, we sit together drinking champagne and eating the delicious deli food. I have switched off the spotlight, pleading that the lights in the trees and the candles on the table are more romantic than the spot. She seems unfazed and I feel a pang of... *what? Guilt? Remorse?* I retreat to the kitchen with the excuse that I need to get the salt and pepper grinders. I study my reflection in the eye-level oven for a second and remind myself who I am.

The rest of the evening follows the plan I had laid out. I get her naked and positioned in front of several of my indoor film-ing stations. She is impervious throughout, willing and eager to please. I realise she needs some coaching, which I'm happy to provide. Her responsiveness more than makes up for that.

As we fall into an exhausted heap in the tangled sheets of my bed I feel happy and pleasantly sore. I look at Alex who is staring at the ceiling, looking angelic, with the flush of someone who has been working out. I smile down at her and feel my heart beating behind her head, as it gently rests on my chest. Not for the first time with this girl I am feeling conflicted. I know who and what I am and that will never change, yet she is certainly eliciting more from me than any woman has before. Even lying together like this in my bed is unusual.

I have entered uncharted territory and I feel both a little out of my depth and exhilarated. I think of the warnings Dave bestowed on me, and the turmoil that has been raging within me due to this girl. And decide to ignore it all. This evening is all about pleasure; thinking can come later and consequences be damned.

Alexandra

In between the sex last night and the early hours of this morning we managed to drink quite a bit, I realise as I wake with a slightly fuzzy head. I smile to myself remembering we had agreed to rendezvous in New York, as we will both be there for the meetings taking place midweek, and to extend our flights to spend the weekend there together. Eloise will need to be managed, or more accurately she needs to stay none the wiser, for both our sakes.

I don't know if Patrick is awake and I dare not disturb him. I have no idea what the time is and I feel like I am still in a bit of a dream state as I watch the pheromones dancing on the dust particles illuminated by the morning sunbeams shooting across from the windows.

This man is a patient and generous lover, I reflect. I lost count of the number of orgasms I had since that first one on the garden table. I blush at the memory. *And who knew that mirrors would be such a turn-on?* I guess Patrick Harrington does, given the strategic positioning of reflective surfaces in his house. To the mild mannered you might think he had decorated his home in this way to create the illusion of more space and light. I now know better.

I start to assess myself in my mind as I catalogued the parts of my body that ached. He gave me a thorough seeing to last night, that was for sure, and I am smiling in spite of myself. I had let myself go and been shown the meaning of pleasure just as he had promised. I feel blood pulsing in my groin at the thought. My feet hurt too. I had remained in my new heels for the duration of our sexual acrobatics and my arches were sore. But if that was what made him happy then I was pleased to accommodate. It was the least I could do.

I slip out from under the covers and walk soundlessly to his en suite bathroom. Easing the door shut as quietly as I can, I set about my morning ablutions including brushing my teeth. As I wipe myself with toilet paper I confirm just how tender I am. I don't care. I picked up my shoes on my way across the bedroom and am now putting them back on for the morning sex I had hinted at.

I slide the bathroom door open abruptly and stride back into the room with my shoulders back and my head held high. I am wearing nothing but the heels. At the sound of movement, Patrick rouses and begins to sit up, propping himself up with one elbow to watch me walk toward him. His sleep-rumpled face breaks into a wide grin when the sight of me and the sound of heels clicking on the floorboards adds up in his head. I reflect his smile, trying hard to look sophisticated and confident even though this is not how I am feeling. The champagne hangover is making me feel a bit tremulous.

When I make it to the edge of the bed I lean forward to grab the edge of the duvet and with one sharp tug I have the feather down cover discarded on the floor beside me. This leaves Patrick as exposed as I am. We are still smiling at each other. He drops his elbow and sinks back into the pillows behind his head, almost in supplication.

I put my knees on either side of his out-stretched legs and shuffle myself up the mattress until I am straddling his manhood, which is already responsive to the view. I move my feet out so they are now under me and I am in a short squat. His eyes widen and then quickly he is leaning over to grab a condom out of his bedside drawer. As he slides the drawer shut again I clock that the contents of that drawer hold more than prophylactics. I make a mental note to check it out when I have the opportunity.

Patrick deftly rolls the condom on and I sink myself down very slightly, taking just the tip of him inside me. I see his face take on a now familiar look of pleasure. I lift myself up and clear of his now straining erection and drop forward onto my knees. I have changed my mind. I am going to try something I have never experienced before. Patrick is quick to recognise the change of direction and is pulling on my thighs to drag me into the perfect position to allow me to sit on his face.

I grab the headboard to allow myself to stand on those heels and leverage my position to full advantage. It doesn't take long before time is frozen and I am lost in the depths of my own hedonism as my body responds obediently, as if all it takes is his command. I let out a loud throaty laugh as I shuffle back and see the victorious look on Patrick's face. I am quick to resume the stance I had been in earlier, atop his hard member. I see Patrick shift his gaze past me to the floor to ceiling freestanding mirror that leans against his bedroom wall. I copy him and lift my gaze to the mirror over his bed. The room feels like it has been designed as a temple to his desires, a carnal playground where two people can appear like twelve at first glance and to infinity when the mirrors work opposite each other. I find myself quickly building to orgasm once again as I rhythmically pull myself up his length and wait just a fraction of a second before pounding down again with increasing force, the exertion causing me to expel feminine grunts. I reach back and use my hands to part my butt checks to allow Patrick to penetrate me as deeply as possible. His hips thrust upwards and I can tell by the look on his face he is close to exploding. I grab the headboard once more and abruptly stop my movements, only to see a look of surprise replace the one of rapture. He grabs me roughly on the shoulders and pushes me back down holding me tightly, his fingernails digging into my flesh. I have lost control of the situation as he forces himself into me repeatedly. I find the whole experience a massive turn-on as the pleasure-pain axis tilts me toward orgasm. Watching his face contort and his leg muscles tense I realise that we are about to have a simultaneous climax.

My thighs quiver and my breathing stops for a few seconds completely before catching up in a series of ragged gasps. Sated, I slump forward to lie beside Patrick and I hear his heart thumping in his chest. That was possibly the most epic sex I have ever had and I want to tell him that, but something stops me.

"I love your cock," I say enthusiastically instead as my breathing starts to slow down. I think this may be the kind of thing he likes to hear, even if it's a novel admission to pass my lips. I feel his chest start to shake before he starts guffawing.

"Alex, my darling, you really are one out of the box," he says through his laughter. I feel the sting of annoyance and roll away from him a little. I hear him sigh as he pulls me back to him, our combined sweat making the skin contact slippery.

"I think you've met your match, Ms Fisher. Let's get dressed and go out for some breakfast with the papers." He gives me a quick squeeze and then extracts himself from me and the bed and the next thing I hear is the sound of the rain showerhead pelting water onto the marble wet room floor.

I take the opportunity to have a sneaky peak into his bedside drawer, which opens soundlessly. I take in the stock of rubbers that he has, as well as the several tubes of lube, a pair of handcuffs, some plaited lengths of what feels like silk to the touch, and a number of vibrators ranging in size. I pick up something and quickly realise I have no idea what it is. It feels like latex, with a thin tip that widens in the middle, leading to a notch and then flaring out into a base. *I guess I will find out soon enough.* I slide the drawer shut and my eyes travel up to the bedside table where his phones sit: the iPhone and Blackberry that are never too far away from the conscientious Mr Harrington.

I can hear the strains of Patrick singing over the shower noise and think I probably have a few more minutes before he turns the water off. I smile at his off key baritone, pleased at the thought that he must be really happy if he is singing. *I'm happy too*, I acknowledge, and could pinch myself at the memory of the last twelve hours we spent together, to check it isn't a dream. I pick up his iPhone, press the home key and slide my thumb across its face to unlock it. The pass code screen appears and I tap in the PIN he gave me for his credit card. The home screen presents itself and I feel a smug sense of satisfaction. He really should be more careful. A small burst of guilt enters my bloodstream but I dismiss the feeling, thinking that this is only fair after his Facebook stalking.

I quickly open his text messages and am puzzled to see that there are only three conversation threads. He is on this thing constantly and I am sure he would have more history stored than this. *Who bothers to delete messages?* Unless, of course, they need to cover their tracks... But then he can't be hiding this from me, as he is none the wiser to my treachery. I am baffled.

The most recent exchange is one from 'Dave - personal', which I imagine is David Grafton who works at Caldwell. I know they are close friends. The next is from me. The last thread is simply marked 'Silvy'.

I open 'Dave - personal' and scroll up and see there is plenty of conversation there. I scan down and it looks fairly innocuous. One message catches my eye about halfway down, sent last week.

'I think we might be fucked. I'm not sure I can stall this for much longer and I'm worried about how much sniffing around is going on. You might want to consider telling Brad ASAP.' I can't even begin to know what this is about but guess that the 'Brad' he is referring to is none other than Caldwell's esteemed CEO.

Patrick's response is curt and dismissive. Then there are a few messages confirming a meet up on Tuesday. And then finally one received this morning:

'So man, now that you've tapped that sweet ass is she 'THE ONE' or what?' Despite the crude reference I am thrilled. I think Dave is his closest friend and clearly they have been talking about me. My heart sings at the thought that he thinks I might be 'the one'. The eligible Patrick Harrington. I know how many women would love to be where I am right now.

Realising time is marching on I don't stop to daydream and quickly move on to look at what he has sent to Silvy. It doesn't take me long to read the messages as there are only two: one from him confirming his appointment and one from her responding to say she 'can't wait to see him.' These texts were sent on Tuesday afternoon. I return to the home screen and lock his phone and replace it carefully just where it had been. I feel a bit sick as I contemplate what I have seen. *Why does he delete his text threads? Who the fuck is Silvy, when I thought he was so enthralled with me? And did he see her and then meet up with Dave on Tuesday night?* I can't make any sense of this.

I lie back and take several deep breaths to centre myself. I can't let my mind race away with this and I certainly can't be anything other than happily satisfied when Patrick emerges. I decide to go on the offensive and remove my shoes before joining him as he finishes his shower. If I act as though I am insatiable that will make me more appealing, as well as ensuring that it is not suspicion that I arouse.

As we head out of the front door I paste a big smile on my face and turn to Patrick. He puts his hands in his coat pockets and shrugs at me, which puts me a little off balance. Here we are about to walk to Harvey Nick's to share breakfast after our first night of lovemaking and he is not even going to hold my hand. For the third time this morning I feel stung, after his laughing at me and seeing the text exchange with Silvy. As I struggle with my emotions I realise that I am starting to feel obsessive and this man is able to affect me deeply, probably without even realising it.

I feel my phone vibrate in my coat pocket and retrieve it as a distraction. It is a text message from Candice.

'So is Non-Com a good shag then?' I chuckle and feel grateful to my best friend for her telepathic connection. I needed to get some perspective and she has reminded me that this is just sex for Patrick and that is how I need to view it too, at least until there is some evidence to the contrary. And maybe there is. He just makes it so hard to judge with the way he had everything set up from the lighting, to the champagne, the shoes, and the music. I know that despite my best logical efforts I have fallen for this man. Last night, there was a moment where I'd thought he felt the same.

"What's so funny, Fisher?" he questions. I seem to be back on his radar as we round the corner and merge into the foot traffic on Brompton Road. I put my hands back in my coat pockets and shrug at him. Let's see how he likes it. Two can play at this game.

"Well?" he says a little louder and with a noticeable edge to his voice.

"Just a reminder about the girls' night tonight, nothing important," I counter, with a touch of steel in my tone. He doesn't look happy with this response but the bustle of people around us prevents any further interrogation.

We walk silently, amidst the noise of the Saturday morning shopping throng. We duck and weave through people and cross the road in front of Harrods to make our way toward Sloane Street and Harvey Nichols. I am trying to keep up with him, trying to stay at his elbow, and not get separated amongst the masses. Suddenly, I feel Patrick's hand clasp my arm and push me backward sharply.

"Stop walking and turn around now," he commands leaning down to my ear, pivoting on his heel and dragging me along with him. I feel like a reprimanded child and move my feet as quickly as the surge of people around us will allow. I glance back over my shoulder to see the sleek form of Eloise Little disappearing into the doors of Harrods. We were mere seconds from bumping into her. My nerves are jangling as Patrick pulls me against the flood of people pushing in the opposite direction.

The crowds start to thin as we get past Harrods but he is still holding my arm and walking at a pace that makes me have to hop step to keep up. I feel the tension emanating from him. I feel annoyed that he seems to think he is the only one bothered by this near miss. I yank my arm free and this slows him down enough to turn to look at me. His face is like thunder. The look softens as he sees how frightened I am.

"Well, that was close, I say." His Irish accent coming to the fore, I note with interest. Maybe that is a sign that he is feeling vulnerable and I instantly feel a little less hostile toward him. We cross back to the north side of Brompton Road and walk up Montpelier Street. He suggests that we stop at Fromagerie Beillevaire and at least get a decent cup of coffee. I had been teasing Patrick the night before that he doesn't cook, as I had found the oven still full of instruction manuals and plastic wrapped wire shelves, as if it had just been installed rather than the truth: that it had been there for more than four years. I wasn't holding out any expectation of us returning to his place to have poached eggs on toast and I hoped this place sold some food along with a cup of java. All that sex had made me ravenous.

Patrick holds the door open for me and the pungent smell of cheese hits me head on as I cross the threshold. I want to gag and it takes all my willpower not to. I watch his face as I walk in and see that while he is smiling at me his smile does not reach his eyes. At this point I don't even care. I need something in my stomach other than the acidic leftovers of the night before. While it was close, Eloise didn't see us so I don't understand what all the drama was for.

I go straight to the counter and order a cappuccino and point at a cheese tart in the glass cabinet. Not even the overpowering odour can stop my hunger. Patrick, standing close behind me, reaches forward to drop a twenty quid note onto the counter and barks his coffee order over my head. He then walks away to claim the two free seats in the window. I watch him sit down with the papers he so desperately wants to read, while cracking the entrance door slightly and keeping it ajar with his foot. I guess I'm not the only one with a sensitive nose this morning.

I decide to make small talk with the barista-come-waiter-come-cheesemonger while he makes our coffees and warms my breakfast. He's French, introducing himself as Jean-Michel in perfect English with a thick accent and a warm handshake across the counter. It is as though he is dropping the first letter off some words. He is young with kind eyes and a cheeky smile. He tells me that he loves the smell of cheese and that it makes a pleasant change from the years he had spent working on his father's pig farm in Bretagne. I laugh with him as he screws his face up in disgust and then opens his arms wide and takes on an evangelical look as he switches from describing the piggery to talking about his beloved dairy products.

I collect the drinks and my pie and make my way to the table where Patrick is seated, head deep in the weekend edition of the Financial Times. He doesn't even glance up as I put his cup down in front of him and take the seat beside him. I set about attacking my cheese and pastry delight with vigour and it's all I can do to stop myself from scoffing, my hunger is so present. I can't understand how the perfect Mr Harrington is not famished.

"Slow down, Alex, for god's sake! Take a pause," he hisses while angrily flipping the page of his newspaper, still not looking at me.

I am stunned and my brain struggles to process an appropriate response. I take a long pull of my coffee and after replacing my cup, let my hands fall into my lap. I want to keep eating. *How have we got to this place?* I feel like I am walking on eggshells yet Patrick hasn't actually enunciated what the problem is. Surely it isn't my over-zealous flaky pastry feast. And Eloise didn't see us, so no harm done on that front.

I don't know what to do. I am stifling my rising panic but only just. I have left his house without my handbag so I have my coat and my phone but nothing else. I am wholly at his mercy. *Just how he likes it*, I think to myself sardonically. No sooner has this thought taken flight, when without warning, he closes his paper and reaches out for my hand. I stare at him as if I am seeing him for the first time. He rolls his fingers as if to entice me but I am keeping my hands where they are, waiting until he opens his mouth and explains his behaviour. I know I am on thin ice but I need more of an explanation than a sudden change of heart. He is a chameleon and it is as off-putting as it is unpredictable. In that moment I wonder what the hell I am doing there. The passion and lust of the previous night and recent morning fade into a distant memory.

"Let's have a wonderful weekend darling. I can't believe we almost bumped into the wicked witch. What a fiasco that would've been." He has visibly relaxed and is smiling at me, still reaching for my hand. My panic and confusion fuses into anger as I register the insulting way he refers to Eloise. I know she is fearsome but she is by no means a witch. She is a clever woman and therefore intimidates men like Patrick who are used to being able to manipulate the fairer sex. *How pathetic*, I think. And as for having a 'wonderful weekend' at no point did I think we would be spending that much time together. I have plans to see Candice this evening. I am beginning to realise that I need space to process my emotions after spending time with this man. It has been so intense and unstable that I am left feeling like a mountain goat clinging to the craggy rock face, trying not to lose my footing.

"Patrick! I care for Eloise and would prefer it if you didn't speak about her like that. You may not get on with her but she is my mentor and friend, so please respect that." I am surprised at myself for exploding like that but I am getting to the end of my tether. He is still staring at me and with all the skill of an actor he keeps the smile in place and tries again.

"Come on Alfie. I was just joking. Jeez. You and I both know that could've been a disaster. How would you have explained that you've been lying to your mentor and friend?" He keeps his tone even as I try and detect whether he is being sarcastic. His eyes are pleading and he has used the nickname I reserve for close friends and family. He does make a good point and I reach for his hand. I am no match for this man and I need to bring the equilibrium back before the situation gets any messier than it already is. I smile and shrug, not trusting myself to say anything just yet.

"Let's go back to my place." He stands and shuffles the papers together. He is not going to wait for me to finish my breakfast so I drain my coffee and put my coat on. This man clearly likes to be calling the shots and this has been a welcome change from Joey, who is amenable to the point of being prone. It is evident to me, though, that I need to stick my oar in at well-chosen moments or risk losing myself completely to this addictive man.

I feel a sense of relief at being let back into Patrick's house and to know I have access to my belongings again. I didn't like the feeling of being wholly reliant on Mr Harrington, a man who was revealing himself as being more hot-headed than I had ever imagined. I guess you don't make it to the C-Suite of one of Britain's largest companies without having a substantial amount of fire in your belly.

As soon as the door clicks shut he has his hands on me, pulling at my clothing, seeking my skin. I am reeling. *How can he switch so quickly between being so annoyed at me and wanting to have sex with me?* I push him away and see the look of a little boy lost. And then in the blink of an eye his temper is back. "What? What's your problem?" His eyes have changed from hurt to angry in a flash and I am momentarily dumbfounded.

"Patrick, please. Let's talk about what happened this morning so I can understand why you got so angry." I try to remain calm.

"It's not brain surgery, Alex. We both value our jobs and I don't want your 'mentor and friend' causing me any issues. Alright? Plus I didn't like how you disrespected me by flirting with that stupid French cheese boy. I don't know why you are punishing me when I've done nothing wrong." His eyes are communicating his mood as vehemently as his sneering words are. He is mocking me, referring to Eloise as my mentor and friend as I had earlier. The use of the word 'me' instead of 'us' shocks me too as I realise he doesn't care about the impact this relationship might have on my career, only his own. And to top it all off he thinks I am being unreasonable on various counts. I decide in that moment to get as far away from him as possible and as quickly as possible. I push past him and head upstairs to the bedroom to collect my things. I return to the entrance hall to find he is gone. *Can I just leave?* I think it is the only way that he will realise he has behaved appallingly.

I burst back onto the street and scurry away from his house as swiftly as my legs will carry me. I don't stop to notice the splendour of the traditional Georgian façades as I rush past the beautiful terraced housing like I had the last time I traced these steps this morning with Patrick. I can't get away quick enough.

I glance over my shoulder as I round the corner to check he is not coming after me. I register that I am actually feeling scared. I hear Adele singing about 'Setting fire to the rain' and it takes me a moment for the music to penetrate my brain and realise that's the ring tone I have assigned to Patrick on my phone. He is calling me.

"Alex, please come back. You're right, we need to talk." He hasn't stretched to an apology but at least he sounds contrite. I stop walking and put a hand on the railing that protects the house in front of me. I need to steady myself. I can't walk and think at the same time. I sigh, expelling stale air from my lungs, trying to force oxygen around my system.

"You need to watch how you speak to me, Patrick. I'm not sure what I am to you but I'm certainly not one of your employees. I'm free to leave when I choose and I won't tolerate being treated badly." I feel bold as the words trip off my tongue. I also feel moved to tears as I think about the sex I had enjoyed with Patrick. It was intense and pleasurable without question, but he had also pushed me to a place where I felt like he was controlling me, stopping right at the brink of humiliation.

This whole experience was causing me to rage against myself as I realise with shame that I am just like my father. I would let this man demean me for the sake of a few moments of pleasure. Patrick was giving me a glimpse into how my father must have lived. It was a feeling that could certainly be addictive, to the point of me ignoring the consequences. I need to wise up, but the pull of Patrick Harrington is so strong it is centripetal.

"Please, Alex. Don't make me beg. You know how much I care about you." Still no apology but getting warmer.

Flashes of the newspaper articles about my dad and photos from the inquest pervade my mind. Faces hide as much as they reveal. My father's epitaph is teaching me much.

"Patrick. I need some space. I would need to leave soon anyway as I'm meeting my friends for drinks and dinner this evening, and I need to go home and get ready. I hadn't realised we might spend the weekend together." I stop short of admonishing him for making assumptions about how I might spend my time.

"Where are you going out tonight?" His tone is almost relaxed as he switches tack but I am starting to appreciate how well he can mask his real feelings. I don't have the bandwidth to try and figure out why he is asking and think it is best to try and ring off on a positive note so decided to answer him without question.

"We're going out in the West End. I think we're having drinks at the Experimental Cocktail Club. We've got a dinner reservation at Joël Robuchon. Look, Patrick, I'm almost at the tube so I need to go. I hope you enjoy the rest of your weekend." I want to hang up in his ear after all that has happened this morning but I don't. I can't. I want to hear his voice.

"Joël Robuchon? Very classy, Alex. Enjoy. I'll call you tomorrow." He exhales audibly letting me know he is still on the line. Perhaps he is finding it hard to hang up too.

"Candice is almost as good as you when it comes to knowing where to go in London. 'Bye, Patrick," I say and slip my phone back in my bag, before slinging it over my shoulder. One more sentence from him and I would have capitulated. I realise my other hand is still gripping the fence railing with all my strength. I drop my hands into my pockets and continue the walk I had started; onward, not back to that man's house, despite every bone in my body willing me otherwise.

Laughing at me after we've just made love. The cheese man. Telling me off for eating too quickly. No amount of money, gifts or fun would paper over the cracks that are already beginning to show. I am starting to see what Eloise must see. But still I am conflicted. If I haven't been thinking rationally before, I am definitely in no state to be logical now, having had sex repeatedly with this man. I need the night out I have planned to get some fresh perspective and feel comfortable in my own skin again.

There is no peace when you're in love, I reflect. It is punishment in motion. A pendulum swinging back and forth through the full range of human emotions. It is exquisite, addictive torture.

Harrington

In between the sex last night and the early hours of this morning we managed to drink quite a bit, I realise as I wake with a slightly fuzzy head. I smile to myself remembering we had agreed to rendezvous in New York, as we will both be there for the meetings taking place midweek, and to extend our flights to spend the weekend there together.

I feel Alex stir beside me and allow myself to feel smug. I lie still as she makes her way to the bathroom. I check my phone quickly as soon as the door clicks shut. Dave is asking me how the sex was. He is referring to Alex as 'the one', which doesn't touch the usual nerve given how satisfied I am feeling. I see that Tanja and that stupid bitch Amber Chilworth have sent me messages. I read them quickly wanting to return to 'slumber' before Alex reappears. Tanja, asking what I'm up to. She has been needy lately, which is annoying, as I had thought she knew her place. I will have to do something about it and file that thought away for taking action later.

As for Amber, well she and her thunder thighs can fuck right off. Her message came through in the wee hours of last night, I realise. She was probably drunk and obviously hoping to be my booty call for the evening. *Fat thighs and fat chance*, I think. If only she knew who I was lavishing my attention on. That would be a lovely triangle to create if it wasn't so explosive. I delete both messages without replying, replace my phone and resume my sleep-like pose knowing Alex will be emerging any second.

I hear the thud as the bathroom door reaches the end of its rollers and open my eyes to see the slender Ms Fisher trying hard to maintain her composure as she sashays across my bedroom floor, wearing nothing but the mesh shoes I bought her yesterday. I smile and my thermostat clicks on, the thought is there even if the execution isn't flawless.

Alex makes it to the end of the bed and strips the duvet off me with a flourish. She takes in my naked athletic form and her smile is the widest I've seen it. Leaning onto the bed I watch her shuffle herself forward so she is in prime position to straddle me. Her face flickers as I watch her make a choice. I read the runes perfectly and grab at her hips to encourage her progression past my midriff and towards my face.

My mouth is a little dry so I start with her inner thigh, the smooth tone of her skin hints at the sweetness that is oh so close. My hand kneads her muscles, and then grasps her mound with its precisely tailored pubic hair. I push her legs wider to help my position but also to reassert an element of control.

I take each side of her pussy in my mouth and suck on the soft flesh. I hear Alex moan for the first time. Encouraged, I use my fingers to explore and to reveal the full delicate pink of her labia and her clitoris. Her trembling legs and stiffening muscles show me that I'm making progress and with a mix of short and long motions my tongue continues its work. I love the sight in front of me, the taste on my tongue and the feel of her hands working my head and shoulders, encouraging me. I have definitely awoken the vixen within this woman and I plan to exploit this to the fullest extent possible. Last night was just the beginning. She has no idea what's in store for her.

At first mildly, then with increasing force, I eat her. Her legs convulse and squeeze against my ears. I can hardly breathe. She doesn't care and neither do I. I find the strength to get my hand up into the fray, my fingers curling upwards and looking for her G spot. Alex is breathing in irregular bursts. This is so hot. I steadily increase the speed as my urgency matches hers and, as she orgasms, it's like my head is clamped in a vice. Her eyes close for a time, giving in to the sensations coursing through her body, before she opens them again to gaze back at me. A few seconds later, her laughter is filling the room in a blast of infectious fun as she acknowledges her body's responsiveness.

Still not sated, and knowing that my erection is still there for the taking, Alex moves herself back to where she had been. She is teasing me, pushing just my tip inside her, her legs wide apart as she squats over me. The immediate view is incredible. I shift my gaze to the large mirror behind her.

I congratulate myself on my interior design choices and, not for the first time, I find myself enjoying the effect the strategic placement of mirrors creates; it is totally immersive and like being at the centre of my very own fantasy. Virtual reality porn. I love watching the mirror-bound doppelgangers and feel like the leader of the band as I start to set the pace.

I sense that Alex thinks her playful resistance is a clever tactic and decide to ensure that she knows exactly who is boss. I grab her shoulders roughly and as I force her down on top of me it is like a circuit connecting. The current is powerful, a thrill, the electricity of the illicit coursing through us. I embrace the surge of desire as I see the lust in her eyes. It is that crazy lust, animal passion. There is no coercion or subjugation here. She wants this and she loves every moment of it.

I use the full thrust of my hips to drive deeper into her and the sounds alone are a soundtrack of sexual frenzy that would be worth recording. Her moans get louder. Alex comes first but not by much. Her hot juices cover my thighs and the final contraction of her orgasm is enough to start my own. So good so good, I feel the pulse of each jet of spunk leaving me. My ass spasms to get the last pleasure hit. She collapses on top of me contentedly, which causes me to feel instantly uncomfortable. I stay where I am to allow my heart beat to slow down, all the while planning a quick escape from this post-coital intimacy. I know that her surging oxytocin levels will make her feel all lovey dovey. I don't do lovey dovey.

"I love your cock," she says, looking up at the ceiling, regulating her own breathing after the exertion. This causes me to erupt with laughter given I had assumed she would be feeling drunk on love. I tell her that she is like nobody else I have met, knowing that she will lap up the perceived distinction from other women. *Do I mean it?* My lies are so convincing sometimes I fool myself.

I extricate myself and leave her lying there, putting a wall literally and metaphorically between us as I enter the bathroom. I deftly pull a razor across my face, smiling at the good-looking man smiling back at me in the mirror. I set the shower running and the near scalding water offers me some relief from my sexworn, aching muscles.

I am humming to myself and I am deep in thought. My heart swells as I think about my persistence and how I always win the prize. Always. And there is still more to play for. I think about the vibrators and butt plug in the drawer beside my bed. The silk ties and the handcuffs. And then I'll move her onto the web. I know a few of my online friends would love to watch me fucking this piece of crumpet in real time. My mind wanders and as my humming turns to singing I hear my velvety voice belting out one of my favourite Irish folk songs.

"And I promise to play the wild rover no more
And it's no, nay, never!
No nay never no more
Will I play the wild rover?
No never no more!"

I catch myself as I sing the chorus again and have an instant of momentary panic as I realise just what it is that I am singing. I hear the door sliding and realise that Alex is going to join me. I'm a bit rattled as I prefer to shower alone, and I am still reeling a bit from the revelation the Pogues have awakened me to. *Am I really in danger of falling for this girl to the extent that subliminally I'm thinking of changing my ways?* It can't be. I will always be a Wild Rover. I allow her under the water and try not to reveal my discontent. I won't ruin the moment right now but she'll know soon enough when she puts a foot wrong with me.

Alex is obviously still tired, but her eyes are dancing with all that has gone before. She tiptoes so she can kiss me in the middle of the forceful shower rain. Initially it is controlled, investigative, but quickly it becomes more frenetic. Our tongues won't be held back and delve deeply into each other, tasting and savouring. She drops lower and starts to kiss and gently bite my neck. My eyes close and I let the sensations envelop me, nerve ends jangling, my erection already fully inflated. My body is betraying me while my thoughts are a muddle. I feel honour bound to capitalise on this situation. Her blowjobs are a bit amateurish but nothing a bit of instruction won't fix. I push her down to her knees.

As we dress and make our way out of the house, I can't shake the feelings of disquiet that are descending on me. I feel off balance as I try to read this girl and worse still, my own reactions. I jam my hands in my coat pockets and set off up the street. She scurries to keep up. There will no handholding. I can't afford her feeling too comfortable. Certainly not when I am anything but.

She is checking her phone and then laughing to herself which only fuels my annoyance further. I ask her what she finds so funny and get a petulant response. I am hit with the reality of why I don't like having women around for too long. I don't like having to moderate my behaviour for anyone and I'm certainly no peacemaker. *Just get to the restaurant*, I think. Strong coffee and some quiet time with the newspapers will allow me to reset my head.

We manoeuvre through the crowds as we hit Brompton Road. I still don't take Alex's hand, even at the risk of being separated. She knows where we're going. We cross the street and the masses seem to swell as we approach Harrods. My heart stops as my eyes pick out a familiar form a short step in front of me. It's Eloise 'frozen face' Little. We are on a collision course. I grab Alex by the arm and spin us around, frogmarching her in the opposite direction. I feel her resistance as she cranes her head to see what has caused this about turn. Then she is falling in step. Clearly she has clocked the old bird.

As we make ground and the crowd begins to thin out, Alex shakes her arm free from my grasp. I turn to look at her and see fear in her eyes. This is all too much. I like to watch drama on TV, not to participate in it. With effort, I change my demeanour and laughingly acknowledge the near miss. I try and placate her by suggesting we get coffee at the nearby fromagerie.

I hold the door open and let her pass me, smiling sweetly at her. Without ceremony she is ordering herself coffee and something to eat. She hasn't even asked me what I'd like, but doesn't refuse the money I lay on the counter, I note with vexation. I order a cappuccino and walk away. I know my disdain will be palpable if I don't get a handle on it quick style.

I take the table in the window and settle myself down, opening the broadsheet and feel slightly better as I read about the continuing Euro zone crisis. Familiar territory. Moneymaking schemes pervade my mind and I feel calmer and more like myself.

Alex's laughter wafts over from the counter and I glance over to see her unashamedly flirting with the scruffy young server. He has greasy hair and a stubbly face. The feelings of relaxation that were building are demolished and my blood is quickly back to boiling. How dare she. This is becoming more trouble than it's worth. The sex is good and I know I can make it great when I've broken her. *But can I get through all this faux-couple stuff?* It's definitely not my bag. While I don't respect the stupid whores that try to spend 'quality time' with me at least I know they are malleable. Alex is proving to be anything but.

She brings over our drinks and places my coffee in front of me. I don't acknowledge her. I want to scream at her, but the thought that she is inciting this reaction in me keeps me silent. Either she doesn't care or knows better than to take me head on. She starts in on her breakfast. I feel like a volcano about to erupt as I hear her gobbling her quiche in an undignified manner. This is too much and I tell her to slow down. Helping her improve her sexual repertoire is one thing but I can't believe I have to teach her how to eat.

I realise I have snapped at her and the childish look on her face confirms this. I finish my coffee and inform her that we are going back to the house. She looks surprised but doesn't argue. I leave without waiting for her, taking in fresh air as soon as I emerge to try and rid my nostrils of the sharp cheese odour. The breathing helps me calm down and by the time we get back to my front door I feel much better. I have stolen a few glances at Alex, and seeing her golden hair falling down her shoulders momentarily captures my attention and stirs my lust.

I let her into the house and without waiting for the door to close I start kissing her, my hands exploring her body as if it's my own personal property. She responds to my kisses to begin with and then pushes me away harshly. She wants to talk. The theatrical mini-series continues.

I'm not in the mood for the amateur dramatics and she moves past me bodily, heading up the stairs. I sigh as I think about how much work is ahead of me if I am to wear her down to total supplication. I head through to the kitchen and drop the unfinished newspapers as well as the 'How to spend it' supplement on the counter. I am seriously pissed off. I had not anticipated her being a problem factory.

I check my phones. There are a few work emails but I can't focus on those until my head is straight. I remember that Dave had text me, asking how the sex was. I feel the chance to debase Alex may restore my composure.

'You know what I like best in a woman? My dick. She's been pounded worse than Omaha Beach was during the D Day landings. My balls are empty.' I hit send and instantly feel better, even allowing myself to smile at my own wit.

I hear her footsteps alerting me to the fact that she is back downstairs. She will be in front of me momentarily and offering up an apology, I'm sure. She's had ample time to think about her immature and unreasonable behaviour.

I wait for her to appear and instead I hear the front door click shut. God damn it. This girl is like quicksilver. I've never encountered this before. I can't pin her down. Usually at the first sign of resistance I weigh the odds and move on. Most women that display drama-queen tendencies are just not worth the effort once you get them in the sack. Fiery or spicy is one thing and often makes for a great lover but histrionics are best avoided at all costs.

I quickly assess the facts. I need to get her back on side. I will dismiss her when I'm ready, not the other way round. Plus I can't risk her shooting her mouth off to Eloise. I grab my phone and start pacing the length of my kitchen. I can handle this. I call her. I listen to the phone ringing and count the rings. She picks up. I breathe out. I'm good at lies but it's much easier to convince a person than voicemail.

I decide to walk the tightrope between being contrite but not actually apologising. She needs to think I am open to talking, but I certainly am not going to say sorry when I haven't done anything wrong.

Her voice is steely as she responds to my earnest plea for her to come back to the house. I realise quickly that I'm not going to win this battle. She may be combative but she won't win the war. I regroup as we talk and realise that I need to try a different strategy. I had intended to get her to change her plans with her friends so I could spend the weekend working on her. This wasn't going to happen so I mellow my tone and ask her where she is going that evening, filing away the response for future use. I let her ring off.

I put my head in my hands. I am exhausted after the turbulent morning and exasperated at not getting my own way. This girl will not outdo me. I decide to head downstairs to the den and settle into my couch to watch last night's footage. Whilst I know that years of practice have made me a sexual virtuoso, I never tire of being inventive, always seeking ways to improve. Seeing Alex naked on screen will hopefully square away the romantic imagery my mind keeps going to when I think of her. I don't know how I have got to this place. I start to formulate a plot, as I desperately need to distance myself emotionally from Alex, but at the same time still ensuring I can take what I want from her. I am now more determined than ever to initiate her into my world and have her so heartsick that she will do anything I ask.

There is no peace when you're in love, I reflect. It is punishment in motion. A pendulum swinging back and forth through the full range of human emotions. It is exquisite, addictive torture.

Alexandra

I am happy to be home alone. It is a relief to be free to be myself and to sit still for a moment without anyone wanting anything from me, giving me heavy looks or making loaded comments.

I feel like I have been in a washing machine on the spin cycle. I am struggling with my own identity after recognising that I, like my father, have a side to me that enjoys being controlled and even belittled. Patrick has unlocked something in me that is both sensual and disturbing. I am so mixed up I now don't know if I am in the midst of a game with this man or if he actually does see me as different, as the one.

The front door thumps shut and the sounds of muffled music fill the space. Joey piles into the room, his headphones around his neck, still clearly piping tunes. He's in his workout gear, still flushed from his run. I watch him as he dumps his iPod on the counter and bends down to take his trainers off. He is a fine looking man with an amazing body. But even more importantly, he has a good heart. He is a good person. With a sigh I blink back the tears, which are welling as my throat constricts with this rush of emotion. I feel like weeping but I don't want him to see me cry. I cross my arms in front of me in a self-hug and pull my knees up under me on the couch. Our last conversation where I tried to push him for a move-out date had not gone well at all.

"Hi Alfie. Wasn't expecting to see you... which is silly, really, seeing it's your flat. I'll be off soon, don't worry." His tone is level; he is being conciliatory, not antagonistic. My urge to cry renews itself.

"It's cool, Joe. How are you?" I want to talk to him, perhaps I even need to. I yearn to laugh in the easy way we used to and I really want one of his bear hugs.

"Yeah, good. I've found a place to move into. A friend of a colleague at work has a spare room going at her flat in Fulham. I met the bird last night and the room is alright so just need to hand over some cash and it's mine. I'll be out of your hair in a week." Every word is like a razor, slicing, cutting, hurting. I need him to move out, I know this. But right now it is the last thing I want to hear. And he is so well adjusted about it. I want Joey to be happy but I thought he would mourn our relationship for a bit longer. I feel my annoyance levels rise as I think about the fact that he is moving in with another woman, and realise with a jolt that I have not processed our break-up at all. I have been too quick to jump into the arms of the intoxicating Patrick Harrington.

"Can I make you some tea? Sit down, let's catch up Levy," my voice is abnormally high pitched as I try to sound casual. He is surveying me.

"Nah, I'm all sweaty. I need to jump in the shower and sort myself out before heading out this evening." His tone remains friendly even though I can see he thinks I am acting strangely. He is watching me and not moving.

"You look great, Al. I hope you're doing well. When I'm settled in the new gaff we'll have a party for sure and we can catch up then." He doesn't wait for me to respond, moving off toward the bathroom. I hadn't come home last night and he would know that. I know he is being good to me when he is probably mad as hell but I still want more from him. The time I've spent with Patrick has really affected me and I can feel myself seeking external validation. It wasn't fair to put that on Joey, but I am safe with him. *Another parallel with my father*, I think bleakly, *the need for constant reassurance.* They call it 'self' esteem for a reason; I want to pull myself together but instead I feel more like I am unravelling.

Joey reappears after an undetermined interval. I can't map time with any accuracy, as I have been miles away, lost in the depths of my own mind. I have been sitting staring into space, still holding myself in a tight human knot. My thoughts are no clearer. They are all screwed up like a ball of string.

"You okay, Al?" he asks warmly. I am so close to tipping I don't know if I can bear his kindness. I know that no matter what, this man will always care about me and there have never been any hidden agendas. His face doesn't hide more than it reveals.

"I guess I could do with a hug," I manage. I don't move and am not looking at him. He strides over and plonks himself down beside me wrapping me up in his strong arms. I lean into him and breathe in the familiar soothing scent of him. I know he can feel my shoulders shaking as I let myself cry.

He holds me as I sob and doesn't say a word, allowing me to vent my emotions. He and I have been here many times before. His clinch loosens and I pull away from him a little to look up at him from under my eyelashes, with eyes still brimming with tears. I feel small and pathetic but I can't help myself.

"Alexandra Louise Fisher, why all the tears?" his tone continues to be compassionate making me want to purge everything even more. My internal voices are raging and I know that I can't be so hurtful as to admit that I am seeing someone else and that he has upset me. Instead, I decide to tell the truth about the disturbing thoughts that are swirling around in my head about my father, stopping short at actually telling him why I am besieged by grief. He listens patiently and watches with concern as tears continue to slide down my face. I am swiping wildly at them with the backs of my wrists as I speak.

"Maybe you need to ease up a bit. Get some balance back, and get some rest. I'm guessing you had quite a lot to drink last night which you know always impacts your mood and your ability to process these kinds of feelings, babe." He is right and hearing him demonstrate how well he knows me only serves to send me into a fresh round of blubbers. He is avoiding the topic of where I stayed last night for which I am grateful. I know that I am asking a lot of him right now, particularly given that it was me who insisted on the break-up and who has been pushing him so hard to get out of both my space and my life. I guess I had forgotten that regardless of who pulls the pin, both parties get oblit-erated when the relationship grenade explodes.

"It's okay to have these feelings, Al. You're a good person and you've had a lot to deal with in your short life. I think that we walk a fine line between the joy and beauty of life and the abyss... Once you've seen horrors and tragedy it can never be unseen, and will always filter through no matter how hard you try to block it out. Ride with it for a bit, it takes so much energy to push against it. Your resilience will come back, and with it equi-librium. Please, please keep trying to be happy. You deserve it. I've got to shoot but I'll text you later, okay?" He is making to stand up.

"It's not like an Xbox game Al, you only get once chance at life," I smile at him and nod, only Joey can be profound and at the same time remind me of his infuriating addiction to gaming as a means of trying to lift my mood.

He has so much insight into who I am and we have so much shared history. He looks really good with his natural style, his hair spiked in a David Beckham-like Mohican, ripped jeans and a crisp blue shirt, untucked, hugging his well sculpted upper body. So different from the 'everything is perfect' Patrick Harrington.

I let Joey go without further ado and assess my options. Hide under my duvet or head out with Candice and the others. My phone beeps as a reminder that I am still in fact connected with the outside world. I check it and when I see what Candice has sent my mind is made up:

'Fish Nets! I'm on my way over with a bottle of bubbles. I fig-ured you and I could catch up before we hit the town. I'm sure you've much to tell me!! xCx'

My second shower of the day is quite different from my first, I think to myself as I towel myself dry. I put on one of my favourite dresses, an emerald green halter neck that shows a little cleavage and a lot of shoulder, dropping away at the back to show the skin from my neck down to just above my tail bone. The satin fabric softly drapes into a skirt that sits modestly just below the knee. A subtle mix of skin and fabric, understatedly sexy but eye-catch-ing enough to give me a boost in confidence. Lord knows I need it. I know it will make me feel better to wear something I feel feminine in. I am not really in the mood to go out but it wins out over being home alone feeling sorry for myself. Besides, I've already had my pity party with Joey.

I buzz Candice in and take a deep breath, bracing myself for the tornado that is about to hit. She breezes in and heads straight to the kitchen dropping her handbag unceremoniously before getting straight down to business by uncorking the Veuve Clicquot bottle that she's carried in under her arm. I dutifully fetch two champagne flutes, pre-empting the order that I know will be coming. She beams at me and grabs me to her in an impulsive hug. The glasses clink as she squeezes me.

"So. Spill the beans. Was it worth being stalked? Is he a zero or a hero?" she is laughing as she quizzes me, her eyes dancing with mischief.

I sit down on one of the kitchen bar stools and accept the proffered flute fizzing with liquid. I bring it to my lips and drain the glass in one go.

"Jeez, was it that good? Or bad? Come on woman. Speak to me!" her impatience is evident as she uses her flailing hands to emphasise her words.

I start at the beginning. She gasps as I tell her about the shoes he had surprised me with. She disappears for a moment to retrieve them from my bedroom, remerging wearing them and a smug smile.

I laugh and continue my story. Every time I skim over the sexual details she shakes her head and forces me to divulge more information. It crosses my mind briefly that Candice might be a better match for the demanding Patrick Harrington than I am. She would certainly keep him on his toes. By the time I am done recounting my sleep over at Patrick's, the laughter and fun from earlier in the conversation have gone. She looks thoughtful and a little pensive.

"I dunno, Fish Bait. My advice would be to run. Run. Run! There aren't enough gifts in the world that can replace your self-respect. He's shown you his true colours." She drains her champagne glass and looks at me with earnest eyes. I feel as though she can see right through me and there is a pregnant pause before she continues.

"Ah, but then by the same token, if he wants to behave like a sugar daddy then let him," she says flippantly. I know she wants to shake sense into me but she also knows how deeply I feel about this man and that any advice she might give will likely fall on deaf ears. Her closing statement is really a reminder that she won't judge me and that I can count on her regardless of what I decide. I really do love my best friend.

We make our way into the West End and surface from the underground at Leicester Square station. As we walk onto Charing Cross Road, the night I had spent with Patrick at J Sheekey comes flooding back to me. The restaurant is just around the corner. I recall the excitement and the anticipation of that evening once more and know I want to feel like that again. I am hooked.

I have implored Candice to keep my new romantic situation to herself. At this stage, I don't know where it is heading so there is really nothing to tell. If I even mentioned having a few dates I know I will pique the interest of the other women. Two of the girls are also Cambridge graduates, with links to Joey. I don't want any gossip to reach him, and, after the mature way he handled me earlier I know that I owe him the decency of telling him directly that I am seeing someone new. *As soon as I admit this to myself.*

The smells and sounds of Chinatown flood my senses as we make our way to number 13 Gerrard Street, the Experimental Cocktail Club. Despite having the street address, the bar is not easy to find and Candice is getting a bit antsy as we make our second pass down the main thoroughfare of Chinatown. Loads of the doors on the street either don't have numbers or they are in Chinese. We stop at a rather dishevelled looking door and realise that the bored looking guy leaning against the frame is actually a bouncer. We navigate past him and make our way upstairs where we check our coats and find the others waiting for us in front of the bar. I take in the exposed brickwork juxtaposed with ornate wallpapers, mirrored tables and the comfy seats. This speakeasy is the latest happening place to be, according to Candice.

I catch my reflection in the art deco mirror hanging over the bar as the chatty mixologist prepares our drinks. I don't yet feel like my old self, in spite of the company, and my face looks a little drawn. I turn my back to the bar. I am sick of the sight of mirrors. I resolve to try and enjoy myself and put Patrick Harrington out of my head, at least for this night.

I make it through the pre-dinner drinks, distractedly making small talk and managing to keep the spotlight off myself. The gaggle of girls make the short stroll up to West Street, led by Candy who relishes any chance to perform in front of an audience. As we are seated amongst the spice jars and hanging kitchenware, I survey the perfect symmetry of La Cuisine de Joël Robuchon. From the floor layout to the black and white wall tiles, to the glassware and the lighting, everything in the restaurant is balanced and uniform. I feel like laughing as I think about the external surroundings and how the consistency is such a contradiction to the chaos in my mind.

I am drinking quickly and too much. I want to get to numb as fast as I can. The two Old Cubans I had at the bar on top of my half of the bottle of Veuve we had at home have made for a good start. I stay on the periphery of the conversation and instead keep topping up my wine glass at regular intervals, just beating the hovering waitress to it each time. She has obviously been trained to be just out of sight but on hand for whatever we may need. I pick at the food. Beautifully presented French dishes prepared tapas style. I am not really going to know if the two Michelin stars are well deserved. It is wasted on me tonight, as my core objective is to dine on liquid.

I can see Candice eyeing me at various points during the meal and she tries in vain to bring me into the conversation several times. I stare determinedly at the large, simple clock on the wall and my brain finally registers that it is just before midnight. I make the universal sign for asking for the bill at Candice. She nods slowly at me before announcing to the group that it is time to wrap things up. The others are staring at me. *What the fuck are you looking at?* I want to scream.

"Ms Fisher, here is the check for this evening's meal. I'm the head waiter here. I do hope everything has been to your liking." A dapper man in an immaculate suit stands before me. He pauses as he waits for me to respond. I am not sure why the bill requires such a ceremony or why it is being presented to me. I look at the printout and widen my eyes at the numbers. We have managed to rack up more than £800 between five of us. I lean over clumsily to grab my handbag, just about falling off my chair. I am vaguely aware that everyone is still looking at me.

"There is nothing to pay, Ms Fisher. Monsieur Patrick Harrington hopes that you've had a lovely evening with your friends." I stare up at him as his words register in my alcohol soaked brain. Anger explodes through my veins. I wanted space from the controlling Patrick Harrington and here he is invading it, and in grand style. The others around the table are clearly impressed and relieved by the gesture even if they don't appreciate who my mysterious benefactor is. Candice, however, is giving him - *or is it me?* - a slow clap.

"Let's get out of here." I can't think of anything else to say to the enquiring faces all trained in my direction. As I move to leave, I glimpse Candice pulling her finger across her throat, warning the others not to ask me any questions. We get out to the street and I know that I need to make a hasty departure. I don't want the Spanish Inquisition. My anger continues to simmer as I think about the predicament that this grandiose deed has put me in.

"Fish Fingers." Candice is pointing at the black car sitting on the curb in front of the restaurant. The driver has put a board in the window with my name on it. This man thought of everything. My inertia is broken as Candice opens the car door and pushes me toward it. I know the other girls are dumbfounded.

"Call me tomorrow," she says, shutting the door and tapping the roof to alert the driver that it is okay to pull away.

I open my eyes and it takes me a moment to realise where I am. Reality crashes into my head along with the blinding hangover. The hangover that lay dormant until I hit consciousness. I am in Patrick's bed, but he is not. I squeeze my eyes shut again and move my hands under the duvet. I am not wearing any clothes. Jesus.

"Hey darling. I was beginning to worry that you'd never wake up. You sleep like the dead." Patrick is standing in the doorway looking fresh as a daisy.

"Don't worry. I slept in the spare room. You insisted on sleeping naked so I helped you out of your clothes. I had wanted to see you last night and have that talk, but I soon discovered you were in no mood for a chat and I'd be wrestling a tiger." I can't tell if he is mocking me. I don't care. All I can think about is drinking a lot of water to fix the fact that my tongue is seemingly glued to the roof of my mouth.

"There's a bottle of Evian on the bedside table, sweetie." Patrick points, ever the mind reader.

Naive spelt backwards, I think, as I look at the label on the bottle. *How appropriate.* I roll over slowly and push my hair out of my face to allow myself to take a long drink. I know I must look dreadful. I am on the back foot and feeling very much on edge. The rage I felt the previous night is not far from the surface. Now, my anger is also battling with remorse and shame for centre stage. Yet I don't know exactly why. I have a massive blank spot in my memory, with no knowledge of what I'd said or done in this man's company. I am at a huge disadvantage here and I don't like it one bit.

"I know you're probably feeling a little delicate. I've got some fruit and yoghurt downstairs. Come down when you're ready. There are fresh clothes in the bathroom and I've booked you a massage for later." He retreats out of sight, not waiting for me to respond.

I sit up cautiously, feeling incredibly sick. Lime and Angostura bitters repeating on me. I drain the mineral water and make my way to the bathroom on shaky legs. Neatly folded in a pile are a pair of skinny jeans, a long sleeved top and a set of underwear. Everything has tags still attached and of course the sizes are mine. I don't know whether to feel immensely grateful or totally freaked out. He has also set out hotel toiletries for me to use, including a toothbrush and a hairbrush. There is also a pair of Havaianas, white flip-flops with 'Cotton House' stamped on the back rim. They too are my size and I guess Patrick is giving me permission to be out of heels for a change.

After showering and donning my new garb, I locate my bag and fish my phone from it. 'The soap opera that is my life continues. I'm alive, not so well but alive. I'll call later.' I want to let Candice know that I am alright while simultaneously discourage her from calling me just yet. My last memory from the evening is of her bundling me into the taxi.

A short time later, I am awash in lavender and whale music as I sit in the reception of the Notting Hill Spa. Tanja is Patrick's regular masseuse or so she tells me. I detect an element of surprise when she collects me to take me through to the treatment room for the massage Patrick had booked for me. It is evident that she had been expecting him and was openly disappointed to discover the treatment was actually for me. As I lie face down on the massage table, I try to process the events of my Saturday night and my thoughts on the conversation with Patrick that morning. He had been heartfelt. Still not apologetic, which I was beginning to understand he was unlikely to ever be, but certainly clear that he didn't want Eloise or anyone else to come between us again.

I had challenged him about all the things that were bothering me; including being honest about the feelings that our sexual endeavours had stirred up in me. I told him that I was afraid that I was like my father. He had taken me in his arms and smoothed my hair, whispering that he would never let anything bad happen to me. I had felt a warmth wash over me as I realised that Patrick really cared about me. He hadn't been put off by my confessions and seemed to truly want to make things right with me. I guess he thought nothing of dropping cash to make a point, or at least to get my attention.

I told him that all of that wasn't necessary, that I was interested in the things that money couldn't buy. The best things in life are not things after all. He had looked at me as if I might be insane, but I had pressed on. He hadn't said much but what he did say was like a balm. He told me that I was special, and that he knew that things were moving fast but that he hoped that I could stick with it because it would be worth it. He had opened up a little and said that he didn't really know what love felt like, as he had never met anyone that had shown him, yet he knew he felt something magical when he was with me. Almost an 'I love you,' I recalled with satisfaction.

The morning's conversation had been intense and I was still feeling jaded from my night out. The massage was firm to the point of being uncomfortable and instead of being relaxing, my time with Tanja was anything but. Her hostility had radiated from her and intermingled with my low energy levels to create a distinctly unpleasant atmosphere. I couldn't wait to get out of there.

Patrick had booked me a car to take me across the park to the spa, telling me the driver would wait and bring me back. I had dismissed the driver on arrival, as I wanted to walk back across Hyde Park. I needed the time, and the fresh air to clear my head. I felt like I was in a space shuttle on warp speed and my thoughts and emotions were struggling to keep up.

Patrick might think that he had the situation under control

but I don't think he had banked on my steely core or fierce independence. I felt like a wild horse that was being fenced in. The only two options were capitulation or jumping the railing and bolting. So really, there was only one option.

Harrington

I am happy to be home alone. It is a relief to be free to be myself and to sit still for a moment without anyone wanting anything from me, giving me heavy looks or making loaded comments.

The film of the previous night made for good watching and I give myself the kudos I deserved for my artful erotic positioning. I guess, if money was ever a problem for me, I could make a sideline in pornography. But then money was never going to be a problem for me.

I am expecting the largest bonus of my career this month. It all hinges on certain situations being tidied up and of course, certain people keeping their traps shut, but I'm not worried. We all have as much to lose as each other and we all took the risk, knowing what there was to gain. In any event, once that money clears in my bank account it doesn't really matter what is revealed. I might lose my job at Caldwell but I have protected myself to the extent that any criminal enquiries would meet a dead end when my name comes up. Cunning like a fox.

The bank had demonstrated that it was happy to trust me to make them vast sums of money, and so what if I flouted protocol a little. I don't always run everything by my boss or the Executive Team. But I am the brain behind the machine and, frankly, I want the glory. No one ever built a monument to a committee.

Watching the ill-gotten footage calms me down and I am once again thinking clearly. Funny how sex has that effect on me. I grab my coat and stroll back to the Brompton Road and Harrods. Enough time has passed that I assume Eloise would have moved on. Harrods is plenty big enough for the two of us and anyway, without Alex by my side it matters not. I can handle that battle-axe if it comes to it.

I make my way to the Egyptian themed lobby and up the golden escalator to the first floor, heading towards Personal Shopping and Womenswear. Susie greets me like an old friend when she sees me coming. I'm sure she sees me as a walking ATM as I always tip generously but I don't care. I like Susie. She is cute, bubbly, and stylish: the essential prerequisites for a personal shopper. I know what is what where fashion is concerned but it is more fun to shop with someone, and given that I am buying for Alex I could do with Susie being a mannequin for me.

I know that Susie would be beyond happy to do more than just model for me when she volunteers to try on the lingerie I have selected. I decline tactfully. While she is nubile enough, she isn't the same proportions as Alex so I don't want to see the beautiful underwear on her body and thereby blot my copybook before my mind has had the chance to see Ms Fisher in it. Susie flits around me like a butterfly as I survey the rails of designer clothing. Sweet and amenable, but that willingness does nothing for me. Anticipation, as the Germans say, is the greatest pleasure. Vorfreude ist die schönste Freude. I want to have my cake and eat it too - but I like to select it from the cabinet myself, not have it served up on a platter.

I emerge from the hallowed building an hour or so later with two bulging iconic green carrier bags. I have selected a pair of so-dark-they-were-almost-black Nudie jeans, a simple but elegant Chloe top in black lace and a lovely sheer lingerie set by Agent Provocateur. Once home, I fold the new purchases neatly and place them on one of the vanities in my en suite. I pull miniature Bvlgari products from my stash in the cupboard. Everything a girl needs for a luxurious shower. I open a new toothbrush and add that to the pile and smile at myself in the mirror, running a hand through my hair with a satisfied shake.

Next on my agenda is calling the restaurant, followed by booking a car. Then my clever plan will be in place, the trap baited, the setup complete. Of course, the staff at Joël Robuchon are more than happy to oblige. I have checked Alex's Facebook page again, going back to the photos of her in Japan to find Candice's surname so I can ensure the restaurant is dealing with the right reservation. The woman at the end of the phone trills when she hears what I am planning. It is short work explaining my romantic surprise and ensuring they know it is Alex that they need to treat like a princess and present with the zero-sum bill at the end of the meal.

Finally, I call Addison Lee and order a car to be waiting on the curb outside the restaurant from 11pm until the passenger arrives. The dinner reservation is for 8pm so while I know three hours might be too short I don't want to miss my mark. I am clear with the operator that I will pay the waiting costs and that the driver is not to leave without the passenger under any circumstances. I am an account client with Ad Lee and they are pretty good at catering to my unusual requests. I know I will probably have to make a call to check that this actually is the case later that evening. The whole scheme relies on that car bringing my catch to me. I know Alex will revel in the attention and that her friends will encourage her to see me. *After all, what woman wouldn't want this kind of fuss made of them?* My plot is foolproof.

I spend my evening checking my various email accounts and reading through the auto-generated emails from the websites I use to find 'intimate encounters'. My favourite is Ashley Madison, the extramarital affairs site. I had set up a profile as a married man seeking a liaison. My personal description talks about how I am mostly happily married but missing that extra 'something'. Women queue up to try to convince me that they are that something. I'm sure the profile photo of me in my dinner suit draws them like flies to shit, given that I look as handsome and wealthy as I am. It shows off my height and good looks without being too close up to make me recognisable.

Some of the messages my profile elicited make me laugh out loud. Some users I block as they are frankly scary, others I enjoy banter with. And then there is the holy grail, an attractive woman low on the crazy quotient who is willing to meet up for a fuck, with no strings attached. Being on this site is genius.

It is easy to dismiss the women I meet; throw the words 'home wrecker' in there. I have the ironclad get-out clause of a wee wife at home. She is fictional of course but they don't know that. *Why do I lie? Because I am so damn good at it, that's why.*

It is after midnight when I get a text message from the Ad Lee driver to say that they are leaving the West End. While it is later than I hoped, I am delighted that everything was coming together as I intended. That is until my well-laid plan skids sideways a little as I watch a very drunk Alexander Fisher emerge from the car and stumble up to my front door. I hadn't counted on this. This girl is a challenge at every turn.

I know I can't take advantage of her in this state so I hastily form a plan B, which is regrettable. While she is clearly intoxicated she is also stunning. The jade dress she is wearing looks so good on her it is as if I had chosen it myself. She is truculent and aggressive as she sways on her heels in my entranceway. It is almost as if she is unhappy with me and all that I have done. I know it is the drink talking, she can't possibly be angry at me after my thoughtful and generous display. With much effort I convince her to go to bed. I am reticent to engage in any conversation even though it is unlikely that she will remember much the next day.

I wake as the room gradually fills with early morning light, filtering through the gaps in the drapes. I am annoyed at having been displaced from my own bed to one of the guest rooms but I am not going to be outfoxed. I make my way to my bedroom and stand in the doorway, watching her sleeping form. I am going to have to speak to her about her drinking. I feel conflicted as I like her to have a drink with me, and it certainly helps with her inhibitions but this is the second time I have seen her a bit out of control. I am a high functioning addict, that is for sure, but I manage to keep my proclivities in check.

As the morning slips away I consider waking Alex. I have booked a massage for her at 2pm. I know that is a nice touch, on top of all the other kind things I have done for her. It also conveniently serves the dual purpose of putting Tanja in her place. The silly witch has been messaging me constantly and demanding to see me. I call the spa and book an appointment in my name and then send Tanja a text to let her know I will be there that afternoon. When a good-looking younger woman in the form of Alexandra Fisher shows up she will get the message. Back off. I am infinitely smarter than her and will not stand for her over-stepping the mark. There is no way she will think to cross me and confront Alex, as the income stream she gets from me is too precious for her. Tanja's behaviour is insulting, and hopefully this little affront will ensure she gets back in her compliant little box.

I return to the bedroom doorway just after 11am to see that my sleeping beauty is stirring. I can see some initial confusion as she registers where she is but I coax her into the shower and get her moving with the promise of food. I am beginning to know what the levers are with this girl.

Alex comes into the kitchen with damp hair and a face devoid of makeup. Even after her heavy night of booze she looks beautiful. I feel my body reacting and stifle a smile. I don't know what to expect from her until she opens her mouth. I do know I am going to have to put in a solid performance and actually 'talk' to restore her faith in me being the greatest guy on the planet.

I watch her eat the fruit compote I have bought for her. I long to touch her but keep myself in check. I am expecting her to be sheepish, but instead I am getting a bit of attitude. *God, she is a handful, and after all I have done for her.* I convince her to come through to the lounge and sit on the settee with me. Her body language demonstrates her hesitance to get too close to me, both literally and figuratively. I know I can win her over with some well-chosen words. I also know that she is getting better at reading me so I have to be careful. But I can't deny I like the challenge.

I get her talking, a well-practised trick of mine. If a woman opens up to me then I have something to work with and can exploit the insecurities that would undoubtedly surface. For Ms Fisher this comes in the form of drawing similarities with her father.

I hadn't thought that she'd be so forthcoming but as I listen to her admitting to feeling ashamed after having sex with me, I know I need to throw the kitchen sink at this if I am to salvage all the work I have already put into this acquisition. I make all the right noises about her father and then act my way through a declaration of my affection.

"My darling, I can't tell you what this is, I can only tell you what it feels like for me." I hear myself saying that I get warm fuzzy feelings when I am with her, that I am afraid of my own emotions and that I am starting to realise what it means when I get that sensation of not being able to breathe when I contemplate losing her. All of this to convince her that I am in love with her. I see the look in her eyes and I know I have her, she has heard sincerity in my voice. Sincerity is everything. Once you learn to fake that, the rest is easy. *I tell you what I do love, and that's the way you lie, Harrington,* I think with self-satisfaction.

I pull her to me and tell her I will never let anything bad happen to her. I roll my eyes as I speak, now that she can't see my face, relieving some of the tension this situation was creating. This is not a position I like to be in. She is vulnerable and raw but she is by no means stupid. I feel like I am in the circus walking a tightrope.

By the time I have Alex in the car and off to her massage, I am like a tightly coiled spring. Even knowing what Tanja is about to get served gives me little relief. I need a release. Before the car is even out of sight I have Fuzzy on the phone. Of course she is available. She will be there as quick as she can. I laugh out loud at my own audacity. To restore my serenity I decide to take Fuzzy to my bedroom and fuck her on top of the sheets that Alex has just slept in. She has never been in my parlour and it will be a consolation, given I will shoo her out afterwards with rapid effect. She is used to a quick turnover but this is bad even by my standards. I have little more than an hour to play with but I'm not worried. I am like the SAS. I'll be in and out before anyone notices. The ticking clock is like a time bomb, for sure, but it also serves to heighten my arousal. Knowing I could get caught is a huge turn on.

Alex might think that she has the situation under control but I don't think she has banked on my steely core or fierce independence. I feel like a wild horse which is being fenced in. The only two options are capitulation or jumping the railing and bolting. So really, there is only one option.

Alexandra

The calendar trips into my birthday month, heralded by the usual April showers in London. I want to plan something special for Patrick; the 21st falls on a Monday so a long weekend would make sense, but before thinking about our birthday weekend, we have the planned New York trip to enjoy.

I am beginning to panic about the lies I am telling. Patrick has pushed me into confirming plans to be in New York, including staying for the weekend. I really want the opportunity to spend time with Patrick in the Big Apple but the risk that Eloise will find out is great. Since I have been working for her, I have always flown back on the same flight as her as the business trip isn't deemed complete until we have disembarked in London. I know she isn't going to take kindly to me deserting her before she considers my work is done.

The Executive suite of the Park Lane office of Caldwell is buzzing with activity. All the Executives are in town for the two-day meeting, along with their support staff. Despite the fact that Eloise is shut away in meetings, I am run off my feet. Patrick is sending me text messages regularly but when we see each other he will ignore me. Even though I know it is the right thing to do, it still irks me immensely.

During a break in the proceedings, I am sitting with Eloise who is passing me papers and talking me through her hand written notes, giving me instructions - all the things she had thought of while she was also participating in the meeting. A master of multi-tasking. Patrick is using the break time for an impromptu meeting with Amber Chilworth who, it seems, is also in town. I see her throw her head back and laugh at something Patrick says and it strikes me in that instant that they are flirting. *Is he doing this deliberately?* I take a moment to appraise Amber. Her hair is pinned up and her face is heavily made up. She is quite good looking but she looks desperate, like a goldfish in a leaky bag. Her shapely body is squeezed into a suit with a jacket that is a bit too tight across her chest and a skirt that is a bit too short. I notice that Eloise is also watching the pair.

I am staying in midtown at the same hotel as Eloise, the Four Seasons. Even though it is walking distance to the office, Eloise insists on having a driver take us between the buildings. Patrick is staying at the Mondrian in Soho. I am to move myself down there on Friday night after Eloise has left for the airport for her flight back to London. I wonder where Amber is staying. I know it is irrational but I can't shake the sense that something is going on between her and Patrick. I don't know what to do. I am brimming with jealousy, which makes me feel neurotic. Patrick and I are getting on so well after our recent heart to heart. I am beginning to feel like he is the sun of my solar system.

I have convinced Eloise that I am staying on in New York for a weekend of shopping with a girlfriend who also happens to be in town for work. I know she isn't pleased but I think I have made enough deposits in the 'trust' bank for no further inquiry to be made. I am on edge though. I know that I am now out in very deep water.

I make my way into the Mondrian Hotel through the lush green garden topiary façade, past the restaurant situated in a large greenhouse space overflowing with greenery and centred around a dramatic hanging glass sculpture. I am under instructions that a key will be behind the desk for me and that I am to be ready and waiting in the bar to go out for dinner at Babbo, the Italian restaurant of the moment, stationed on the northwest corner of Washington Square Park in Greenwich Village.

I have duly followed my orders and am dolled up, ready and waiting on a bar stool with a tonic water in front of me when Patrick breezes in to pick me up. I am happy to be with Patrick again, and at the restaurant I listen as he has a knowledgeable chat with the sommelier about which Super Tuscan to order to compliment the rib-eye steak for two. As they discuss the merits of the Sassicaia, the Tignanello and the Ornellaia I feel as if my heart might burst. Here I am with such an accomplished man and he loves me and we have a lovely weekend ahead of us.

Patrick continues to demonstrate his carnal life force, his lustful hunger seeming boundless. Our sex has taken on a new level of intimacy and I feel more relaxed and cherished as we engage in increasingly varied sexual congress. There are still moments where I have fleeting thoughts of humiliation but it seems Patrick is being careful and patient now that he knows more of my history and how disturbed I am about the parallels with my father.

The next morning, I smile at the kissing salt and pepper dogs on the table at The Standard Grill as we sit companionably in the patio area of the popular Meatpacking District eatery with our eggs Benedict and coffee. Like Candice, Patrick seems to know exactly where to go to be part of a scene. After eating, the idea is to walk off our brunch by scaling the stairs up to the nearby High Line, the historic freight railway line elevated above Manhattan's West Side. As we leave the restaurant the heavens open, putting paid to our well-intentioned plan. Patrick leaves me under the eaves of the restaurant while he tries to hail a taxi along with all the other hopefuls caught out by the sudden rain.

He gives up holding a newspaper over his head, laughing at the futility of it in the downpour. As if by miracle, he stops a yellow cab and runs back for me, grabbing me by the hand to run from the safety of the covering to the car. He opens the car door and then stops me, in a euphoric gesture of romance. A kiss in the rain. I am overcome by the feeling that no one else in the world matters as we embrace, water streaming down my face and thunder clapping in the sky.

We make our way uptown to Fifth Avenue, abandoning our nature walk for a stroll around Bergdorf Goodman. Hand in hand, he leads me around the vast floors, stopping to point out items of interest, watching my reaction, as he surveys the best and the finest. At the Alexander McQueen collection he drops my hand and starts to amass beautiful pieces of ready-to-wear designer clothes. The sales clerk, spotting a walking wallet, is on him immediately, offering him her card and a drink. She takes me in, still looking slightly bedraggled from the rain, and turns her charm on me too knowing she has to win us both over to make a big sale.

With rat-like cunning, she follows Patrick around and takes the hangers off him to place the tailored clothing in a changing room for me. She ushers me through and proceeds to help me try everything on. I wonder at the lives of the rich that they need help to get dressed. The woman fetches several pairs of heels to match with my outfits which I know will please Patrick. She has even corralled an oversized handbag, a sequinned clutch, a delicate scarf and some fierce looking jewellery to complete each look. I feel like Julia Roberts in Pretty Woman as I emerge from the changing room to twirl in front of Patrick, who is now comfortably sitting on the expertly positioned couch, sipping an espresso.

The sales assistant is telling me that everything looks amazing, fabulous, striking, wonderful. The adjectives roll off her tongue with faux-sincerity. I choose a short cap-sleeved dress and a metallic corseted top and take them to the counter to be rung up. I hadn't intended to spend quite this much money but out of the numerous things I have tried on I love these two garments. I watch in horror as other items I have tried but not selected are wrapped before me. I try to argue, but Patrick soon reassures me that it is his treat. I am stunned. The parallel to Julia Roberts is back but this time I feel like a prostitute, not a pretty woman. I decide to be gracious and feel just like the disingenuous lady who is serving us as I wax lyrical about how marvellous I think Patrick's choices are.

By the time we make it back to the hotel, laden with shopping bags, it is starting to get dark. At least I have some new purchases to back up the shopping story I fed Eloise. En route, I convince Patrick that we should stay in and watch something on TV and order room service rather than shower, change and head out again in the big bad city. He is initially reluctant but after a long day he sees the sense in my proposition. I follow him like a lamb to the concierge desk so he can cancel our dinner reservations. The woman behind the desk is not very tall, petite in fact, with dark hair cut short. Her eyes are dark set in a triangular face. She is slightly boyish looking. She is beautiful. Her name badge tells me she is 'Natasha'.

I know Patrick is appreciating her the same way I am and instantly I feel the now-familiar burn of green possessiveness as the woman turns on like a light as Patrick smiles at her. I realise as they look at each other that they have made each other's acquaintance already during his stay. He looks at me and tells me to make my way upstairs to the room and that he will be along momentarily. I feel like I have been dismissed. I don't want to argue in front of this rival, and walk away feeling as if the other woman has won. She is immaculate while I am dishevelled; she is enjoying his attention while I have been disregarded. I see us as he must and can hardly blame him.

I decide to take a shower to try and quell the rising feelings of inadequacy. When I emerge wrapped in a towel, with damp hair trailing down my back, Patrick is there and one smile is all it takes to win me over again. He has the menu for Lombardi's, and is excited to announce that we are having pizza for dinner from America's first ever pizzeria, that happens to be just around the corner. He will go out and pick up our takeaway feast once I choose what we are having.

I share his enthusiasm to try to mask that there are any negative thoughts in my mind. I don't want to be confrontational about the scene in the lobby with Natasha and decide that it was nothing. He was probably thinking I needed to take the weight off my feet after a long day while he changed our plans.

I realise I am exhausted as Patrick clears up our pizza mess and the ending credits of the film we have been watching roll. We have been snuggling on the couch dressed in the hotel's matching white towelling robes and I have been dozing off. The bottle of wine we had shared adds to my sleepiness. I am quick to swallow the two Ambien Patrick offered me, as he tells me that sleeping tablets will help with the jet lag. *So thoughtful*, I think, as he carries me through from the lounge space to the bedroom, settles me down and gently smoothes the covers over me. No sex this evening, I realise, which was probably a first for us, to be sharing a bed and not sharing each other's bodies.

As I succumb to the medicated sleep, my last lingering thought is that perhaps we are stuck in second gear. I feel deeply about Patrick, I know this, but it is almost as if my basic needs are not being met.

Harrington

The calendar trips into my birthday month, heralded by the usual April showers in London. I want to plan something special for Alex; the 21st falls on a Monday so a long weekend would make sense, but before thinking about our birthday weekend, we have the planned New York trip to enjoy.

I am keen to get back to the Big Apple even if it means a busy few days of meetings and the threat that Eloise 'the she-devil' Little finds out about the secret that Alex and I are keeping from her. During a meeting interval, I have Amber Chilworth up in my face laughing like a drain and doing her standard hussy routine of being a little too close and a little too loud for my liking. Given my recent thoughts about this brass, I categorise talking to her in the same way I do kissing after sex. Both are a waste of time. But in this case, I know that both Alex and Eloise are watching us. I enjoy the double whammy of making the young one jealous and the old one furious. Alex is sitting with Eloise working through the recess of the Executive Team meeting as usual. *Does that woman ever take a break?*

I have decided to stay in the Mondrian Hotel in Soho. While I am a risk taker and could have shared the same hotel as Alex to have her in my bed each night, I know my limits. All the other Executives are housed there too and the place will be crawling with Caldwell employees. It isn't worth it and in any case, I am relishing having a few evenings to myself ahead of sharing my space with Ms Fisher on Friday and Saturday night.

I am getting a little bored of having to walk on eggshells with Alex, and the correlations she keeps drawing between herself and her father are causing me to alter my approach to having sex with her. I prefer to be free to pursue the carnal thoughts that enter my head. Sure, it gives me an angle to work in terms of my quest to deconstruct this girl but it is tiresome in my wearier moments. People are just as happy as they make up their minds to be.

I go to the Tom Ford store on Madison Avenue after the first day of meetings, given its proximity to Caldwell's Park Lane offices. I select a new suit and a couple of ties. Retail therapy is my second favourite way to let off steam. My patience is wearing thin after enduring hours of meetings with my colleagues, going around in circles trying to resist their attempts at advocating a firmer line when it came to risk management. They are not listening to my balanced arguments at all.

My new purchases are to be delivered to the hotel for me, after the in-house tailor has made some minor alterations to the suit trousers. After stopping in to have the truffle mac'n'cheese at The Waverly Inn, I make my way back to the Mondrian. I am in two minds about whether to head to bed or to hit the hotel bar and check out the Thursday night talent.

I am lost in thought and following my feet across the oak panelled wood flooring as I enter the lobby. I make it all the way to the lifts before an authoritative voice informs me that Tom Ford has delivered my items and that they are hanging in the wardrobe of my room. I glance up and am surprised to see a small pixie-like woman before me in a concierge uniform. That deep husky voice doesn't compute with what my eyes are seeing. I have to hear her speak again. Alongside her name badge, I see the crossed gold keys of Les Clefs d'Or on her lapel. The international symbol that assures travellers they are dealing with a seasoned professional, one who is dedicated to serving the guests' every need. *I certainly have a few needs that require serving*, I think to myself as my dick hardens, the possibilities dancing behind my eyes.

Natasha looks up at me and it is the easiest thing in the world to reach for her shoulders, pull her close and start to kiss her, right there in front of the closed elevator doors. Her tongue explores my mouth and I press my erection against her so that she knows exactly what I am about. She takes a step back and tells me that she finishes her shift at midnight so will be along to my room shortly thereafter. It seems she has a way to supplement the income from her regular job. She spots me and in a calculating move that is going to pay off, recognises me as someone who would be amenable to her proposition. I up the ante by asking her to bring a friend. I smile and nod; I have little over an hour to wait.

As the witching hour passes and my guests arrive and make themselves at home in my suite, I think about my luck as I watch the two woman before me. Sasha checks Natasha's outfit, adjusting her suspenders before the two turn to face me as if asking for my opinion. The vision is magnificent. Both women are dressed in New York City police shirts, largely unbuttoned and deliberately tight. Their breasts are pushed front and centre but barely contained by delicate contrastingly feminine black bras. Black fishnet stockings and suspenders lead the eye up to black lace knickers that show off the splendid contours of both pairs of buttocks. Implausibly high heels and police hats frame the picture. Their makeup is bright, excessive and playful. Hanging from the girls' hips are handcuffs and truncheons, props that aren't going to be just for show I am certain. Sasha dons some mirror shades and the fantasy is complete.

The two women assume the act with relish and treat me like I am a criminal from whom they are trying to elicit a confession. They each take their time pleasuring me before the three of us merge into a single mass of limbs, hands, tongues. Mouths search for erogenous zones and a chain of cock to mouth to pussy to fingers assembles and then realigns before reforming. *As threesomes go, that was pretty wild*, I reflect as I spot a pair of handcuffs left behind as I leave the room the next morning, headed for the office. The mental imagery gives me the strength to face another day of going into battle with my co-workers.

The preceding days of meetings have rattled me more than I had anticipated, I acknowledge to myself as we are seated at the best table at Babbo that evening. Alex is doing a wonderful job, along with the sumptuous surroundings, to help me regain perspective. Her ability to identify what made me tick is quite extraordinary. *Legitimacy, amongst other things*, I think as the waiter treats me like the VIP I am. I feel a sense of calm as I watch the skilful server deftly reduce the rib eye to beautiful proportions on the centre table close by. Alex and I share the lobster spaghetti and are languidly making our way through the expertly decanted bottle of Tig as we wait for our steak. Italian hospitality with an American twist.

The sex we have after dinner that evening has me feeling better still. We end up in a conversation about what turns me on and Alex says she is willing to let me introduce her to the world of vibrators and pleasure aids. Lucky for her, I have either planned ahead and never leave home without a bag of tricks, or I have purchased a selection of new paraphernalia on my travels. As ever, my hotel choice is based on several factors, and the Mondrian scores points for being proximate to the flagship Kiki de Montparnasse store, the perfect place to stop in for exclusive and limited edition instruments of pleasure. It was one of my first stops on arriving in New York. Like a boy scout I am always prepared.

I try to hold back, but for the first time I sense that Alex doesn't want me to. I am too turned on anyway. We share some intensely intimate moments as we bring each other to climax using the toys, our mouths, hands and genitals.

We eventually untangle our bodies only then to close together once more. My hands and kisses cover every inch of her as a thank you. Twice during the remains of the night our caresses escalate and we fuck like rabbits. Eventually we doze off, my arm around her shoulder, our legs wrapped like vines. I feel an eerie sense of contentment that lasts through to the next morning.

I enjoy showing Alex around New York and even the pouring rain doesn't dampen our spirits. Forced indoors out of the weather, I decide to take the opportunity to spend some money at Bergdorf Goodman. The infamous windows and their fabulous dressings capture Alexandra's attention but I pull her inside and out of the wet. I love the air of pedigree as we wander the floors amongst the luxury goods. We spend a significant amount of time at Alexander McQueen, and I spend a not-insignificant amount of money adding some classy apparel to Ms Fisher's wardrobe.

But a great night followed by a good morning slips down the charts past average as we head back to the hotel. Although Alex is close physically, I sense she was actually miles away, but I can't fathom why. How easily our moods influence each other.

In the lobby, I'm presented with a choice between Alex and Natasha; the split second to make my mind up feels like a month of Sundays. Here is a wolf dressed in sheep's clothing in the form of the elf-like concierge; her neat uniform belies her true character. Well, she certainly likes to dress up; that is a given. And then there is the increasingly troublesome Alexandra Fisher. I have just dropped a small fortune on her after a fun afternoon of trying on designer clothes and she has been less than courteous in response, almost as if it is now expected that I will provide for her. I contrast the two women dressed up in my mind.

I ask Alex to retire to the room. That will at least buy me a little more time to decide what my next steps were. I can have them both. Natasha has a scenario all ready to persuade me and it doesn't take long to twist my rubbery arm. I have all my chess moves lined up as I return to the room with the promise of the best pizza in Manhattan and a rom-com movie, trumping Alex's earlier suggestion of room service and TV. This woman should know better than to restrict me to staying in on a Saturday night. I see the ruse through, cuddling on the couch, while watching some mindless chick flick.

I feel a small pang of conscience as I hand her the sleeping pills which she swallows without protest. I hear myself telling her they will help with her jet lag. Not an ailment I suffer from. I guess that's as much for the frequent travelling as it is from my nocturnal activities. I can function on very little sleep, better than most people do on the recommended eight hours.

I turn the bedroom light out with promises that I will just watch the late news and be joining her shortly. I know the medication won't take long to take effect. I am straight on Blackberry messenger, as my excitement mounts, to alert Natasha that we are good to go. I feel a spring in my step and my eyes trail the rose vine design on the carpet as I make my way down the saturated blue corridor between the rooms. The door to the Penthouse is ajar, and I enter with the authority of a man who has come to take what he is owed. I overlook the fact that I had been told the Penthouse was unavailable for my stay. My shoes click on the marble floor as I walk into the opulent loft-like space.

As I look over Natasha's naked shoulders at the lights of the downtown Manhattan skyline and push myself deep inside her tiny frame, I know I have made a good decision. Her hands are in front of her as she pushes back against me from the railing of the private balcony. Her golden keys have unlocked the door to this suite along with my desires.

Before slipping into bed beside the slumbering shape of Alex, as the light started to glow in the dawn sky, I decide to take half a sleeping tablet myself. I am exhausted and don't want to tempt insomnia due to the various thoughts and memories swirling in my mind. I certainly am no fan of my conscience pricking me. Ah, women. They make the highs higher and the lows more frequent.

As I succumb to the medicated sleep, my last lingering thought is that perhaps we were stuck in second gear. I feel deeply about Alex, I knew this, but it is almost as if my basic needs are not being met.

Alexandra

I hate my birthday. Everyone makes a fuss but I am quite happy not to be the centre of attention. Plus this year it will be all the more complicated by the fact that I am sharing my birthday - literally - with Patrick Harrington.

I am hiding my plans from my friends, my boss and my ex-boyfriend. Patrick and I have opted to stay in the UK as Patrick has a gruelling series of business trips shortly after, and was happy with the idea of a fabulous weekend away without getting on a plane. I had asked him to let me organise it and he has been more than happy to defer to me, though only after providing me with a short list of acceptable hotels. I am choosing between the magical Oxfordshire Le Manoir aux Quat'Saisons, the stately Babington House in Somerset and the enchanting Gravetye Manor a stone's throw away in Sussex.

Patrick's instruction is to arrange a driver to take us there but I have a better idea. I know that Mr Harrington loves to drive and is a big car aficionado; boys and their toys, and all that. I decide to rent a Bentley for the weekend as a surprise. And not just any Bentley: a brand new midnight-black continental GT convertible.

The surprises won't stop there. I have been back to the independent jeweller, Longmire, the cufflink connoisseur, after Patrick had marvelled at a pair of ladybird cufflinks they had on display in their window on a recent weekend stroll around London's celebrated luxury shopping streets. At £4,240 they are an expensive gift but I feel like I need to redress the financial balance after all the generosity Patrick has shown me in the time we have been together. *If I can't treat him for his birthday, when can I?*

After he has seen the car, the next revelation will be a surprise lunch with Dave Grafton and his girlfriend on the Saturday afternoon. I figure Patrick will want to see his best friend on his birthday weekend and given Dave lives in Buckinghamshire, it will give us the perfect stop-off point to drive the Bentley to en route to the hotel, along with an opportunity to show it off.

After all the effort I have put into planning, I am beyond excited when we wake up on the Saturday morning to fine weather, knowing that Patrick and I are soon to be racing along in a state-of-the-art vehicle with the top down. I can barely contain myself when the driver calls me to say he is coming down Edgware Road and will be at Patrick's place in about twenty minutes to drop the car off, almost an hour ahead of our scheduled departure time. I hurry the usually über-organised Mr Harrington into finishing his packing and insist that we leave as soon as the driver arrived. He is a little flippant, telling me that they are used to waiting. He is clueless as to my grand plan.

It is my turn to be surprised when I walk Patrick out of his house to show him the car he will be driving for the weekend. He is speechless for certain, but it is with shock rather than excitement. He goes through the motions of signing the insurance paperwork and showing his driver's licence, growing visibly more and more uncomfortable by the second. He is very dismissive of the kind chap who had delivered the iconic car, and I am at a loss as to how I have so spectacularly missed the mark.

I wait on the sidewalk with my bag while he locks up the house. We have barely spoken. I climb into the front seat as Patrick sets about putting the roof down. At least our thinking is aligned on that much.

"So, what do you think? I thought you'd like the chance to drive one of these as a treat, I know you think there is no need to own a car in London, but this is a special occasion." I am trying to illicit some sort of reaction from him. I know I should leave well enough alone as this might ruffle the feathers of this peacock.

"Alexandra. I wish you had consulted with me first. Now the car company will think I can't afford to buy one of these, and we both know that's not true. I'm embarrassed. I could have a garage overflowing with super cars if I chose to. Jeez." Tears prick in my eyes and my throat closes up as I listened to him belittle my well-intentioned surprise. I programme the address for our lunch destination into the satnav and sit in silence as we make our way out of central London. The car certainly turns heads but instead of enjoying it, I am desperately wishing I wasn't on display. I am hurt and furious. I am trying to be thoughtful, and while it might seem like peanuts to the wealthy Patrick Harrington, this birthday weekend is costing me an arm and a leg. And all because I am trying to show him that money didn't matter to me. The irony is not lost on me.

We have hardly got past the reaction to the car before it dawns on me that the unerring Patrick Harrington does not like to be blindsided. *I should have known better*, I reflect, knowing Eloise was just the same. I guess there is something about the Executive mould that makes them need to be perpetually aware and in control.

Dave and his younger-than-expected girlfriend are waiting outside when we pull up at the Beaconsfield outpost of the Crazy Bear Hotel and Restaurant.

"For fuck's sake, Alex," Patrick hisses as he slams the heel of his hand onto the intricately stitched leather steering wheel with the distinctive 'B' winged logo in its centre. He pulls into a parking space near his friend and I watch his face switch expertly from irritation to magnanimity. If I hadn't heard what he had just said, I would believe that this man is thrilled to see his best mate.

I sit through lunch, almost mechanically, um-ing and ah-ing at appropriate points in the conversation, but I am distracted. I glance around at our setting. It is almost grotesque in its flamboyancy. An eccentric mix of padded leather panelled walls and shiny mahogany tabletops. I have let Dave choose the venue, given this is his home turf. But I am beginning to see that, with Patrick, nothing can be left to chance and I need to be all over every detail.

Patrick isn't drinking, due to driving, which seems to add further insult to his perceived injuries. I should be the one that gets to feel injured. Dave's stupid girlfriend shakes my hand on meeting me and says with a knowing smirk, "Nice to meet you, Amber. I've heard so much about you." Patrick looks horrified. Dave laughs and corrects his dunce-like girlfriend by repeating my name three times with increasing volume as if he was in the throes of orgasm: "Alex-and-ra, Alexandra! ALEXANDRA!" They think Dave's uncouth display is hilarious. Patrick and I are momentarily united by our contempt. I hardly know Dave and I have taken an almost instant dislike to his arm candy girlfriend. This weekend is derailing before it has even begun. At least I know Patrick will like my gift come Monday, our shared birthday.

I am immensely relieved when my phone interrupts our post-lunch coffee and I excuse myself to take the call outside. It is Joey ringing to catch up and see what I was doing for my birthday. I put my hand over the screen to hide the picture of the good-looking Joey that comes up when he calls me and tell the table that it was my mother. Once out of the restaurant, I continue with my lies and tell Joe that Candice had planned a spa weekend and that I am out of London for the weekend. The last part is true at least.

As I laugh and expel some tension as Joey and I chat, I realise how much I miss him. He has moved out as planned and it has hit me harder than I expected, even with Patrick putting increasing demands on my time. I walk around the parked Bentley, taking in the dominant bonnet line and the prominent matrix grille of the pedigree motor. I feel like kicking the tires. Here I am again trying hard to win the approval of the exacting Patrick Harrington. The more I try, the less it works. *Is this who I have become? And how dare that simpleton mistake me for Amber? How do I reconcile that?* It isn't possible that the moron has actually met the impudent Ms Chilworth, yet it was a definite needle; of that much I am sure.

I am grateful for the fine day once again as we get back on the road and leave Dave and his halfwit girlfriend as they wave goodbye exaggeratedly. Having the top down means that the noise of the engine and the wind makes conversation difficult, and that is a welcome relief. I have so much turning over in my mind. The petulant reaction to the car, being called Amber, and Patrick's demeanour toward me when all I have done is try to

185

arrange an amazing mini-break for his pleasure. I have chosen Babington House as our destination. It looks luxurious, but then of course all the options Patrick had proposed do. What had been the deciding factor for me was its location. I had thought that being the furthest from London would give Patrick a good chance to stretch the Bentley's legs on the open road. As the monotony of the M4 sets in and his face remains hardened I begin to doubt myself. *Have I made a grave mistake? Maybe this whole relationship is a mistake.* I shake my head trying to clear the negativity. I need to sweep the miscalculations of the day under the carpet and focus on ensuring the rest of our time together is special. I know that sex will fix things even if my thoughtfulness has been disregarded thus far.

The goodwill returns in a flurry once Patrick is in the comfort of our garden room. He envelops me in a sensual hug and I know that I will be able to amplify the positivity and get us back on track. As he unpacks his laptop, it occurs to me that he is once again going to try and persuade me to participate in online sex. Something he has been suggesting for some time, chipping away at my resolve. I sit with him and watch fatalistically while he logs into his web account for 'Fuxx Club' knowing that my lack of protest is tantamount to acceptance.

"Dirtyharry21. Makes me laugh every time," he says, punching in his password. He is so happy with himself that it stirs the bile in my stomach.

It isn't swinging per se, it is voyeurism and excitement without cheating or switching partners. *Where is the harm in that,* he reasons? His argument is couched in a way that makes me feel that failure to comply will mean he will actively seek to cheat or swing as a consequence. As if my nonconformity gives him permission to pursue the alternative. It is with a jolt that I realise that along with an ego the size of China, he has no obvious limits or boundaries. Maybe with such wealth comes the notion that anything is possible. And if there are consequences, money will fix it. Tiger Woods comes to mind.

He is clever to position this act of depravity as part of this weekend away as if it were only something we would do on a special occasion. He pushes my guilt buttons by playing on the birthday angle. This is what he really really wanted, and with me. While I struggle with it immensely, eventually I give in, knowing with certainty that I will lose this man if I don't yield.

Patrick takes me from behind, gently at first, while I bend over the leather-topped desk with his laptop and web cam taking in the full view, and I bite back my tears, everything inside me screaming 'no'. *Why am I doing this to myself?* I stare hard at the reflection of the girl that looks like me in the mirror and then back at the couple in front of me, on screen, looking eager and excited. They are fully clothed but pawing at each other while they watch us having sex. I am overcome with repulsion toward these strangers, and toward myself. All the world is a stage, according to William Shakespeare. *Just act the part, Alex.*

Patrick has at least given me the courtesy of selecting the pair that will watch us fuck, but this token act of goodwill is like lipstick on a pig. The web chat stream is coming thick and fast as they tell us how great we look, and tap out words of encouragement as Patrick's rhythm and intensity builds and he pounds himself into me. As my orgasm takes hold and I feel my juices run down the inside of my leg, I observe that I have lost myself.

At least we are back on an even keel, I think, as I lie alone in the roll top steel bathtub that afternoon. The only minor bump we encounter for the rest of the weekend away is some rambunctious kids during breakfast the following morning. I watch as Patrick's face clouds over and I curse myself for not checking the child friendly policy of the hotel. We spend Sunday playing tennis, which I make sure he wins, and we enjoy a couple's massage. I have a few hours to myself while Patrick works out in the gym and does some reading in the library of the main house. Work and its demands are never banished completely.

Our birthday morning arrives and, with it, unrelenting rain. My shame and regret are continuing to mingle just below the surface and I watch the condensation slip down the windows, as if emulating my spirits. We have made it to the all-important moment of exchanging gifts. I have wrapped my gift, the small and somewhat obvious-to-its-contents box, in a larger container to throw Patrick off the scent. He looks at me, perplexed, as the birthday paper reveals a large spotted cardboard box. I nod to encourage him to look inside. Dawning acknowledgment starts to spread across his face as he extracts the small embossed leather box, dwarfed by the larger receptacle. "Oh boy, Alex, you didn't. Tell me you didn't," he is almost whispering.

He pops the tiny chest open and gapes at the contents. Two ladybird cufflinks, richly decorated with hand painted red and black enamel, finished in 18-carat gold. I know he is aware of how much these have cost me, and as his eyes start to well up I get the feeling that he is finally appreciating all that I have put together for his birthday, even if some parts of it aren't so well received.

He wipes at his eyes with his fingertips to eradicate his tears. I feel the subtle shift that I was coming to recognise quickly as his emotional rev counter pushes into the red zone of annoyance. I watch him, clearly struggling within himself. He passes me two neatly wrapped gifts. One is a long box that I know must contain shoes. I saw it when he had packed the trunk of the car before we left London and then again as the porter took our things when we arrived in Babington. I remove the shiny silver foil wrapping to reveal a mauve Jimmy Choo box. Inside is a pair of knee-high black python skin stiletto boots. I know these are expensive and that the hotel, including meals and spa treatments, is costing him a bomb but a bit of quick mental arithmetic tells me he is lagging in the birthday spend maths. I know this is the source of his unspoken ire. Like with the car, I have made him feel inferior where money is concerned. Big mistake.

I gush appropriately and am quick to put the boots on and sidle up to him, knowing that he will definitely want to add this footwear to the growing list of bedroom-worn heels. He has the good grace to smile before he gently pushes me away, encouraging me to open the remaining gift. A much smaller box covered in the same satiny foil. Removing the paper revealed another box also with 'Jimmy' on it; 'Jimmy Jane' this time. I stare at the logo of two swirling 'J's and am none the wiser as to what I am holding. As I open the box to reveal a long slender silver bullet-like object, Patrick starts to speak. I can tell he is overcompensating and I know this is not going to end well.

"It's limited edition, you know. It's made of platinum and will last a lifetime, unlike ordinary vibrators. It's worth a lot of money," he adds, almost as an afterthought, as he tries to boost his total.

I can't stop myself from frowning as reality snaps into my consciousness like a whip. The gifts he has given me are self-serving and indulgent. Not thoughtful in the slightest. I set about opening his card to buy myself time. The world tilts on its axis as everything I thought I understood shifts around in my head. There in his neat handwriting are the words 'You are the thoughts in my dreams. You are the vision in my eyes. You are the sound in my ears. You are the words in my mouth. You are everything I need. You are everything I want.'

Once again Patrick Harrington has managed to be both true to form in his ability to stupefy me, and better than I had ever imagined. All wrapped up in one bewildering birthday bonanza.

Harrington

I love my birthday. Everyone makes a fuss and I am more than happy to be the centre of attention. However, this year it will be all the more complicated by the fact that I am sharing my birthday - literally - with Alexandra Fisher.

Alex insists on being in charge of proceedings, which makes me very uncomfortable. I am flat tack at work and not really in a position to oversee her arrangements so leave it at giving her a short list of acceptable hotels. We have agreed on a UK break, as I am due in New York and then office hopping in Asia shortly after my birthday.

I only just manage to find the time to purchase two amazing gifts for Alex, making it home in time to stash them before she arrives. She is staying over before we leave for our break away. I have given her a set of keys to my place. While it had been my idea, it is all starting to get a bit comfortable for me. I guess I can't blame her, though, as we have fallen into a pattern of saying 'I love you'. Well, at least she has and I respond with 'me too', which always makes me laugh because I do love myself. Or the oft-used male response of 'ditto' rolls off my tongue, thank you very much Patrick Swayze. If she has noticed that she is sailing solo on the 'I love you' boat she hasn't commented. I keep her happy by dropping the word 'girlfriend' into the dialogue just enough to please her while keeping my vomit response in check.

Alex is clearly excited and in high spirits on the Saturday morning. I don't really understand why, simply putting it down to her relishing the opportunity to spend a dirty weekend with me, until she drags me outside to see the car that has arrived. I am expecting a run of the mill black saloon car from the Addison Lee fleet. Instead, dominating my narrow street is a shiny black Bentley convertible. Alex is clapping her hands with glee and poking me in the ribs as the delivery guy hustles around me with papers to sign and instructions for using the car. I am apoplectic with rage and know that I have to keep my mouth firmly shut to ensure the anger bomb doesn't detonate. God help me. The smarmy guy is still talking, pointing out levers and buttons as if I have never seen or driven a super-car before. I want to tell him that I earn his annual salary in the time it takes me to take a shit.

We finally get on the road and Alex forces me into articulating my annoyance when she won't stop gabbling on about it being a special treat. I tell her that I can have a street full of these cars if I choose to. I am furious. The admiring glances we get as we idle at lights and inch forward in the central London traffic does little to quash my resentment. I am no stranger to people appreciating me and my acquisitions, in the form of women, toys, clothes, you name it.

The car's mechanical symphony calms me down a little as we make it onto the M40 and get out of the congestion of London's surface streets. I know we are stopping en route for lunch and wonder why Alex has selected an as-yet-undeclared venue that isn't actually en route to Babington. As I follow the verbal cues from the satnav and find myself in Beaconsfield I feel my stomach lurch. My unease peaks as I see Dave and his airhead lady friend standing outside a restaurant. For the second time that day I have been caught off guard and I don't like it one bit. I shake my head to clear the mist of anger and let a mask of benevolence slip into place.

Despite the appalling service, mediocre food and the nauseating stream of consciousness coming from Dave's girlfriend, I actually manage to enjoy myself a little. I write the morning and its mishaps off as I acknowledge that Alex has only been trying to please me. I know that I can be a nightmare at the best of times, and while I never would have chosen this place with its confused baroque-meets-gothic decor, it is quite reassuring to be reminded that living in central London is the only place to be. These commuter-belt villages might be leafy but that is about all they had to offer. Dave is a fool for investing in property out here.

The peace is short lived as a not-familiar-enough-to-place-it pop song interrupts our conversation. It is Ms Fisher's phone. She answers it at the table and as I watch her unfurl like a flower in the sunshine I know exactly who it is. She hastily makes a retreat to take the call outside claiming it is her mother, but my suspicions are confirmed as she has not been quick enough to shield the caller's identity. I see the headshot of Joseph Levy on her iPhone.

I watch Dave's vacuous girlfriend leave the table and decide to wait a moment before following her to the bathroom. I don't really want to be subjected to an interrogation from Dave about my relationship with Alex, and at this point Ms Fisher has a running tally of black marks on her scorecard. I am seeking release and know exactly where to find it. I skip down the black and white granite staircase just in time to see a velvet door slip shut. It is just as well I haven't left it any later to follow her as the entrance to the bathrooms appears to be a wall to the unknowing. I walk into the ladies' bathroom.

I take a seat on a clamshell velvet armchair and wait. It doesn't take long before she emerges from a stall and with one look she knows what I have come for. As I push her back into the cubicle and she gets to her knees I relish the feeling of killing two birds with one stone. Alex and Dave both deserve this for their recent indiscretions. I tell her to hurry which isn't an issue for this crotch vacuum. As the dumb slut's hands seize my buttocks and move my cock deeper into her hungry mouth I feel myself calm down. Getting this ditz to play my skin flute ensures I regain my composure.

I make it back to the table just in time to argue with Dave about who should settle the bill. I don't care that it is my birthday; I don't like to feel beholden to anyone. Once his girlfriend finally reappears, all smiles and recently reapplied makeup, he demonstrates his ignorance by teasing her about taking a dump. I feel unflustered for the first time that day. Even the fact that

Alex is still outside on the phone doesn't bother me. I have plenty more tricks up my sleeve to make her pay for the ways she had slighted me.

As soon as we are in our suite at Babington House I start to fire up my laptop and connect to their wi-fi. It is all I can think about after being stimulated by the fellatio in the bathroom at Crazy Bear. I have been suggesting to Alex, asserting increasing latent pressure on her, that we try online swinging for some time now. I am a member of a web club where I like to watch other couples have sex and where I sometimes arrange to meet up with the more attractive women if the fancy takes me.

I figure that this may be the final straw for Alex but I don't care. At least not that much. I have yet to be on the other end of the web cam and the quest to do so excites me as much as the actual proposition does. One of Alex's original protestations was that she didn't want to be part of an orgy. I had patiently explained that this was not an orgy. One person is masturbation, two is a couple, three is, well, a threesome, four is two couples swinging, and five is the same with a looky loo. It took six people before it qualified as an orgy. We will get there but all in good time.

I watch her battling with herself. I know that she is opening up to new experiences and she trusts me; after all, she knows how much I have to lose. I push the envelope by wrapping her in a bear hug and whispering sweet nothings in her ear. I feel her body respond and know that it is mine for the taking.

I undress her quickly, not wanting to risk taking too much time lest she change her mind. I position the laptop to capture our sexual endeavours, ensuring our elected couple have a front row seat. I thrust deep into her welcoming pussy which tells me that any resistance is a show. She wants this as much as I do.

Along with her heels, I leave her wearing her chunky necklace. The beads swirl to form a mesmerising geometric pattern as I increase the speed of our coupling. I feel the walls of her vagina grip on my cock, the grip of her thighs around my own hips, and the look of ecstasy on that pretty face, now consumed by fire. I withdraw and flip Alex over so that she is holding the desk now, looking into the laptop and the web cam as I re-enter from behind. I feel for her hipbone for leverage and start again to fuck her harder, watching her face intently in the mirror. Her eyes close for a time, giving in to the sensations that were coursing through her body, before she opens them again and stares back at me with a mixture of love and hate. This alone almost causes me to come but I don't want this to end. I try to slow down, but she won't let me, using her thighs and her arse to pump me, to bring on the climax that we both so badly want.

My hands reach around onto her breasts as we come, virtually together. I savour the release of my orgasm as I shoot my hot semen deep into her, and then, emboldened by the extra hardness from that last moment of restraint, I feel the quiver of her thighs signalling it is over. For a fleeting moment I think that I could spend the rest of my life with this girl, as long as my infinite conditions are met. This is a good start.

We hold the pose, as if to allow our voyeurs to take photos, for a few delicious moments, before I withdraw and we start to reassemble our dishevelled clothing. That was epic and I tell her as much. I figure a little bit of reinforcement is required to ensure that I can build on this coup d'etat. I have to keep washing her brain. I am reluctant to disconnect and log out but decide that she probably can't be coerced into a second round just yet. I know our audience is not disappointed by what they've seen as I read their comments. Next time I'll have Alex respond with sexy chat as we fuck to heighten the whole experience for everyone involved.

We limp through the rest of the weekend managing to avoid tackling the myriad issues head on. Alex seems to be learning quickly enough that confrontation is not the way to deal with me. I beat Alex convincingly on the tennis court which makes me feel good. She may be younger and technically a better player but both my power and stamina outplay her skill. I book a couples massage as a reward for her participation in my sexual fantasies, after which I leave her lollygagging while I do a cardio session in the gym and try to get through some ever-present work.

I wake up to my favourite day of the year and not even the rain dampens my good spirits. Of course I should have known that it would be Alexandra that is the killjoy as I unveil her gift to me, a box inside a box. Not for the first time this weekend it feels like Mercury was in retrograde. I feel myself brought to tears when I see the expensive Longmire cufflinks she had bought me. I want them, for sure, but the extravagance of the present makes me feel indebted to her. Not a feeling I tolerate lightly. My inner turmoil is magnified by the knowledge that this girl is hopelessly in love with me; to buy such a big-ticket gift when I have been embarking on a campaign to undermine her confidence and beat her into sexual submission is more than my conscience can bear.

Despite the fact that Alex will think my tears signal that I am overwhelmed by her generosity, I push them away as an external signal to myself that they are unwanted. As if changing the subject, I bestow my presents upon Alex. I have bought her an amazing pair of snakeskin boots that will impress anyone but the members of PETA. As she leans down to zip them up her lovely pins, I feel my nether regions stir. She is at my side in an instant, making eyes at me but I am polite enough to let her finish opening her gifts. The second box contains a platinum everlasting vibrator. The choice of material means that you can heat it or cool it for extra sensations. While I know it is a gift for her, I am looking forward to her penetrating me with it.

I have written her birthday card with words that I know will keep her enamoured of me. The gifts are amazing, I know, but I also realise I have to appeal to both her superficial nature and her depth. Sometimes she rivals Rodin's thinker, other times she makes a puddle look deep. I have hit the bull's eye as I watch her reading and re-reading my card. I decide in the blink of an eye to take her with me to Mustique for Christmas. It may be months away but I know I should book it so we can travel together before the airlines get gummed up. I won't actually invite her just yet, and anyway, if things go sideways I'll just cancel the arrangements. I am relieved that she is turning out to be smart enough to present me with a constant mental challenge, balanced with the right amount of sexual deviance to keep my interest piqued.

Once again, Alexandra Fisher has managed to be both true to form in her ability to stupefy me, and better than I had ever imagined. All wrapped up in one bewildering birthday bonanza.

Patrick

I stare at the brown paper envelope and feel sick to my stomach. It contains large colour photographs, slightly blurred and grainy but crystal clear in what they portray. Me, naked in a variety of different sexual positions with a number of different women. Their faces are indistinguishable but I know who they are and what they are. Hookers. Other pictures show me entering and leaving establishments that a man in my position shouldn't be associated with. *Too late for that.*

The sender has not included a note. Scrawly hand writing across the envelope refers to the contents as 'The Harrington Sexual Misdeeds Dossier'. I am clueless as to the intention of the sender. They have not asked for money. Or anything else for that matter. *Is it a veiled threat to ruin my reputation, and along with it, my dreams of ever becoming Caldwell Bank's next CEO?*

I run my hands through my hair and wonder, *which one of the countless women I have slept with could possibly be behind this?* I found the envelope wedged into the mail slot of my front door. It was hand delivered to my house. *Could it be a work associate?* I know I have burned my fair share of bridges and stepped on plenty of toes in my time. *Who hates me enough to go to these lengths to do this to me?*

I start to mentally index the most likely culprits. I don't want to acknowledge to myself how endless the list could actually be. I focus on recent incidents and try to think about perceived slights.

Dave. Could he have found out about his pea-brained girl-friend deep-throating my cock? I dismiss him quickly as I know he would front this with me, and to be fair the reality is that he would need to be seriously in love with that dullard to risk our friendship. Bros before hoes was the newsletter we had always subscribed to. I don't even bother putting his girlfriend in the frame as she doesn't have the brain cells required to compile this material, she is using the few she has just to maintain her bodily functions. Must be nice to live a life unburdened by genius.

Faezeh. Perhaps I had been too callous and dismissive during our recent encounters. She is smart enough to pull this off, but then I also know she is hopelessly smitten with me and wouldn't risk her fantasy of the potential of a real relationship with me. She asks me 'how high?' any time I asked her to jump. Our rela-tionship is crude, for sure, but I know I throw her enough bones for that dog to be happy. Despite the fact that I have perhaps crossed her boundaries, I rule her out.

Tanja. Thinking about boundaries, she had disregarded the limits of our arrangement. I had set her up for a fall sending Alex for a massage in my place, but she deserves what she got. I have been through this before with other hopefuls. Same shit, dif-ferent bucket. Her presumption that she can demand anything more from me when what we had in place was purely transac-tional is misplaced at best. I struggle to see this pretty little thing think past her next appointment, let alone have the patience and wherewithal to put this dossier together.

Lizzy. When it comes to means, this woman could definitely have had someone trail me and she is savvy enough to mount this type of campaign. But then she too has plenty to lose. I don't see the motive for her. Sure, she is in love with me and when I think back to the quick fuck we had at the Connaught Hotel I may have offended her. But then she knows I have plenty of nudie pictures of her and some Blackberry messenger conver-sations her husband would be shocked to see. There is no way she would cross me when she likes her New York 'society wife' lifestyle. Surely, she wouldn't have done this knowing it would jeopardise her perfect life. I know women can be emotional but this would be the equivalent of shitting in her own nest and if I know her, and I do, she isn't a fan of mess.

Maria. Thinking of mess, maybe my seductive cleaning Madame has it in for me. I try to still my rising panic and think logically. I send her business and have her girls working in every way she offers. *Why would she bite the hand that feeds her?* I gave her one, as she rightly wanted me to. Maybe I took it too far with the erotic asphyxiation but she put my tie around her neck. She asked for that, and she enjoyed it. I can't help appreciating replaying that highlight reel in my head. Before our play date, I had always treated her like family.

Siobhan. Speaking of family, mine is troublesome, that is for definite. Jealousy is evident in my brothers but it is my sister that seems unable to disguise her loathing of me, even when she would surely be homeless and destitute without my money. I think of the venom she spat at me on my last trip home and feel myself growing tense. I hate her just as much as she hates me. She is greedy and devious, an unpredictable cocktail. I mull it over as I try to work out if she would have enough energy to mastermind this kind of treachery. She certainly doesn't have the stamina required to get herself to the hairdresser, let alone stage-manage this kind of surveillance remotely. I strike her off my mental list of suspects. It has to be someone closer to home, or maybe more rightly, someone at work.

Amber. I have not shown her much attention at all of late, and she has not had any physical action with me for weeks. I'm sure she is missing it and I know that she loves the game, the thrill of living dangerously. I wonder, too, if she may have found out that I am bedding Alex, and that it is Alex who is getting a smidge closer to intimacy with me. Still arms' length, by anyone else's standards, but much closer than Amber would ever have the privilege of enjoying.

I don't know if I can strike her from the roll call of the accused I am reviewing, but my gut feeling is telling me it isn't her. Again, a woman with much to lose herself, and she knows that I wouldn't hesitate to destroy her in order to save myself. The power distance is too great for her to try and bridge it in this way. If I am to go down, I will take her down with me. As disturbed as I am by this unwanted photo journal, I know that I can think my way out of this. I have not come this far and got to where I am without determination and sheer willpower. My mental Rolodex spins round to the next name.

Silvy. Perhaps she had cottoned on to the fact that she is not the only prostitute I use. Hell, maybe these hustlers all know each other. *But why would she care?* She always gets paid, in shiny fifty-pound sliders, and it isn't like I am a bad client. She appreciates my body and the pleasure she gets from it, and I know this as sure as I know my own name. Nothing we do is too much; it is her trade at the end of the day. If she has a grievance she should take it up with the Streetwalkers' Union. It doesn't exist? Well, cry me a river. Get a new job. While she knows me well enough to know my sexual preferences, the reality is that she doesn't know me well enough to understand what I do for a living. Plus she spends so much time on her back just to afford that Knightsbridge apartment. I doubt she would part with her hard earned cash just to get at me.

Eloise. Now, here is someone with a sharp axe to grind. She has it in for me, there is no question about that. She knows that I aspire to be the next CEO. But this is not her style at all. She is deadly, noxious, yes, but she is also very clever. There is no way she would be so clumsy as to post a tatty envelope through my front door. Eloise 'holier than thou' Little would be more likely to out me to Brad Stone and have him fire me in a publicly humiliating way. She would do it by the book. Jeez, that woman wrote the damn book. I'm not sure I can cross her off my list but the more I try it out in my mind the more it doesn't sit right with me. So, I am left with one more name to consider.

Alex. I cast my mind right back to the beginning. It is like a mosaic, a thousand tiny pieces that make up the complete picture. I am really struggling with this. I showed her the journey I am taking and she was a willing passenger, along for the ride. *Or was she?* In order to have this kind of dirt on me she would have had to know so much more about me than she let on. She would have had to be at the centre of mission control for more years than I cared to work out, I calculate, as I flip over the photos again and try to mentally date stamp them. I reflect that my sex life is split almost equally between the things I can't remember and the things I don't want to.

If Alex has any inclination that I have been sleeping around, she has not mentioned it. It isn't like she would even need to say anything; her body language is often my guide. And really, does she think that I am going to forsake sleeping with any other woman *ad infinitum*? Show me a beautiful woman and I'll show you a man who is tired of fucking her. I need the variety and I need to feel free.

I keep trying to reconcile the facts in front of me with the Alexandra that I know. I can't believe she is such a good actress that she would be able to fool me and weasel her way into my affections in order to try to plot my demise. I would be in a world of hurt if this type of thing were ever exposed to the powers that be at Caldwell.

I am never going to settle down, but I have to concede to myself that I have been thinking that if I can train her, I might be able to get used to the idea of her being the most important woman in my life. After my mother, of course. Alex can have it all: the glory of being with me, the lavish lifestyle, amazing sex and all she would have to do was look the other way occasionally. Well, as often as I deem it necessary.

This is nuts. I can't let myself believe that this girl who had resisted me at the outset, that had kept me more enthralled than most woman ever had, that had planned our birthday retreat, can be the mastermind behind all of this. She has spent a lot of money on luxury gifts she knows I wanted, even if she missed the fact that I didn't want her to buy them for me.

If anything, as I think about it, I reassure myself that it wasn't her. I am no closer to determining who my enemy is, but what I do know is that Alex is in love with me. She is only human. And I have found a place in her that I am almost willing to call home.

Maybe our relationship isn't as crazy as it seems.

Fisher

I stare at the brown paper envelope and feel sick to my stomach. It contains large colour photographs, slightly blurred and grainy but crystal clear in what they portray. Patrick, naked in a variety of different sexual positions with a number of different women.

I am unaware that I am crying until I see a fat teardrop land in the middle of the photograph I am holding. I look up at Eloise, who, to her credit, is keeping her face impassive. I know I won't get any sympathy from her and I prepare myself for the onslaught as I ask, with trepidation, "How did you get these?"

Eloise talks at length. She describes how she had never trusted Patrick and had been slowly and surely building a dossier of evidence against him. I stare at the pile of paper; the top sheet show neatly typed paragraphs. Someone has gone to a lot of trouble to document their findings. She explains to me that she had known that he was grooming me, like a pimp, using mind games and mental manipulation to assert control. "That man eats, drinks and sleeps thinking of ways to trick women into doing what he wants them to do. He preyed on your emotional vulnerability, offering you a sense of love and giving you a false sense of confidence. I can just imagine the lies he fed you.

It's all about influencing your perception of reality. It's gaslighting." The way she speaks is so matter of fact; she is totally oblivious to my heart breaking.

Eloise tells me that while she knew he was deviant from years of working with him, even she was shocked by the extent of his perverse behaviour. She labels him a narcissist, a sex addict, a gambler and a sociopath. Her words rain down on me as I try to take it all in. I say nothing, listening as she flicks through photos and talks me through the bulging catalogue of his indiscretions. Eloise had employed a private investigator to follow Patrick after she suspected nefarious dealings at work. What she had uncovered when she lifted the rock confirmed her suspicions beyond anything she could have imagined, both in terms of his borderline business dealings and his twisted sexual appetite.

"Caldwell is an old institution, and a great one, but it's turning into a bucket shop thanks to that man. Patrick has turned the Investment Bank into the Wild Wild West, the 'Cult of Caldwell'. He's had a bunch of quantitative traders dreaming up products, layering in complex hedges, to sell off to corporate clients, like lambs to the slaughter. He's finding ways to squeeze more and more margin out of the same clients. The smaller businesses don't know what they should and shouldn't buy. He takes a competitive advantage and pushes it all the way. His theory is that if we are extending the bank's balance sheet to these businesses, we should be making as much money as possible out of them. He's gone way too far."

At this point in proceedings I don't care about his reckless attitude to risk, but I do wholeheartedly agree with her last statement. I can't look at the pictures another second longer. I reach over for the report and before I can start reading, Eloise puts her hand on top of mine. The gesture is not lost on me. "Alex, I am sorry. I had wanted to give you some insight into this, but I also knew that in order to use any of it I need to move slower than a glacier. I need to be one hundred percent certain of what I have. If we let things unfold for a little longer I think I can dole out enough rope and Patrick will hang himself." I see her wince, uncharacteristically, as she realises the terrible faux pas she has made. She carries on, regardless.

"I watched the way he looked at you. I was devastated that Saturday I saw you two outside Harrods together, and then the New York trip sealed it. I knew he had you. I'm sure you probably spent your birthday weekend together too. I didn't buy the girls' spa weekend at all, Alex." I am past crying now as the pain of the truth she speaks jabs at me, finding the scar tissue that barely protects my heart. My annoying sensible inner voice is adding to my distress, dropping unhelpful thoughts into my mental pandemonium, as the holes in the multiple layers of Swiss cheese line up. I feel the urge to be sick as I wonder if there are pictures that Eloise isn't showing me. Photographs of me. I sit with my eyes screwed shut for a moment, swallowing down the nausea. I am about to have a meltdown of nuclear proportions if I let those thoughts thread themselves into a story in my mind.

Eloise lifts her hand off mine and lets me slide the report closer so I can read it. In her inimitable style, she is showing me where to look but not what to see. We sit there in silence as I read. It is slow going as I try to make sense of the words on the page before me. This transcript is thorough. This investigator had been in situations where he was close enough to take pictures, and had validated what he had seen through monitoring Patrick's work email account, Blackberry and the bank's online messenger system. I am chilled by the Big Brother nature of it all. The report includes minute details of his dalliances with Amber Chilworth; it teaches me that Silvy was a prostitute; it describes Tanja, his 'happy ending' masseuse; I am also introduced to a host of other women including an Iranian 'fuck buddy' who works for the Financial Times and Elizabeth Edelstein, a married mother of three whom he had met on his Christmas vacation. It seems his criteria are simply female and breathing. But it is the most recent entry that sets my internal tectonic plates shifting. Natasha, the concierge at the Mondrian Hotel. I feel like a jigsaw puzzle that has been torn apart as my fears are confirmed. This behaviour hadn't stopped once he had declared his love for me.

Revenge fizzes and pops inside me. It is all I can think about. I have everything in front of me needed to ruin the man in these photographs. As if reading my mind, Eloise tells me that she has revealed this to me to ensure that I don't get in any deeper than I already am with the vile Patrick Harrington. With a rare note of concern, she assures me that she would handle this, and that all I need to do is extract myself from the relationship. She will ensure that he loses his job, his reputation and everything he holds so dear. All knots eventually get the comb.

I nod meekly. Easier said than done where my role is concerned. I have been sleeping with the enemy. It feels like there is a steel knife in my windpipe. I can't speak even if I wanted to. I had turned up at Eloise's house this morning with my laptop bag, thinking I had been summoned there to work on something that was too confidential even for the office. It had happened before. Confidential is indeed the operative word and I understand why we are sitting at Eloise's kitchen table. I appreciate the fact that she is sparing me the agony of having to maintain a façade at work. This is not a bombshell she could have dropped in Caldwell's Head Office. While she knows me well enough, judging how I would react to news of this magnitude would be impossible, particularly if there was more coming, and she had something on me. I feel volatile as I try to process these revelations, as though lighting a match would result in a catastrophic explosion.

I think about Patrick and what I have believed, how susceptible I have been to his charms despite all the warnings. I realise that lies hurt less than the truth does. I want to vomit. I can actually taste the shock in my mouth. I am well aware that Eloise has probably only hit the tip of the iceberg as I think about his iPhone and the fact that he always deletes his text message threads. Clearly covering his tracks. And then there is his relationship with me, but I can't go there.

As if the photographs and the report are not enough, Eloise has one final card to play. "Alex," she says gently, which sets my heart racing. "Patrick's home technology was set up by Caldwell's Executive support technology team. While we can't and won't access anything on his personal computers, what we do know from his Internet usage is that his download rate is excessive. Not surprising as I can only imagine the filth that man likes to watch." She is not even trying to hide her disgust.

"What I really need to tell you is that his upload rate is just as high and my guy tells me that he streams video online. I would be very careful about how you approach this man. He is manipulative and conniving, and he undoubtedly has something that will ensure you don't cross him. My guess would be video footage."

I am suffocating; it feels like there isn't an ounce of air to breathe in the room. I am suffering. I am tangled up in a sticky web of deceit. I have been high off my love for Patrick, now I am drunk from the poison of my hate. The reality of my world has been shattered in the twenty minutes I have been in Eloise's house. It seems it didn't take long to tear another black hole in my universe.

Outwardly, I am holding it together when all I want to do is scream, weep, cry like a baby, be held by my mother, and somehow have the horrible ugliness of it all wiped from my memory. The parallels with my father are sickening. I need a Neuralyzer, standard issue for the Men in Black, to erase the memories of the past hours, days, weeks, months.

I cannot see a way forward. I don't know how I am going to get myself out of Eloise's house, or even get up from her table, let alone go through the motions of a break-up with the overwhelming Patrick Harrington.

Eloise is canny. She knows that Patrick has only just left on a ten-day business trip to the States and the Far East, and that will give us time to get our ducks in a row. Or perhaps more accurately, it will give me time to recover from the atomic blast that this dossier has unleashed on me.

Eloise is eyeing me, trying to assess where I am with my processing. She has clearly seen the vengeance in my eyes. I can listen to reason on that, or pretend to for now anyway. I want Patrick to fall. And fall hard. Be publicly disgraced in the same way I have been privately humiliated. I want him to lose everything. But most of all I want to be as far away as possible from any association with him before that happened. Eloise, as usual, is right. Glacial pace. No missteps. We can't arouse his suspicion and let him get off with anything less than total ruination. He is as formidable as she is.

"He is like Teflon, Alex. Nothing sticks. He had the audacity to be sleeping with the company lawyer when we were handling that big integration project a few years ago. I remember knowing he was evil when I heard that he had persuaded her to be by his side, and you know what that means, on Mother's Day when she has two small children." I can see that she thinks little of this woman, but she doesn't go as far as to say it, knowing that this lawyer and I are peas in a toxic pod.

"In the immortal words of Lincoln, 'you may fool all of the

people some of the time; you can even fool some of the people all of the time; but you can't fool all of the people all of the time.' He will make mistakes. We have to ensure that we bury enough land mines to ensure that he blows himself up." This time her analogy steers a safe course away from any similarities with my father's death. *How have I gotten myself into such a spectacular mess?* What you see is certainly not what you get with the unscrupulous Patrick Harrington. But then, faces hide more than they reveal. My father continues to teach me this from the grave.

I finally risk using my voice. It sounds hollow and muted. I still am not sure if I can trust Eloise implicitly but at this point she is a safer bet than the egoistic Patrick Harrington. I tell her that I have a set of keys to his house, including a fob to disable the alarm system. I tell her that I know his PIN code and some of his passwords. She is still making a study of me but clearly these confessions show her that I am still capable of logic, of thinking clearly amidst the emotional maelstrom.

"We need to be careful. I know you don't wish to hear this, but what he does when he is not on Caldwell time is actually his own business. Lucky for you, he is very rarely actually off the bank's clock. It goes without saying that everything I've done to date is legal, all within the safety of the employee/employer relationship." As she speaks I have misgivings about whether what she says is strictly true, but I guess she is treading a fine line between what is acceptable and knowing that he will not, can not, blow a whistle on her. If I know her, she will have someone else hit the kill switch in any event. Eloise may orchestrate his demise, but she will be happy to watch it from the sidelines for the sake of her own reputation.

If Eloise is aware of my pain she isn't showing it and she sure as hell isn't moderating for it. "Alex, promise me that you won't do anything, other than terminate your relationship with this man. We still don't know how many clowns are in that car. You can still have a good life, an amazing career. Don't let this change the course of your life entirely." I nod. At this point, my life is in tatters, my future a dense fog with no apparent way through.

"Why have you let Amber continue in her role?" I want to deflect the scrutiny from myself. And I am genuinely interested; Eloise doesn't tolerate moral turpitude and she will see Amber's transgressions as a personal slight, given the impact it could have on her.

"Mistakes require correction, not punishment. Amber is very capable and does an excellent job. Sure, her personal life is a mess. Her husband left her and she's not coping with that. She lets everyone ride her, just like a bus route. But she gets stuff done, even if it's with a lot more baggage than I bargained for when I hired her. In any event, it all serves my ultimate aim. I can force her hand to bring a sexual harassment suit against Harrington if need be." Eloise is coldly calculating and, as expected, she is covering all bases. I wonder about her reference to correction rather than punishment and think about what that means for me. I figure she doesn't see what Patrick has done as a mistake. This is beyond premeditation; it is a way of being.

Eloise sees me out and I wonder how my legs are working, my body responding when my mind feels like shutting down. I feel traumatised, like someone has ripped off my protective cocoon, exposing me to the world and all its hurt. While I am no stranger to this feeling, I hadn't expected life to catapult me back here so soon. I start walking and it takes me a while to realise I have headed north. Instead of heading home, I am walking to Patrick's house as if on autopilot.

I know how much he wants to be the next CEO of Caldwell and we both know how close he is. I am sure that Caldwell's board will never consider a man with these kinds of skeletons in his closet as a viable candidate. Once inside, I make my way to his home office and sit down heavily at his grandiose desk. Being in his pristine house gives me some respite from the feelings that continue to brew. A small violation in return for the many. It takes me a few moments to start up his laptop I search for any files with my name, and I look through the files in the date order they were created. Nothing. I feel no sense of relief as this is probably not where his private viewing material is stored or uploaded to the web from.

I stuff the pictures in a brown envelope from his desk drawer. Caldwell's logo is laughing at me from the front. I pack my stuff up in haste. I briefly consider wiping the surfaces of my fingerprints and laugh loudly, manically at myself. I feel crazed. After re-arming the alarm, I walk through the front door and pull it shut, surveying the street on either side of me. It is the middle of the day and there is nobody around. I push the envelope back through the mail slot and leave in a hurry. By the time Eloise realises I have taken the photos it will be too late. I'm not thinking straight, but I don't want to be. I want this man to hurt as much as I do right now.

I walk, and walk and walk. I make it to Fulham Broadway and wander into the tube station, grateful that the next District Line tube will take me to Putney. The rhythmic movement of the train lulls me into thinking it is an ordinary day. My mind is wiser and now knows better. It goes back to the beginning, searching for evidence, trying to grasp for some sense in the midst of a waking nightmare.

The porter startles me as I make my way into the building. I am on another planet. He tells me he has signed for a delivery for me and it is at my front door. He starts to make conversation which I ignore. I am incapable of small talk and am so close to falling apart; I am holding on just long enough to make it inside the refuge of my flat. I climb the stairs, the news barely registering until I round the corner. There is a large vase of blue hydrangeas on my doorstep. My favourite.

'Alex. I miss you and I love you. You're amazing. P x'

For the first time that day I feel a sense of reality, of calm. Love is an act of faith and the contradictions and conflicts are what make it grow. This force, that moves the world, is at once creative and devastating. Sure, this is no walk in the park, but my life has proved to be far from ordinary. I have had plenty of servings of life's shit pie. I try to reason with myself; surely if something is worth having, it is worth fighting for. All I know is that I love him too much to walk away.

Maybe our relationship isn't as crazy as it seems.

CPSIA information can be obtained at www.ICGtesting.com
Printed in the USA
LVOW07s0730151214

418855LV00004BA/143/P